Books by
RICHARD MARTIN STERN

THE BRIGHT ROAD TO FEAR
THE SEARCH FOR TABATHA CARR
THESE UNLUCKY DEEDS

These Unlucky Deeds

by
RICHARD MARTIN STERN

CHARLES SCRIBNER'S SONS · NEW YORK

COPYRIGHT © 1960 RICHARD MARTIN STERN

This book published simultaneously in the
United States of America and in Canada—
Copyright under the Berne Convention

*All rights reserved. No part of this book
may be reproduced in any form
without the permission of Charles Scribner's Sons.*

A–11.60 [V]

Printed in the United States of America
LIBRARY OF CONGRESS CATALOG CARD NUMBER 61-6902

THIS BOOK IS DEDICATED:
>TO *Dot, of course, with love;*
>AND, *with affection, to Meg and Floyd, our mentors and guides amidst the flora, and fauna, of the county.*

THE CHARACTERS in this tale do not exist. They are not, I hope, straw people set up to be knocked down, but neither are they facsimiles of any real persons, living or dead. The fact is, of course, that I have tried to invent, as convincingly as I could, the kinds of characters who might credibly dwell in the community I have described which is also the result of invention and not geography. As Gladys pointed out, Quidnunc County is not on any map. Perhaps it is just as well.

I list the main characters, my inventions, below. If you enjoy making their acquaintance, I am content.

GEORGE HANKS, artist, monologist, animalistic philosopher, observer, catalyst and occasional participant in mortal confusion. Think of Puck with muscles;

MARTIN and MADGE FULLER, he an aircraft engineer, who have breathed the Quidnunc County miasma for only a year, time enough to contract the infection, but insufficient time to develop antibodies in the bloodstream;

MILDRED and BEN PIERSON, actors, the Method School in real life;

BOB and JOY LEWIS, advertising agency Vice-President, exponent of the hard sell, and wife;

SAM and LOUELLA (BLOOM) BARNES; Sam is a broker, Louella a best selling historical novelist, and the result is Wall Street morality versus 17th Century Divine Right of Queens;

WALLY and MONA PETERS, he another writer, to whom Quidnunc County is Main Street, Sheridan Square, and the womb;

PAUL WARREN, publisher of both Louella Bloom and Wally Peters, and husband of

ROZ WARREN, who began it all.

PREFACE

"THERE ARE, YOU'LL FIND, roughly four kinds of people here in Quidnunc County. The base is made up of the aborigines, the kind you'll find in any collection of villages and small towns anywhere in the country, the solid folks who farm and run the small businesses, the drug stores and the groceries—even, yes, the supermarkets—and the candy stores and the hardwares; they're the plumbers and carpenters and electricians, the people who earn their livings and aren't at all ashamed that they may work with their hands—you follow me? They look down on the rest of us, call us carpetbaggers, and we look down on them—a stand-off.

"Then there are the family types who have mortgaged their souls to buy development houses. They're strict conformists; they're the ones the *togetherness* ads are directed at; the ones who *have* to keep up with the Joneses—picture windows and wall-to-wall you know what and green toilet paper to match the tile of the shower.

"The third group would be just as much at home in Greenwich, or Grosse Pointe, or Shaker Heights, or Burlingame, or Pasadena, and we don't, maybe luckily, maybe not, have many of those. They run to small families and Andover-Kent-Groton *cum* Harvard-Yale-Princeton and the Wall Street Journal. Nice people, maybe a little stuffy.

"And then, number four group, and God knows what to call them. Exurbanites—nasty word. Somebody even dug real deep once and came up with Upper Bohemians—by which he meant, I imagine, anybody who makes enough at painting or writing or acting or producing, that kind of thing, so he doesn't have to cadge drinks in a Village bar. The name doesn't matter. You'll gravitate to them, from the looks of you, and maybe that will be good, and maybe it will be bad. Some people fit, no matter what they do to earn a living. Some people don't fit, and sooner or later, if they're smart they get the hell out. There is a kind of built-in bitchiness in group four that is meat and drink to some and plain poison to others. How do you recognize them? Group four, I mean? I'm damned if I know. Not by their clothes; they left their pony-tail hair-do's and their turtle-neck sweaters back in the Village, most of them, anyway. Not by their cars. Not by any one thing I can think of offhand. They live in all kinds of houses, mostly old, but not necessarily. Oh, yes, there is one thing, a kind of negative quality, but maybe you'll see what I mean. You won't find any wagon-wheels on their front lawns. Children, bless you."

GEORGE HANKS, *late one night, to*
MARTIN *and* MADGE FULLER

These Unlucky Deeds

Wednesday

WITH THE COUNTY'S PRACTICED ALACRITY the word spread, by phone, by face-to-face conversation at *kaffeeklatsch* and supermarket, by apparent, if not actual, telepathy: Roz Warren was back home from wherever she had been, the secret annoyingly well kept these last six months; and, what was more, the snapper on the tale, Roz—Roz!—had a baby.

It was George Hanks who, later, pointed out that Roz's return was not the beginning, human gestation being the unhurried matter that it is; but merely a point in time some months after what might be called the inception. And as it all turned out, George's comment proved to be perceptive, almost prescient.

THE NEWS, of course, meant various things to various people. Louella Bloom Barnes, deep in her idealized version of the seventeenth century which she much preferred to the twentieth, hardly missed a beat.

She was in her first floor study of the fine columned white house that faced the river, the house her best selling novels had bought and restored, formal gardens, parquet floors, broad staircase sweep and all. She hung up the phone after Mildred Pierson's call and went back to the typewriter with only a small trace of annoyance at the interruption. Five manuscript pages before lunch; five more during the afternoon—this was Louella's working schedule, and she adhered to it strictly.

2

MADGE FULLER DROVE HOME from the supermarket after dropping off Mona Peters; a bi-weekly affair, this, since Mona, as everyone knew, simply could not drive an automobile, the buttons and pedals and switches and things terrified her. But Mona could, and did, talk, gaily, amusingly, usually inaccurately, occasionally with simple childlike candor at which you really couldn't take offense. Madge put the groceries away in cupboard and refrigerator and freezer with automatic care. And then she sat down and stared unseeing out of the window that overlooked the river, and began to cry. "Oh, damn," she said. "Oh, damn, damn, damn!"

3

JOY LEWIS, like Louella, got the word over the phone in Mildred Pierson's flawless diction, and it occurred to her as she listened that Mildred could have been playing one of the more emotional scenes from *Medea*, but, of course, Joy wouldn't for the world have said this aloud because she never, never inflicted pain deliberately. And when the torrent of words had stopped, Joy said merely, "Is the baby pretty? Being Roz's, she certainly ought to be."

There was a short silence. Then, "Really," Mildred said. "You're impossible, Joy. Nothing affects you. Nothing." Which was just Mildred's way of talking, and you couldn't take offense at her any more than you could at Mona because Mildred was an actress, a very sensitive actress which was, as the critics kept pointing out, the very best kind.

Joy pondered the news in her thoughtful way. And then she

went to the freezer and took out one of the thick steaks she had been saving for a special occasion. Bob loved his steak. She also set out the martini things, although it was only mid-week and they usually reserved their drinking for weekends. She spent a long time in the bathtub and an even longer time dressing and arranging her hair. And then, at last, she was ready for Bob's return. Or at least, she thought, as ready as she would ever be with what she had to work with.

4

OF THE MALES AFFECTED in this essentially matriarchal community, only Ben Pierson got the word before evening. Ben was an actor, too, although not, of course in Mildred's class; Ben took whatever TV parts were offered, and had no objection at all to working at Equity minimum, a practice Mildred found unthinkable. Between engagements, while he waited for the phone to ring, Ben chopped wood, or did small chores around the great, gloomy house (painted dull black, no one knew precisely why; and turreted and bow-windowed, an outstanding example of what George Hanks called *Edwardian Excrescence*) or labored endlessly in his immaculate garden, and thought. Ben did a great deal of thinking.

Mildred's voice, summoning him to the nearest turret to hear the news, was almost expressionless, which was strange, even startling, because Mildred's voice customarily held undertones of hysteria. And Ben loped dutifully up to the house and stood beneath the turret and listened and said nothing, and then returned to the garden where, inexplicably, he plucked three healthy roses from a bush one after another and demolished them, scattering their petals like snow before his mind became aware of what his hands were doing.

5

AND GEORGE HANKS HEARD, too, of course, almost as soon as Paul Warren had delivered Roz and offspring home from the airport. But, then, George Hanks was a special case, and how he found things out no one ever seemed to discover. Osmosis, perhaps. George's reaction to the news was thoughtful, and he put down his palette and stuck his brushes in turpentine and wiped his hands and went out to his car. And so George was, actually, the first to welcome Roz home.

It was a fine house that later became somewhat notorious—white clapboard with dark green shutters, set well back from the road, protected by two enormous and handsome white pine trees, a house of substance, of taste, of permanence. Roz herself opened the door, and her slow smile appeared, unchanged after all this time as Roz herself appeared unchanged. "I thought you'd be first," she said.

George nodded. "But, of course. The motto of my family, like that of Kipling's mongoose, is 'Run and find out.' Do we kiss, or just touch hands?" The kiss was cool, perfunctory, on both sides. "Now show me the infant," George said, and he followed Roz up the gleaming stairs, and he stood beside the crib and studied the child for some little time in silence.

Roz watched him quietly. "They all look alike."

"More or less," George said.

"Some people," Roz said, "think they can find resemblances. I think they're wrong." Watching him still, she wondered, as she had wondered before, if her words even reached him. One of Paul's authors had told her that of all languages Spanish was the easiest to learn to speak and to read and the hardest to master, and she had found it so. And George Hanks was like the language, easy to know but with his intricacies still unsolved even after—

"The question," George said, "is whose child is it?"

"Mine."

"Produced by schizogenesis?"

Roz was silent.

"You'd better be ready for the question, pet, because it's going to be asked many times and in many ways."

"Advice? From you?" The slow smile appeared again.

"Much woman," George said, and he bent down then and extended one thick forefinger into the crib. The baby goggled at it; one tiny hand, reaching, grasped the finger with surprising strength. George moved it gingerly. Over his shoulder he said, "But this time you've given a hostage to fate." He disengaged the finger with vast gentleness, straightened to his full height. "And now give me a drink and I'll bring you up to date on local gossip."

"I was hoping for that, too," Roz said.

Not the beginning, as George pointed out later, but a point in time that would be remembered.

6

AND IT WAS AT ABOUT THIS TIME, too, that Sam Barnes, Louella's husband, the Stock Exchange closed for the day, rode the subway uptown to Grand Central, had his customary single drink of scotch in the Oyster Bar, and carried his neatly folded newspaper aboard his train, where he read the scant evening news with half of his mind, while with the other half he wondered if tonight Louella would, by any chance, emerge from the seventeenth century into the present, or whether her eyes, studying him across the dinner table, would, as usual, appear to be measuring him for a sword and silk stockings and finding him lacking. It was sometimes difficult being Mr. Louella Bloom, the husband of the famous novelist, especially when Louella was working. And, as solace, he brought out for secret inspection those deliciously guilty thoughts of Roz Warren who, six months ago, had simply dropped out of sight. Why?

7

IN THE RCA BUILDING Bob Lewis, Joy's husband, shirt-sleeved and cigarette weary, went over the new Barker Manufacturing Company presentation for the umpteenth time with the agency art director and the copy chief. "It'll do," Bob said. "It'll have to do. It doesn't send me, but—"

"Tell me," the art director said, "just tell me how you put sex in a pump."

The copy chief said, "Everything makes Bob think of sex. If he ever takes a Rorschach test—"

"Okay," Bob said. "Okay." He leaned back in his chair. There were times when he wondered why anyone in his right mind chose this way to make a living. Madison Avenue—only it wasn't; the agency office was closer to Sixth, but the appellation still held. It was Ulcer Gulch no matter where its location. He said as much.

"Better," the copy chief said, "than playing piano—"

"I know," Bob said, "in a whorehouse, only sometimes I wonder." He sat up. "All right. Take it away. Let's hope they buy it."

"Get a good night's sleep," the copy chief said, "on your own side of the bed. You'd better be bright-eyed and bushy-tailed tomorrow."

"That will be easy."

As he rolled down his sleeves and got into his jacket, picked his cocoa straw hat from the rack, it occurred to him that it had been a long time, six months at least, since he'd given much thought to sex in the way the copy-chief meant it—filled with eagerness to get home, that was, with anticipation, every sense alerted and his mind working with enormous craftiness at turning up ways and means where none seemed to exist. Joy—Joy was all right. The only trouble was there was nothing exciting left in Joy. The excitement had all drained away down the sink of familiarity. Roz Warren, now—he wondered where she had gone, and why, just disappearing like that. Trouble was, a man couldn't go around asking. Not without attracting too much attention, anyway. Two, three times, always at parties and always after a few drinks, he had even been right on the verge of bracing Paul Warren and asking him straight out. Good thing he hadn't; what gossip that would have started. He wondered if Roz would ever turn up again. Or somebody like Roz. If there was anybody else like Roz.

8

MARTIN FULLER CONSIDERED CALLING Madge before he left the office and decided against it. If he left immediately he could beat the traffic. He supposed he was being selfish, waiting until he got home to spring it on her without warning. ("By the way, I'm flying to London tonight. You don't need to drive me. I'll leave my car at Idlewild. I'll be gone three, four days, probably no more.")

In a way, Martin supposed, he lived a life of continual selfishness. Madge was always there, always waiting, never complaining, and so, bit by bit, he took advantage. It was hard, almost impossible, not to. Other wives connived, as Mona Peters did; or threw tantrums in Mildred Pierson's pattern; or just withdrew as Louella did so thoroughly. Some wives churned deep down inside and on the surface showed nothing, or next to nothing—Joy Lewis came to mind; and these women, were, perhaps, even dangerous because the explosion, when it came, would have the factor of long containment to give it overwhelming force.

Madge fitted none of these categories. Madge was—Madge. She gave him, Martin, a completely free hand, never prying, never probing, merely accepting. If he had to fly to London, why, he had to fly to London. ("Have a good time. I'll miss you." And that would be all.)

And it was out of this fact of acceptance that the guilty feelings arose, and yet he did nothing about them. Madge made it too easy for him to do whatever he had to do, or even wanted to do. Madge's trust in him was bottomless—witness that Roz Warren affair, Martin's one and only lapse. Even now, after all this time since Roz had left the county, those memories were fresh and plain, and uncomfortable. His trouble, he supposed, was that he was basically a weak character. If he was given latitude, and he was by Madge, he took advantage of it.

Driving out the elevated highway, headed north towards the bridge, well ahead of the traffic as he had known he would be, he thought of Madge with sudden tenderness, and humble appreciation. But he did wish that once, just once, she would raise her voice and tell him that she was sick and tired of merely being, of waiting. And yet he knew, too, that if she did he wouldn't like it. Something would be spoiled. After all these years.

9

WALLY PETERS CAME OUT of his tiny study and went downstairs. There was no sense in sitting longer staring, merely staring at the typewriter. On page 210 the story he was working on was off the rails, and he had spent most of the morning and all of the afternoon trying not to admit it, but the fact was inescapable. He had to go back and re-do, maybe thirty pages, maybe fifty, maybe—God, forbid!—as much as a hundred pages. At times like this there was a kind of near-hysteria that began to build when he thought of the schedule he had set himself and the status of the bank account and the bills that were either due or would be coming due—and, of course, no assurance, no real guarantee that the book when finished would sell after all. One thing was sure: it would never sell the way it was going.

Maybe he had written too fast. Maybe he had written too slowly. Maybe he hadn't thought the story through in the first place, or maybe he had pondered it so long it had gone stale in his mind. Maybe. Maybe. Maybe. Once, eight years ago when he had sold his first book and started on his second, cut himself loose from his copy-writing job, ventured into the vast loneliness of free-lancing—once, then, he had thought that with experience the self-doubts would diminish, even disappear. He knew now that they never would. The knowledge made them no easier to bear. Maybe he was all through, dried-up. Maybe. Maybe—

Mona was sitting at the dining table nibbling on the end of a pencil. She had a piece of paper in front of her. She said, "The Kerrs are going to Europe." And then, after a little silence, "Did you hear me?"

"The Kerrs are going to Europe," Wally said. He told himself not to be hysterical. Fifty pages to re-do; if he could turn out seven pages a day, he had lost only a week. At ten pages a day— he was kidding himself that he could do even seven, and the gloom returned.

"And Mildred has a thirteen week Hollywood offer and she's considering it. Why can't you get a Hollywood offer?"

"Because I'm not a very good writer," Wally said. "And Mildred's a good actress."

"You're just feeling sorry for yourself. You do that." Mona examined the pencil. "Why don't we go somewhere? Mexico? Europe? Any—"

"Same answer."

"It's cheaper living in Mexico. And we've never gone anywhere, not even for a trip. Everybody else does. Now don't sulk. Sit down."

"I want a drink. I need one."

"You drink too much," Mona said. "Besides, there isn't any more gin. Mildred was here and I had to give her a drink. I couldn't just let her sit. Honestly—" She set the pencil down with a little thump. "We owe everybody, simply everybody. People ask us to parties, but we never—"

Wally said, "Is that what we're working up to? A party, for God's sake?"

"We can't travel," Mona said. "We can't even take a little trip. The least we can do is keep up our social obligations. And what does a party cost compared to Mexico? Or Europe?"

"There's an answer to that," Wally said, "but I can't find it now. Is there any sherry?"

"Not a big party, only ten, twelve people. I drank the sherry while Mildred drank the gin. Now listen to the list."

"Look—"

"Sam and Louella, of course. They've had us so often. And Bob and Joy. Martin and Madge. George Hanks, of course, and he'll bring somebody, he always does. And Paul and Roz Warren—"

"Who?" And then, slowly, "Say that again."

"Paul and Roz," Mona said. "Roz is back—"

"I didn't know."

"Well, she is. And what's more—" Mona smiled. It was almost a giggle. "What's more, she has a baby. That's why she went away, to have it. Nobody thought of that. But it's just what Roz would do. Can you imagine her letting anyone see her, anyone at all, with her belly all swollen? With that figure?"

"I'll go up and get some gin," Wally said.

"There, you see? When you want something we can afford it. But—" Mona stopped. There were times, she knew, when she tended to allow herself to go too far. The point was already gained. There would be a party. The trick was merely to beat Wally down, not kick him after he had fallen. He resented that. She giggled again as Wally opened the front door, and she raised her voice to be sure he heard. "Whose baby do you think it is?" She was already reaching happily for the telephone.

Wally walked all the way to the village instead of taking the car. What with one thing and another he thought fresh air and exercise might do him good. Only once he paused and stared at the river, as unseeing as Madge Fuller had been, and he was thinking no longer of the story that had to be re-done, or even of the party, but only of Roz, and a baby. "Dear God!" he said.

10

PAUL WARREN SAID GOODNIGHT to his secretary and to the receptionist in the book-lined front office. He had his briefcase which contained, as always, a manuscript to be read. He hoped it might be a good one, but, then, publishers always hoped that and were usually disappointed. But the reports from the readers had been enthusiastic and that might mean something. Still, even if he was enthusiastic too, any book remained a gamble. Unless it was written by a Hemingway or a Yerby or, yes, a Louella Bloom.

Riding down in the elevator he wondered if he should call Louella and ask her how the new book was coming. Sometimes Louella liked that kind of indication of concern. Other times, though, when Louella was stuck the way all authors seemed to manage to get themselves stuck, she resented any questions, considered them patronizing. It was hard to tell whether he should call her or not. And the question was, really, academic anyway.

He was not going to call Louella tonight. Nor was he even going to open his briefcase to take a single look at the manuscript it contained. Not tonight, with Roz just home, and as beautiful, as breathtaking as ever, baby or not. Until today, there at the airport gate, he had not realized, not allowed himself to realize, how much he had missed her.

11

BOB LEWIS SAID, "What goes on? Martinis? In the middle of the week?"

"Martinis go with steak," Joy said in her calm way. "I thought we might burst out a little after we get the children to bed."

"And you," Bob said. "What is that, a new dress?"

"You've seen it before. Three or four times."

Bob shook his head. "What is this, a party? I don't get it." He missed the change in Joy's eyes, faint, but there.

"The party," she said, "is Saturday night. At the Peters'—"

"Oh, no. Mona finally conned him into giving one?"

"The usual people," Joy said. She recited the guest list, or most of it. She added, as she turned away, "And Paul and Roz Warren. Roz is back. With a baby. I'll call you when the children are in bed." She was tempted to look back, but she was afraid of what she might see in his face.

12

ACROSS THE DINNER TABLE Sam Barnes said, "How are the Roundheads and the Cavaliers doing?"

Louella said, "You don't have to pretend that you're interested."

"But I am. You know that."

Louella sipped her wine. "Sometimes," she said, "I wonder how you would have made out if you'd lived then. The men fought. They gambled. They wenched." She shook her head. "I can't really see you, Sam, except in a Brooks Brothers suit and a head filled with stock quotations."

"I might have been quite a gay blade. Other times, other customs."

Louella smiled then. "Swordplay? Dice cups? Midnight assignations? You?" And then, "Speaking of wenching, Roz Warren is back. She has a baby." She bent to her plate. She failed to see Sam's hand as it reached for his wine glass. The hand was unsteady. The glass almost, but not quite, overturned.

13

MADGE MET MARTIN AT THE DOOR. They kissed. Martin said, "I should have called you from the office but I was afraid I'd be caught in the traffic if I waited." Putting it right out like this was a kind of penance, by this much apology for the selfishness. "The thing is we've got trouble in London, two ships grounded, and—"

"When do you leave?" Madge said. Merely that.

"Tonight, midnight. You don't need to drive me."

Madge nodded then, closed the door behind him. "Have a good time. I know you will. You like London." And then, "Will you be back Saturday? There's a party at the Peters'—"

"I'm sorry," Martin said. "I don't know. You could go with George—"

"Bob and Joy," Madge said. "Louella and Sam. Ben and Mildred. And Paul and Roz. She's back. She has a baby. Let me take your briefcase." She turned away quickly, the briefcase in her hands. "And I'd better pack for you. Then we won't have to hurry with drinks or dinner."

Martin said, feeling the sense of penance strong, suddenly almost overpowering, "I can pack. I'm a big boy. You don't have to do everything for me. You—"

"Go talk to Johnny," Madge said. "Tell him about London. He'll be—excited." She was gone, up the stairs, almost running.

And later, over coffee, Martin said, "Look, about that party. I'll try to get back. Maybe—"

Madge stood up. "I'll take care of the dishes. You don't have to help. Just sit there and—relax."

INTERLUDE

THERE WERE TIMES WHEN Roz Warren, in one of her rare introspective moods, brought out for re-examination a talk she had had once with Martin Fuller because it had seemed to her then, and seemed to her now, that that single conversation cast a considerable amount of light on the person Rosamund McCartney Warren, in a sense summed her up without excessive flattery or unnecessary censure.

They had been in bed, a place, Roz thought, where probably more truths were spoken than most people believed, the social barriers down, the small deceptive niceties set aside. In bed one could ask questions, and get answers. And she, Roz, had asked Martin one of the oldest questions of man, or woman: did Martin remember the night of the Barnes's party which was the first time they met?

"Actually," Martin said, "I don't remember much about it, or you. Since you ask. You're fishing, of course."

"Not very flattering," Roz said with that slow smile that Martin, and others, would always associate with her. "I rather imagined that I had made an impression."

"It's hard to explain," Martin said. "You did, of course—far and away the best-looking female in that or any other gathering—"

"Go on. I can forgive anything else you might say now."

"You don't mean that, of course," Martin said.

"Don't I?"

"You're an enigma," Martin said.

"That's nice."

"Be quiet. What I mean by enigma is this. You're the only

16

really—breathcatching female I've ever seen or heard tell of who isn't primarily concerned with her looks. You have them—the face and the body—and you use them, but they're only a part of you, they're not everything. I don't think they're even the most important part of you. You walk past a mirror, and sometimes you stop to look, but just as often you don't. It depends what's going on in that mind of yours."

"There is a school of thought that maintains nothing ever goes on in that mind of mine."

"And," Martin said, "you like it just that way, don't you?"

"That means what?"

"You're an awful bitch, Roz."

"Flattery, yet." She watched him quietly.

"In a way," Martin said, "it is flattery, although maybe it sounds like a George Hanks kind of compliment."

"It does. I'm not sure it becomes you."

"Are you angry?"

"Not yet. I'll let you know when I am. I'm suspending judgment until I hear your definition of a bitch." There were times when she allowed this quiet, contemplative, controlled part of her to show, the part that was usually hidden deep. "Speak up, darling."

"Fair enough," Martin said.

Roz said, "In anybody else, almost anybody else, I'd say that this was a ploy, a way of—what is the phrase?—breaking things off by a clumsy attempt at insult. You're not going to disappoint me, I hope."

"I don't think so," Martin said.

"What do you mean when you call me a bitch, darling?"

And Martin had said, "You are wonderful, Roz, almost unbelievable. You are the triple-distilled essence of female—Lilith comes to mind. You are *Woman*, in italics, a kind of freebooter with the moral scruples of a cat, and with a cat's singleness of purpose. Whatever you want is right. You're Aphrodite with a kind of inner serenity that I don't think even Aphrodite managed. You are complicated and uncomplicated at the same time, if you see what I mean. Complicated, because your appetites aren't limited, they're catholic. Uncomplicated, because you never let go of something until you've achieved it. When you're hungry, you eat. When you're thirsty, you drink. When you're angry, you act. When you want to go to bed, you do that with the man of your current choice. You never forget what you started out to do, whether it's politics, or cleaning the house, or slapping down some other female who's annoyed you, or charming a new author into Paul's stable—"

"Or luring you into my bed?" And the slow smile returned.

"All of it," Martin said. "That's what I meant by calling you a bitch."

"I thought that was what you meant, darling. I wanted to hear you say it. But you disappoint me when you say you didn't notice me much that first night."

"There it is again," Martin said, "never forgetting the original point. There were too many people, and I was trying to take them all in at once. I hadn't learned then to take them one at a time."

"Madge still hasn't learned," Roz said. "You know that, don't you, darling? I don't know why I'm warning you."

"Neither do I," Martin said. "And that's another side of you. But it's true."

Martin's judgment, Roz supposed, came as close to accuracy as it was possible to come, which was a trifle strange because you didn't expect character analysis from an engineer, even one with an English professor for a father. On the other hand, it was George Hanks who understood Roz too, in his way just as thoroughly as Martin, and when you looked into George's background you found all manner of odd pursuits from truck driving and professional football and television wrestling to enormously successful magazine illustrating and the occasional painting, for his own amusement and pleasure, of delicately superb nonobjective canvases that were pure emotion—and where in this pot-pourri of interests came knowledge of people and what made them tick?

Bruce Walling, for example, MD and psychiatrist and all, had delivered his judgment once upon a time, too, also in bed, and Roz, in a rare show of impatience, had ticked him off scornfully. "You speak of compulsions," she had said, "but all you're doing is giving something a name and pretending that you've explained it. Any number can play that game. For example, was it compulsion that brought you into my bed, some deep-seated quirk arising out of the fact that you sucked your thumb when you were a baby, or didn't suck your thumb, and so you're in love with your mother and through her either love or hate all other women?"

"You don't understand," Bruce Walling had said. "You're deliberately—"

"Or was it," Roz said, "that after mentally undressing me at every party for the last few months you finally worked up enough nerve to find out if I'm as good a roll in the hay as your dirty little mind has been imagining? I trust I haven't disappointed you."

The periods of introspection actually accomplished nothing, nor did Roz expect them to. She was what she was, and from time to time it was interesting to stand off, as it were, and examine the whole picture of herself. She wondered occasionally if other people did the same, merely obeying, for purely practical reasons, the injunction *Know thyself*.

Once, at college where she had paid her own way by working in a dress shop and posing for a photographer of calendar art and, later, correcting papers in Freshman mathematics, all of this because she knew with a deep certainty that Rosamund McCartney either gained an education or gave up Rosamund McCartney's dreams—once, then, studying herself she had come up with a theory that amused her.

She was, she had always been, different from other girls. "The McCartney girl, the cat that walks alone." She had heard one of her grade school teachers say this, and she had examined the statement and found it true. (Strange that Martin Fuller, years later should come up with the cat analogy too.) The theory, then, a pure exercise in imagination, went like this:

By a process of adaptability, evolution, if you will, some people were born without vermiform appendices, some girls without maidenheads, some people with spines already fused, fifth lumbar to sacrum. Was it not also possible that some people were born with a pre-frontal lobectomy already accomplished, that part of the brain where the moral sense would normally develop isolated and unable to exercise control? Well? Why not? Something, certainly, had been left out of Rosamund McCartney. Except in a purely practical sense, as, for example, when an action led to punishment, the word remorse had never for her had meaning.

Her father, now dead, had stormed in futile rage. He had been unable to comprehend that his daughter, unlike the animals on his farm, could never, never be brought to heel. "You are a Godless child," he had told her once, only once.

And Roz had said, "If God is the way you picture Him, I couldn't care less." And she had added, "I think probably He is. If He exists."

Her mother, now also dead, had tried the opposite approach of cloying solicitude and appeal to a sense of compassion that did not exist. "You hurt your father. You cause him sorrow."

"And so my sitter is sore," Roz had said. "I won't cause him that kind of sorrow again."

And yet, out of her first earnings after college, out of the original sixty-five dollars a week, and later out of the two hundred and fifty the publishing house eventually paid her, she had sent home to the farm every month a check in lieu of a letter. She never understood why; in her considered opinion this single action could probably be categorized as one of Bruce Walling's compulsions—although labeling it so did nothing to explain it.

She had never had close friends of her own sex, neither girls nor women. And in her candid way she had explained this once to George Hanks, and George had understood. "When I encounter another female I consider my equal," Roz told him, "I bristle."

And George said, amused, "Knowing you, I imagine it doesn't happen often."

"Quite seldom," Roz said with complete honesty. And then, "The others, the ones who don't have my looks, or my figure, or my brains—they aren't worth fooling with because sooner or later they make me uncomfortable by gaping at me as if I were some kind of freak."

"You are unusual. You'll admit that."

"So are you, darling. In some ways we're quite alike."

"But with certain interesting differences. Shall we explore them?"

Her laugh was soft, pleased.

And because of her independence, among the women of her acquaintance it was said, and believed, that Roz Warren thought like a man, which was neither complimentary, nor true. Martin had summed it up accurately when he had said that she was *Woman,* in italics, with all of the physiological and psychological urges the title implied. The baby was final conclusive proof.

Conception had been deliberate and not at all casual. She had approached that mating with a feeling almost of humility as if all that had gone before had been mere preparation, study and exercise in the mechanics, and the delights, of intercourse. And after the event she had waited, calmly confident, until the fact of pregnancy had been established. Not until then had she even mentioned the possibility to Paul.

"Brace yourself," she told him after dinner, over coffee and the small cognac they both enjoyed. "I'm going to have a baby." *I,* not *we;* neither of them noticed the use of the singular. "And I'm going away to have it." Mona Peters' analysis was correct. "Because I'm not going to have the other women laughing behind their hands at the size of my belly. I thought Mexico. There are fine doctors in Mexico City. I've looked into it." And then, "Do you mind?"

Always he had stood in awe of her. She was the stronger, the more intelligent. He had never met a woman he considered more beautiful, and the possession of her as *wife* continued to amaze him even after all this time. There were moments when, suddenly seeing her across a room or walking towards him on the street or stepping nakedly resplendent from her shower, he found himself viewing her as an impossibly lovely stranger instead of an intimate, and at such times he pitied all other men whose wives had lost this quality of freshness.

He was not blind. He could read on other men's faces what went on in their minds when they looked at Roz; it amused him sometimes to see their clumsy attempts at concealment. If he was actually being cuckolded, and he rather imagined that he was, he took care not to find out for sure, because as long as there was doubt, and as long as Roz belonged to him, nothing else mattered. If he left the office early, if he returned from a business trip at other than the scheduled time he was meticulous about telephoning ahead, serving notice on the fine white house and whoever might be in it that the lord and master was approaching. Their marriage was the fact, substantial, solid; anything else there might be was transient, as fleeting as a picture painted on water and as quickly forgotten. His wife, and now to be the mother of his child—it did not occur to him for a single instant to doubt that it was his child she was carrying. And if she wanted to go off to Mexico to wait out her pregnancy and to give birth—
"I'll miss you," he said. And he got, as he had hoped he would, the warm, slow smile as reward.

"It will be mutual, darling," Roz said.

They spent that evening in talk, and this, too, was a continuing source of amazement to Paul, that two people, after five years of marriage could still find subjects of interest to be explored. They had one highball, scotch for Paul, bourbon for Roz, in celebration. They had a second highball for no particular reason at all except that the atmosphere was warm, and companionable. It was Roz's suggestion that they carry a third drink up to bed. "Being pregnant," she said, "doesn't—mean anything yet. In case you just happened to have ideas tonight." And she had added, "I'm going to be gone a long time."

"Funny you should mention it," Paul said. "I've—"

"I could see it in your mind, darling. I've been watching it grow all evening."

And now, months later, she was back, and with the child, a girl. "I named her Paula for you," Roz said. This was as they were driving in from the airport. "It's on her birth certificate, so, you see, there's nothing you can do about it."

"Why would I want to?" Paul said. And then, "God, it's good to have you back." And he smiled. "The verbal gymnastics I've gone through evading county questions. The news will be the local sensation."

"That's nice," Roz said. "I intend to be a model of matronliness. That will probably be a sensation, too."

Thursday

1

THE THREE DAYS before the Peters' party were an odd strained period as if the people concerned had, by some kind of telepathic agreement, established that particular Saturday night as a point in time, a kind of midsummer New Year's Eve towards which all attention was focused. Something was bound to happen.

Speaking of it later, George Hanks said to Martin, "You missed the waiting period, and I'm sorry you did because you would have smelled trouble too and we could compare notes now."

"You'll have to be plainer than that," Martin said with a flippancy he did not feel. "The Hanks lucidity seems to have come unstuck."

"Look," George said, sitting there, a can of beer in one large hand. He wore paint-stained denim shorts, and sandals, and a tee shirt that strained at his enormous shoulders. He was unsmiling, even grave in an un-George Hanks manner. "You've seen a dog, or a cat when a thunderstorm's brewing? Restless, jumpy? Well, try to picture not one but a dozen dogs and cats, all strangers to each other and all penned up together with static electricity in the air so heavy you could taste it."

"I was at the party, remember," Martin said.

"But that was the culmination. I'm talking about what went on before. Did you know, for example, that Ben Pierson followed me down to a Jersey bar that Thursday night for the specific purpose of picking a fight with me? With me?"

Martin said, "I knew Ben wasn't very bright, but—"

"He wanted to kill me," George said. "He was quite serious about it, if a little awkward." He finished the beer, collapsed the can with absent ease. "Maybe it will give you the idea."

"Did he tell you why?" Martin said.

"Not coherently, but I understood."

Martin was silent for a few moments, reluctant to speak the name. But he had to say it at last because by then facts could no longer be ignored. "Roz," he said.

George folded the beer can double, tossed it to the ground. "Of course." And then, "We're all members of the club, friend Martin. Ben, Bob Lewis, Wally Peters, Sam Barnes, you, me, all of us. And the wives are members, too, don't think for a moment they aren't, voting privileges and all."

Martin thought of Madge. He opened his mouth. He closed it again.

"Don't look so shocked," George said. "Because you aren't. Not really. Sooner or later the balloon had to go up. Anybody with the brains of a mouse could have seen it the day Roz came back, with child. Most of us just kidded ourselves. Now we can't kid any more." And he added, "I repeat, I wish you'd been here those three days. Because the roots are there somewhere."

Martin said, "Then at least I—"

"Don't be naive," George said. "I said the roots were there, not the flower or the strange fruit. You were back on Saturday, in plenty of time. You could have killed her just as easily as any of the rest of us. We're all in it together."

2

THOSE THREE DAYS NOW, the waiting period, the time of a strain that was subtle, but nonetheless there. George Hanks was, perhaps, more perceptive than the rest, a strange thing because when most people considered the bulk of

George, his solidity, they tended to think in terms of psychical insensibility to match the blacksmith muscles. But there were others who felt it, too, if not so clearly, and each reacted in his, or her, own way. The period began on Thursday morning, county time.

By then, having advanced the clock five hours, Martin Fuller was already in London and eating a luncheon his stomach said he did not yet need. His host was an assistant Managing Director of World Airlines, Ltd., a man named Brookings, friendly enough, but also firm. And there was Johnny Richards, a field service representative of Coast Aircraft, Martin's company. Brookings said, "We can't take chances. You'll appreciate that. Passengers expect to be taken in comfort and safety from one spot to another—"

"Obviously," Martin said.

"And if the fault is in the aircraft—"

Martin shook his head. "We haven't established that." He looked at Johnny. Johnny nodded emphatically.

Brookings said, "Now see here, old boy. One aircraft had to use emergency procedure in order to lower its undercarriage when it came in to land. One aircraft after becoming airborne was unable to retract its undercarriage. The fault, obviously, is within the hydraulic system. Our maintenance people—"

Johnny said, "Some of them are first rate mechanics. Some are gourdheads, same as any place else, grease monkeys who think that if it doesn't fit all you need is a bigger hammer."

There was a little silence. Brookings smiled faintly. "Refreshing, this candor," he said. "I'm accustomed, you know, to dealing with your sales staff, which is a very different thing indeed." He glanced around the table. "More coffee? No? Then—" He laid his napkin on the table, beckoned for the check, signed it, stood up. The smile was gone. "It is in your hands," he said.

Martin nodded.

"I trust," Brookings said, "that you are not concerned with saving face for your company. Because, you know, we shall accept your recommendations if they appear at all reasonable. The safety and performance of the aircraft, are, after all is said, the manufacturer's responsibility."

Martin nodded. "That's why I'm here."

"And there is, too, the matter of time—"

"As soon as we know for sure," Martin said. He hoped it would be soon, but he had learned long ago that trouble could not be hurried. Not in aircraft, because, despite all precautions of careful design and fabrication and assembly and testing, despite all inspections and overhauls and protective regulations, despite the knowledge of the men who designed and the skill of the men who flew—despite all of this the margin between safety and disaster seemed at times to be impossibly vague. And he had learned, too, long ago, that there was no evasion of responsibility.

Responsibility had been a frightening thing at first, far different in actuality from the way he had pictured it. Responsibility had turned out to be so final, so irrevocable, and if it carried rewards and satisfactions, it had also carried failures, and at first the failures, however minor, had seemed catastrophic. He remembered coming to work at the main plant one early afternoon during the last year of the war.

Bill Parsons had been his boss then, the fighter Project Engineer. There was a stack of parts, formed sheet metal parts, untrimmed, standing in the corner of Bill's office which Martin used at night. Bill said, "You were a busy little fellow last night, it seems. What time did you get home, anyway?"

Martin was unable to take his eyes from the parts in the corner. "About four." And he wanted, but did not dare, to ask why the parts were there; in his stomach and in his chest there was a kind of sick feeling just looking at those parts.

"You know anything about these?" Bill said.

"I did a sketch for them. I got the night planner to order them in Experimental." Just sitting there, the sick feeling strong, his lips and his throat dry and the palms of his hands vaguely damp.

"What are they?" Bill said. "Stainless steel, which takes a priority these days, just what in hell are they?"

Martin said, "Every ship at the terminal was tied up by Army Inspection. The terminal called me. The exhaust manifolds were burning out at the elbow in service. These were a temporary reinforcement patch to get the ships at the terminal accepted. Army Inspection bought it."

"The Army Chief Inspector turned it down this morning."

"Oh," Martin said.

"The sheet metal shop in Experimental," Bill said, "dropped whatever they were doing. They worked half of swing shift and all of graveyard turning these things out by hand. Experimental is screaming for somebody's hide."

Martin looked at his hands. Bill waited, watching. Martin said, "I thought it was the thing to do. The ships were tied up—"

"The planner conned you into it? Or the terminal?"

There had been pressure from the terminal, yes. But with the planner it was the other way around; Martin had talked the planner into ordering the parts. The responsibility was his alone. "I guess it's all mine," he said.

No one who had not been there could imagine what the factory was like on night shifts with all of the offices closed, all sources of information dried up, no conferences possible, no way to spread responsibility. On the night shifts you did the best you could, and hoped.

"The manifolds," Bill said, "are all taken care of. We've had Unsatisfactory Reports from Okinawa to France. New manifolds are coming in. Army Inspection won't settle for less. So we threw away a few thousand dollars making parts we can't use—"

"What do you want me to say?" Martin said. "I had no way of knowing, or finding out about new manifolds—"

"Simmer down," Bill Parsons said. "I'm not blaming you. You did the best you could—"

"But it wasn't good enough." And there was the crux—the knowledge of failure.

Bill Parsons turned to look at the parts. "It might have worked at that," he said, "if we hadn't had anything else."

It was hard to describe the sense of relief. Martin said nothing.

That night, after the day shift was gone, Martin and the planner together carried the useless parts out to the scrap heap. Martin bought the planner a cup of coffee. It was all he could think of to do.

He still wondered sometimes even now how the patches would have held up in service. And at times, usually lying awake at night, he remembered the sick feeling in his stomach and chest, the sense of catastrophe.

He had had it since, many times, but the feeling was no longer overpowering as it had been that afternoon in Bill Parsons' office. It was now a familiar thing, a concomitant of his job, part and parcel of responsibility. And he had learned to harness it, use it as a force to sharpen, rather than to dull, his mind.

He had learned, too, and this was something not even guessed at when the mental tools he had brought to Coast Aircraft had been shiny and bright and unused, that there was no sharp line between credit and blame, between the right way and the wrong way of doing things, that the concept of a panacea, a sudden complete solution to any problem was an illusion of inexperience, no more than this.

Between panic in the face of trouble and the feeling that somewhere there lay an instant painless remedy, was the middle way of patience and judgment and care, and calmness. This was knowledge laboriously acquired, but now ingrained, a part of him.

Driving out to the service hangar at the airport, Johnny Richards said, "The design stinks. The hose attachment, I mean. And maybe the hoses themselves are no good. And I don't blame these guys for getting jumpy. I wouldn't like to fly, either, when I had to worry about whether I could get the landing gear down when I got where I was going, or, for that matter, whether I'd lose the whole hydraulic system before I even got there."

"We'll see," Martin said.

"Why, hell yes, we'll see. That's why I screamed for you, isn't it? You're the expert. You shout frog, I jump."

Martin had to smile.

"Maybe," Johnny said, "it's some little damn thing I've missed. Maybe—"

"No," Martin said. "It won't be that simple. You'd have caught it."

"I'm not infallible. When I get in over my depth I yell for help. You're the one who can't make a mistake."

And yet, Martin thought, he had made many of them, none, so far, catastrophic. But the margin was, sometimes, so vague, so narrow. And not only in his work, but in other affairs as well, human affairs which were just as complicated as, and perhaps even more complicated than, all of the combined intricacies of aircraft manufacture and service. And for human problems, as for aircraft problems, there were no easy panaceas. And the responsibility was in its way just as great, his responsibility, to Madge, to Johnny.

He had spent most of the seven hour flight from Idlewild thinking about this. There was no panacea, no easy solution, but at least there was one first step, now that Roz was back. He had to talk to her, tell her that what had been between them had ended abruptly when she had left the county. That much was clear, and plain, and unavoidable. And he had to tell her as soon as he possibly could. And, knowing Roz, he didn't think she was going to like it. But it had to be done. Before Saturday night, if possible.

3

AFTER BREAKFAST that morning, Wally Peters went up to his tiny study and shut, and bolted, the door. There was a window, but he kept the window closed and the shade drawn even during the heat of summer. His desk faced a blank wall. Sometimes, when people asked him about his working habits, as people always seemed to ask writers, by their questions making it clear that they thought they were dealing with freaks, he would say that the tiny study, shade drawn and door bolted, represented a back-to-the-womb movement, and wasn't that what everybody wanted?

And maybe it was true, although the practical reasons were also valid. Thurber had said once that there were advantages to blindness for a writer; and that was probably true. Without sight a man would not be tempted to look at trees, or the sky, or his watch, to count the spots on the ceiling or trace the pattern of the rug or merely stare at the lettering of the typewriter keys in a kind of self-hypnotic trance—anything, anything at all to keep from committing words to paper. Because the thoughts, the concepts in a writer's mind never came out in their full glory, their meaningfulness, and the disappointment at the inadequacy of words was something you never quite got over. And so the process of writing was always a contest between eagerness to set the story down and reluctance to see the result. Hence the blank wall behind his desk, offering as little distraction as possible. But even at that he could stare for hours, and see nothing.

And this morning he knew from the start that any attempt at work was useless. Still he tried because he had to try, even cranked a fresh sheet of paper into the machine and typed the page number at the top—167, forty-three pages back into the story that was off the rails. And then he sat and thought, not about the story he was writing, but about another story he would never dare write.

Sometimes, but not now, he glamorized his brief affair with Roz Warren, added small touches and lines of dialogue that put him in the proper dominant male role. It had not been at all like that. He had behaved in a ridiculously adolescent fashion, fetching drinks for Roz at parties, commenting on her dress and appearance, dancing with her whenever it was at all possible merely for the unsatisfying pleasure of physical contact.

He was not without wit, and he could often make her laugh—an accomplishment not dissimilar to walking along the top of a fence to impress the little girl next door. Paul Warren was his publisher, as he was Louella Bloom's, although there was a vast difference between Wally's and Louella's statures, and Wally exercised far greater ingenuity in finding excuses to visit the white house than he ever had in making up stories to write and sell.

He knew all along that Roz saw through him, even if Paul did not. Even if Mona did not. But the knowledge was no deterrent. Roz, beautiful, desirable Roz with her slow smile, was a kind of magnetic pole, and Wally, out for a walk or drive, aimless, he told himself when he left the house, would vacillate, a compass needle gone wild; but in the end steadying almost inevitably on a course for magnetic north which was the white house.

He knew he was being ridiculous. He was supposed to be a grown man. He also knew that nothing, nothing would ever happen between himself and Roz, and so where was the harm? A man could think lascivious thoughts, couldn't he? As long as nothing came of it? But something did come of it.

It had been a Saturday, and Paul ought to have been home. Paul was not. He was at a booksellers' convention in Washington. "I didn't know," Wally said. "I—"

"Never mind," Roz said. And there was that slow smile. "Come in. Maybe you can help me. I tried to get the plumber, but they're always busy when you want them."

The thermostat was up, and the hot water circulator was running, and the gas flame in the furnace burned high, but the radiators gave off faint heat. "Well," Wally said, and he stared at the dials which seemed to show ample pressure, conscious that Roz watched him, even seemed to expect him to find a solution. "Maybe," he said, "if we bleed the radiators—" Miraculously, it worked; freed of air, the system eagerly accepted water to be heated, circulated.

Wally took heart. He expounded the basic theories of hot water heating systems. At length.

Roz listened, smiling. "I probably won't remember," she said, which was untrue. "So I'll have to call you if it ever happens again." Which gave him visible pleasure. And he was rather sweet. And basically so shy, in many ways like a little boy. Standing there now, basking in pleasure because he had been able to help, in his face and eyes a yearning, and in his mind a knowledge of his own cowardice—all of this Roz could see, and pity, and find curiously attractive. "Tell me," she said, "why have you never asked me to go to bed with you, Wally?"

Even now, months after the event, he still found no satisfactory line of dialogue as answer to that shattering question. At the time he merely stood, his mouth open, no words coming out.

"You've been wanting to," Roz said. It was gentle accusation. And then, with the slow smile that forgave his inadequacy, dismissed it as unimportant, "Never mind." And she took his hand. "Take me upstairs."

And now she was back, and the torment had begun again, and he sat and stared at the blank sheet of paper with its single, ridiculous number at the top meaning nothing, a symbol of sheer bravado. He tore the sheet from the machine, crumpled it, tossed it in the wastebasket. He pushed back his chair and stood up, uncertain still. As he unbolted the door he told himself that he still had a choice—he could turn left, towards the bathroom, get a drink of water, say, and then go back to the machine pretending all along that this had been his goal; or he could turn right, towards the stairs. But he was only kidding himself again, and the knowledge was bitter.

Mona was on the telephone when he came down the stairs. A fair share of Mona's life was spent on the phone in long, aimless conversations. She watched Wally walk towards the front door, and she cupped the mouthpiece of the phone with her hand. "Where are you going?"

"Out," Wally said. "Just out."

As he walked down the drive, Mildred Pierson drove in. Wally waved at her and thought nothing more about it.

4

WHEN THE DOORBELL RANG, Mona had a brief moment of panic arising out of the necessity for decision—stay on the phone, or answer the door, because it was clearly impossible to do both. Always decisions were difficult for Mona. She was a shopper who could spend an exhausting day in New York stores, even on the rare occasions when she had money to spend, and come home empty-handed because she had been unable to make up her mind between this dress and that, or maybe it was a pair of shoes she really wanted, and weren't those bags simply beautiful? She could, and did, spend hours trying to decide which dress to wear for tomorrow's party, and in the end, long after Wally was dressed and waiting, discover that she had to, she simply had to change everything, from the bottom out because she just couldn't be seen like this.

Unpunctuality, therefore, was one of Mona's trademarks. For a time it had been common practice in the county to invite Wally and Mona for six o'clock if you wanted them, say, at eight. But the practice was discontinued because there was no accurate way of predicting just how late Mona was going to be. And everybody liked Mona. She was so sweet, and so flighty, so like a gay little girl, really—which, in fact, emotionally she was.

It took a George Hanks to be brutal to Mona. He had met her and Wally at his door at nine o'clock one night when they had been invited for one of his superb dinners at seven. "We've had dinner," George said. "Sorry. Maybe you can come some other time." And he had closed the door in their faces.

But you couldn't really stay angry at George, either. George was a character and you just had to put up with him, Mona explained later. Wally, who craved peace above all else, never spoke of the incident to anyone.

Mildred Pierson rang the bell a second time and then walked

in, and so, through waiting, Mona's decision was made for her. She hung up the phone with visible relief. "Honestly," she said. "I like Joy Lewis, but when she starts to talk on the phone you simply can't get her to stop." And then, "Let's have coffee, shall we? I have simply thousands of things to do. For Saturday night, you know. But I can take time for a cup of coffee."

On the sofa, coffee at hand, Mildred said, "Where was Wally going in such a—purposeful fashion?"

"The dear boy," Mona said. "He really should be upstairs working, but sometimes he gets an idea that he simply can't write another word, and so he goes for a walk."

"Really," Mildred said in her actress's voice.

"If he stays here," Mona said, "he's underfoot, always asking what we're going to have for lunch when I haven't decided what we're going to have, and, anyway, he always gets his own lunch and he knows that perfectly well." She added, thoughtfully, "And I simply don't see why he has to leave the kitchen such a mess."

Mildred said, "Ben went for a walk, too."

Mona smiled. "Did he? Maybe they'll meet."

"He puttered," Mildred said, "just puttered in the garden. He was thinking about something. I can always tell."

"Ben thinks a great deal."

Mildred searched Mona's face for mockery, found none, chose to ignore the remark. "I have an idea what he was thinking about. He wanted to take the car, but I told him I was going to use it." She was silent, thoughtful. "I think they may meet. I hope they do."

Mona shook her head. Her little girl's face was puzzled. "Where, dear? And why do you hope that?"

"That," Mildred said, "was what I wanted to talk to you about. I don't want to carry gossip, but I think it's about time someone told you the facts of life."

Mildred, at her sepulchral best, was just too, too dramatic. Mona giggled. "I know all about the birds and the bees."

"Do you?" Mildred said. "Do you, really? Because I don't think you do at all."

5

SOMETIMES GEORGE HANKS USED a model in his work, sometimes he did not. Much depended on precisely the effect he wanted to achieve in an illustration; some effects were better drawn out of imagination. And, of course, the market made a difference, too. What was right for *Cosmopolitan*, for example, was not necessarily good for *The Saturday Evening Post*, or, for that matter, *Playboy* or *Esquire* or a cigarette advertising account.

George worked, successfully, for them all, and if, in the opinion of the art critics and the frequently untidy people who labored at the Art Students League (where George himself had once, briefly, studied) he was considered a mere artisan and worse, a man who sold his talent for a mess of pottage, the knowledge caused George no torment. Among other things, he believed strongly in paying one's own way in human society, and the concept that artists were precious, unappreciated superior beings to be supported by a Philistine public moved him to undisguised scorn. He had never applied for a Fulbright, a Guggenheim or any other grant.

Oh, once upon a time he had seen himself as Picasso, of course, or Gauguin in a garret. And he had done his share of two-dimensional one-eyed abstractionist portraits. He had gone through a blue period, and a red period, and a period of black-on-black—he had worn a large bushy beard during this last—but the difficulty was that he had never been able, really, to take that work seriously. After the first enthusiasm waned, there was always the mute canvas remaining as testimony of that spent enthusiasm, and sooner or later he had found himself laughing aloud at the solemn pretentious pomposity the canvas expressed, and it was this laughter of his own which violated George's code of behavior and led him at last to his present, pleasant work.

If he had ever tried to put a single name to that code of behavior, which he had not, he would probably have called it professionalism. It was not to be found in books; it was a personal thing, built up out of many experiences.

He had grown up large, for one thing—larger than lifesize, someone had said once. He was not overly tall, an even six feet in his bare feet; but immensely broad, and solid, at his full growth some 240 astonishingly nimble pounds. And, within the limits of the human body, indestructible.

Early youth was a bad time for George. It was difficult to learn, for example, that his physical strength was far too great to be used. He could, and on several occasions did, cause other boys fairly serious bodily harm without in the least intending it. The result was a kind of inner withdrawal, not extending to athletics but to the times away from them. He liked to sit alone, watch things, think about them, sketch them. From the beginning sketching had been as natural as seeing. He liked to tell himself stories and illustrate them secretly, working with infinite pains until he was satisfied with the result. Until he was well into college he was always a trifle ashamed of these lonely tendencies.

At college, on a football squad not distinguished by its Simon-pure amateurism and consequently stocked with large, active and durable young men, George never, never allowed himself to take part in the locker room horseplay that went on from time to time. He was afraid he might hurt someone. On the field it was different. There you used your force and your speed and your skill unstintingly, because that was what you were there for, wasn't it? In a sense, the feeling of professionalism had already begun. And yet, even at college, football was a game.

Going to the pros was like walking through a door and closing it behind you forever. It was not that he, like so many highly publicized All-Americans, found the transition almost impossibly difficult. He did not. He was competent in any company in his first pro year. By his third year he was superlative. And the difference lay partly, of course, in growing physical skill and strength and increased knowledge of techniques, the ability, for example, to diagnose a play almost before it began and react instantaneously in his explosive way. But a part, a large part of the difference lay, too, in a change in attitude, or, at least, a hardening of a conviction until now fluid.

Football was no longer a game. It was a business, a vocation; to the men who practiced it successfully as important a vocation as, say, law or medicine or the selling of stocks and bonds. If you took your work seriously and did it well, and the second was impossible *without the first,* you could hold your head up in any gathering, look any man in the eye without shame. If some people were contemptuous of professional athletes, why, that was unimportant, even amusing, because uniformed opinion is always somewhat ridiculous to the man who knows.

That the business of pro football was temporary, age the limiting factor, was also unimportant. It was a means of paying your own way while you prepared yourself for other things—for some, law; for others, business; for some, of course, nothing but dreams of past glory. For George, no longer ashamed of his lonely tendencies, it was art in one form or another that was the goal.

And off-season pro wrestling helped, too, and to that he brought the same attitude. Take your work seriously; never yourself—it was a dictum many Very Important People could, and did not, remember with profit. Professional wrestling was a fake? Nobody argued the point. Acting on a stage was fake, too, and if the two pursuits had not the same social status, where, actually, was the basic difference? Within the limits set by the script, what went on inside the ring was real—not the grunting and the stomping, the grimaces and the snarls, but the quickness of hand and eye, the swift knowledgeable application of leverage—and if the public thought otherwise, the men in the business knew better and could take pride in their performances, secure in the judgment of their peers. The basic attitude of professionalism was the thing that mattered; most people, whatever their occupation, never stopped thinking like amateurs.

And it was as true in magazine illustrating as in anything

else. If people smiled at the thought of George Hanks wielding a tiny paint brush, why, that was all right; George thought it was pretty funny himself that whoever arranged these things had gotten his signals crossed and stuck an artist's mind in a longshoreman's body.

And let the art critics and the art intellectuals look down their noses if they chose. George was used to that, too, and harbored no malice. Nor did he repay contempt for contempt, *per se*. His views of art were basically traditional, but that was not to say that he was scornful of those who thought, and practiced, differently. His scorn and contempt, were reserved for those who called themselves artists and were merely pretentious dilettantes whether they copied Rembrandt or flipped paint at a canvas with a putty knife. It was the attitude, not the direction of the art, that was important.

Every man chose his own jury, and by the judgment of that jury could, and did, consider himself a success or a failure. And the jury of George's choice, informed opinion within his own field, did not look down. They looked up. A magazine art director had once put it into words. "The difference between your work and most others," he had said, "is conviction, emotion, call it what you will. Your pretty girls are what we all carry in the back of our minds and never seem to see on the street." And he had smiled. "You believe in them, don't you?"

"Why, hell yes," George had said. "I lust after every one." Which was not precisely true, but close enough.

He had a model this Thursday morning. She had taken a train up from New York, and he had met her, driven her back across the broad shining river. And she prattled. "I just love the country. Don't you?"

George disliked prattlers. "Which one?"

"Why, why this one, of course."

"Which part? It's a big country."

"I meant here, out of the city, trees and things."

"Oh," George said, "is that what you meant?"

And the model, whose name was Gladys, glanced at him and

wondered if he was kidding, or if anybody could really be that square. From other girls at the agency she had heard quite a bit about George Hanks. They all said he was a character. But in her profession it did no harm at all to be able to say that she had posed for George Hanks, and so she was silent, if a trifle uneasy.

The silence did not last. "What do you call this—this part of the country? I mean, it has a name, doesn't it? Like Manhattan or something?"

"Welcome to Quidnunc County," George said.

"That's a funny name. I've never seen it on a map or anything."

"It isn't on a map," George said. "It's the original Indian name." His lips did not even twitch.

His studio was large, and comfortable, and it was obvious that he lived in it as well as worked, and lived well, which, of course, he ought to do with all the money he made. "You can dress in there," George said. *There* was a bedroom with adjoining bath, the furniture of the kind, and with the soft mellow glow, that you saw in some of the antique shop windows on Lexington Avenue or 57th Street, the expensive antique shops. Gladys was impressed.

"I brought three swim suits," she said. "I didn't know which one you'd prefer."

"Put one on and we'll take a look."

And when she appeared in the first suit, George studied her without enthusiasm. "No," he said.

And to the second one also, "No."

To the third, after scrutiny, "Oh, hell. Take it off. I'll paint one on you in the picture."

He worked fast, with a sure touch. The model—he thought of her this way, not as a girl named Gladys, not even as a person—had a good body, good breasts, and legs that had knees; and not, thank God, the kind of caved-in hips the photography boys chose for their fashion ads. And she held a pose well, even with a fixed smile on her rather vacuous face. (The smile and the face he would alter in the picture, but so deftly, so subtly, that Gladys, seeing the finished product, would wonder, even marvel at her own loveliness.)

George was considerate, too, always remembering in his professional way that posing was hard work, that muscles tired. They took one break. George smoked a cigarette and studied his easel. They took a second break. "Want some coffee?" George said. "Or a drink? Whatever?"

"Do you have any sherry?" Gladys said. "I'd love a glass of sherry. I don't like for a girl to drink too much, do you? I mean a girl has to watch herself, and if she drinks too much—"

"Sherry," George said, "coming up." He brought it to her, with iced coffee for himself.

"May I—" Gladys began.

"See how the picture's coming?" George said. "No. I'll show it to you when it's done."

"After you paint the swim suit on?" Gladys giggled, sipped her sherry. Her eyes watched George over the rim of the glass. He was a character, no doubt about that.

It was then, the sherry raised to Gladys's lips and the iced coffee glass in George's big fist, a clubby scene, that Ben Pierson strode in.

Ben was a tall man, and thin, with a fine deep voice, and awkwardly solemn gestures. On television he was usually cast as a judge, occasionally as a butler. He knew, and sang well, Spanish Loyalist songs. To George Hanks, Martin had said once, "There's nothing wrong with Spanish Loyalist songs. If I'd been at all interested in politics or world affairs in those years, I'd probably—I'd almost certainly have been sympathetic to the Loyalists. But I wasn't. And it was twenty-five years ago, and I wish to hell Ben would find a cause that's current if he has to have a cause."

"You miss the point," George had said. "Everybody else is excited about nuclear fall-out or world disarmament. But Ben has to swim upstream. That's what gives him his charm, if you can call it charm."

"He's a depression radical," Martin said, "and his ideas are twenty-five years from making any sense."

George said, "He doesn't live entirely in the past." And there was that happy gleam in his eye again. "He has his current enthusiasms. One, at least."

"What?" Martin said.

"Roz Warren. He belongs to the club, by that much a conformist. Ben's trouble is that with Roz, as with the Spanish Civil War, he can't believe the final shot has been fired. But it has."

Martin thought of Roz, and of Ben. "That I can't believe."

"Which part of it?"

"That she, Roz—Migod, with Ben?"

"Ben wears trousers."

"Now, look," Martin said. "I won't—"

"That Puritanical streak in you," George said. "Root it out. Cast it away. Then life becomes simpler." And, "We were talking about Ben."

"I think," Martin said, "that we finished—clobbering him."

"Not quite," George said. "Most people tend to dismiss Ben with a smile, a real-life Buster Keaton, a man utterly and completely humorless. I don't. He's an object for laughter, yes. But he is the classic form of comedy, by which I mean that there is tragedy, too."

"You're way beyond me."

"I think not," George said. "I think you're protecting yourself from reality again, refusing to look deep enough. There's a strong martyr streak in Ben. He's been trying for years to destroy himself. Maybe some day he'll succeed."

On this Thursday noonday Ben looked as if he had already partially succeeded. He was breathing hard. His eyes had a not quite sane appearance. He looked at the naked girl, the sherry glass in her hand. He glared at George. His entrance line was, "So," delivered in that fine deep voice.

"I didn't hear you knock," George said.

Ben fought hard for control. "That is not important. The important thing is that I'm here, and I find—"

Gladys said, "Well." She was suddenly, shamefully, aware of her nakedness. There was a kind of circuit-rider righteousness about Ben. She turned and almost ran into the bedroom, slammed the door.

George said, "Go away, Ben."

"I will not go away. I'll say what I came to say. And more."

"You're wrong," George said. He set down the glass of iced coffee. He moved with the quickness that was always startling in a man of his bulk. He caught Ben's thin arms in his large hands, lifted Ben from the floor without effort, carried him to the door. "I'm in no mood to argue," George said.

He deposited Ben on the doorstep, closed the door, shot the bolt. For a moment he stood there, frowning in his puzzlement, wondering just what it was that might have set Ben off. No matter. He walked over to the bedroom door. "Come on out, Toots. We won't be bothered again. Let's get back to work."

6

WESTERN UNION'S CALL awakened Madge Fuller in the last few minutes of sleep before the alarm went off that Thursday morning. The over-stylized voice read Martin's message, which announced merely that he had arrived safe in London. Madge thanked the voice, hung up, and lay back against the pillows for a brief moment of relief. Always she worried when Martin flew off on one of his trips. It was silly, she knew, but there it was. Statistics or no statistics, when your man went away the world was a large and empty place where anything could happen. Sometimes, even when your man was home—

The alarm went off, and she was grateful to it for stopping that train of thought. She got out of bed, dressed quickly (she had no patience with women who faced their husbands and families at breakfast in wrappers or worse) and went downstairs to start breakfast before she called Johnny.

And after she and Johnny had eaten, and he had gone off to do whatever boys did in summertime, and the dishes were done and the beds made and the house in order, she sat down in the living room and looked out the window over the broad river and wondered what she was going to do about Roz Warren. Now, in broad daylight, the night resolutions seemed less feasible.

Lying awake after Martin had gone (to the last he had insisted that there was no need, or sense, in her driving him to the airport) she had evolved what seemed like a reasonable idea. While Martin was away and so would not know, would never know, she, Madge, would pocket her pride and go to see Roz, woman to woman. She had even made up the dialogue. "I can't compete with you. I don't have your looks. I don't have your brains. I don't have something else that's probably more attractive than either of them—the fact that you're forbidden, that you're stolen fruit. So I'm asking. I'll plead, if you want me to. You're back now. Please, please leave my husband alone."

At this point she anticipated denial, and she was prepared to deal with that. "We can be honest. Just the two of us alone. There's no need to try to pretend." And then the hardest part of all, "I don't think I can really blame Martin. If I were a man I don't think I'd be able to take my eyes off you, either. But that's just the point. You have all the men you can possibly want. Will you leave mine alone? Please."

Now, in daylight, the scheme no longer seemed so logical, so certain of success. On the other hand, what else was there to do? Just wait? And hope? Turn her back on reality and hope that the problem would disappear?

She could talk to Martin, of course. That, undoubtedly, was what someone like a marriage counselor would recommend. Madge had never to her knowledge met a marriage counselor, but she could imagine what one would be like—either a severe, humorless, no-nonsense female in flat-heeled shoes and frustrations; or a mild, fatherly-type man with a now-now-everything's-going-to-be-all-right attitude. In either case, the advice to talk to Martin would be wrong, the wrongest. This Madge knew with deep conviction.

There had never been anyone but Martin. Oh, one or two puppy love forays, but they did not count. Since high school in California there had been only Martin. And for him, she knew, there had been only her—until Roz. And when you had known a man so long, and so intimately, and he known you, there grew up something between you that had no name, but was as solid, as real as life itself.

It was not merely love, as Madge understood the word, as people used it. Love was bright and gay and fierce, a fire blazing when it was first lighted. This other was different, qualitatively different, as Martin would say. This other was that same fire, but banked now and no longer recently lighted; it burned low and steadily and gave off a warmth the high flames could never approach, and in that steady, long warmth things happened that were almost beyond belief—as clay in a kiln turning at last, miraculously, to pottery, durable, functional, beautiful.

Madge did not pretend to know all the things that went on in Martin's mind. But some of them she did know, because she could feel their echoes within her own. Sometimes it even seemed that she could see herself through Martin's eyes, and it was on the knowledge gained in this way that she drew now.

To Martin, she, Madge, was there, always there, a base secure, a foundation on which he could build, as he had built, as he would continue to build, never forced, as most men were, to drop his eyes from time to time to see if that base was still secure. Some wives, most wives, and particularly those here in the county, thought that Madge made it too easy for Martin, never complaining, never prying, never scolding—behaving, in short, as if women had not been emancipated, an affront to modernity and equality of the sexes. Several of the local wives had told Madge as much. Several of the husbands had told her the same thing, but for a different reason—the husbands, envying Martin's domestic bliss, had hoped by infiltration to cut him down to their own status. (This was Martin's analysis, not Madge's. She had told him what the men had said, of course. After a time it had become incredulously apparent to the county that what was told to Madge would automatically be told to Martin. And vice versa. It was incredible.)

Out of the steady warmth of the banked fire this structure of their relationship had emerged, like the pottery durable, functional, beautiful. For her, Madge, to tell Martin that she knew of the Roz affair would be to chip away at the structure, flaw it. (If she knew that, what else might she know? Had she, all this time, pried and probed without seeming to? The doubts would begin.) And once the first crack were started, who knew where it would end? In Madge's mind there was not even the temptation to talk to Martin about Roz, whatever the marriage counselors might think. And so what was there to do?

The river lay flat and shining and she watched it for a time. When she and Martin had first come here, only a year ago, she had loved the river. Funny, she hated it now. It was, somehow, evil.

She stood up at last, walked to the telephone, sat down. And this was funny, too, but she didn't even know the Warren's telephone number. She had to look it up. She dialed with slow reluctance, and the phone rang three times before Roz's voice answered. In the background there was another voice, muffled, a man's voice, of course.

Madge said, "This is Madge Fuller, Roz. I—"

"You," Roz said, "in your way are welcoming me back, too?"

Madge took a deep breath. "Martin's in London," she said. "Before he comes back I'd like to—talk to you, if I may. Alone."

There was a little silence. In the background the muffled, man's voice began again, a timpani introduction to a new movement. Roz said, and her voice was no longer brittle or defensive, "Will tomorrow be all right? Tomorrow afternoon? Say at four?"

"Thank you," Madge said, merely that.

"Do you drink tea?" Roz said. "Or have you fallen into the county martini habit?"

"I drink tea," Madge said. And then, again, almost humbly, "Thank you." She hung up. It was done now. No drawing back. She looked at her watch. Twenty-four and six—thirty hours to wait. It was going to be hard to think of anything else.

7

LOUELLA BLOOM BARNES believed in regular exercise, particularly when she was working. Rain, shine, sleet or ice she walked, not always at the same hour and not always in the same direction, but always in the same way—head up, her not inconsiderable bust jutting forth like a double bowsprit, striding briskly. "Quite a sight, our Louella," George Hanks had said once to Martin. "If only we had rubberneck buses out here, she'd be one of the points of interest. 'And here, ladies and gentlemen, comes Louella Bloom, the famous novelist. There she goes.'"

Louella did not see well at a distance of more than twelve feet, but vanity forbade glasses except, of course, when she was driving (Louella was a determinedly safe driver, merely causing, rarely being involved in, traffic accidents) and when she was reading, or working.

She was an omniverous reader, with a well-stocked, and heterogeneous library—Richard Eberhardt and E. E. Cummings cheek by jowl with Raymond Chandler and Santayana, as an example. Her collection of seventeenth-centuryana was the delight of Parke-Bernet in New York and Christie's in London. What Louella read, she remembered, in detail and with accuracy. If she distorted events for purposes of story, she was meticulous about announcing the anachronisms in the introduction to each novel. (It was Paul Warren's opinion that nobody bothered to read these apologies, and sometimes they took up as many as four pages that could otherwise have been eliminated, but if that was the way Louella wanted it, and she did, then there was no more to be said. No publisher in his right mind argued with an author who could string best sellers together like beads in a necklace.)

Louella had a dark, lush, beauty (in her youth, Rebecca in Ivanhoe had been her ideal) and the uncompromisingly honest mind not infrequently found amongst Jewish intellectuals. "She is quite a girl," George had told Martin. "Don't ever underestimate our Louella. Maybe she takes herself a little too seriously, but don't let that fool you into thinking she's a stuffed shirt—or maybe stuffed bosom would be the better phrase. She isn't. She's a pro. Not many people are."

And he had expanded the personality sketch. "She lives in a kind of dream world, true; but, then, if she didn't have worms of some kind crawling around, she wouldn't be a fiction writer. She specializes in big-breasted females and castles and horses and men with swords, but she does them better than most—with real enthusiasm, probably because she's writing about herself, an idealized Louella. I think she keeps Sam around partly as an abrasive, and when she gets sore enough from rubbing against him, she goes off deeper into that dream world and writes a book about the way things ought to be—dashing hero mad with love and lust, and in Louella's mind they are, or ought to be, synonymous, and herself on a pedestal but not really out of reach. Again, don't get me wrong. About her feelings towards Sam, I mean. He doesn't measure up to the heroes she writes about, of course, but that doesn't mean that Louella is indifferent to him. Who knows what goes on between any husband and wife? Sam is hers. I have an idea she'd fight to keep him. God knows why. Sam is an ass."

On this Thursday morning, Louella turned right at the end of the long drive, and strode briskly along the river road. She passed Wally Peters walking in the opposite direction, and they nodded, one strolling writer to another. She passed the Peters's house and noticed Mildred Pierson's car in the drive, and thought, with accurate near-contempt, that gossip was being exchanged over coffee inside.

Louella was of, and yet not of, the *kaffeeklatsch* circle. That is to say that when she was not working Louella occasionally indulged—talk of clothes and gardens and village affairs had a certain limited appeal. But when she was working she held herself aloof. The result was that she was on the periphery, no part of the hard core, a kind of auditor at the scandal course.

She walked on, breathing deep, taking pleasure in the exertion. Joy Lewis, backing her car out of the driveway, almost ran Louella down. There was a brief period of minor confusion. Then, "Sorry," Joy said in her calm way. "I was thinking of something else than my driving. Not very smart of me, I admit."

Louella agreed that one should always exercise caution when behind the wheel of a car. She also pointed out that no harm had been done. She prepared to resume her walk.

Joy said, suddenly, unexpectedly, but still in the calm voice, "What are we going to do?"

Louella's black eyebrows rose. "Do? About what?"

"Roz Warren." Joy's hands on the wheel were not quite relaxed; it was the only sign she gave of emotion.

"I don't think," Louella said, "that there is anything anyone can do about Roz Warren." She paused thoughtfully. "I had a cat once, a beautiful cat, intelligent, affectionate, everything a cat could be. She came into heat, and squadrons of tomcats came around, lurked in the bushes, yowled at night, and daytime, too, and, I'm sure, provided everything tomcats could provide, and still my cat stayed in heat. It was appalling, the carryings-on. I think every tomcat in the neighborhood, and there were more of them than you'd believe, tried, and failed. Miss Potter stayed in heat, and the tomcats stayed around. Eventually I had Miss Potter spayed. It was the only solution."

"It's a thought," Joy said. "Only it's probably illegal to kidnap her and have it done, and it probably wouldn't do any good anyway."

"As I said," Louella said, "I don't think there is anything anyone can do about Roz Warren. And I don't intend to try."

Joy studied her hands on the steering wheel. "Short of murder," she said, her voice still calm, "you're probably right, there isn't anything." She looked at Louella then, studied her. "Suppose," she said, "just suppose that Sam were involved. What then?"

"I've never liked hypothetical questions," Louella said. "And now—"

"Wait," Joy said. And she was silent for a few moments, weighing reluctance against need for support. The scales tipped without hesitation. "Well, he is. Sam, I mean." And with the first faint display of emotion, "That's one of the county's troubles. Everybody knows all about everybody else. It's only when it comes to yourself that you're sometimes ignorant, or naïve." She raised her head again. "I don't mean just you, Louella. It happens to all of us. I knew about Sam and Roz long before Roz went away. Everybody did, but you. And now she's back."

There was a brief silence. "I don't believe it," Louella said then. "And I don't like your saying it. There are names for that kind of thing."

Joy said, "I won't pretend I told you for your own good. I wasn't being noble. I was, I am being desperate." Her voice was calm again. She rubbed one hand lightly on the rim of the wheel. "Suit yourself, Louella. Believe what you want to believe. I'm sorry I almost hit you with the car."

Louella continued her walk, but not for long. She strode back to her fine house, and closed herself in her study, sat down at her desk which, like Wally's and for the same reason, faced a blank wall. Five manuscript pages before lunch; five more during the afternoon—this was her working schedule, and she adhered to it strictly.

By dinnertime this Thursday she had not managed to put a single word on paper. She had not, as a matter of fact, even been able to think about the seventeenth century.

8

AT LUNCH in Hoboken in a little place the copy chief remembered from Prohibition and was, fortuitously, still there and open this Thursday, Bob Lewis uncoiled gradually. The Barker Manufacturing Company presentation had been a strain. One martini helped. A second helped more. "That son of a bitch of a cousin of the president," he said, "the sales manager who thinks he's a hot shot on advertising—" He shook his head.

"I thought," the copy chief said, "that once or twice you were going to clobber him. Never mind. You made him look silly in the nicest possible way. I think Old Man Barker got a kick out of it."

"Do you?" Bob said. After that kind of ordeal you felt empty, drained, eager for encouragement of any kind, whether it meant anything or not. He knew that the copy chief understood this, and he didn't care.

"I think," the copy chief said, "that we're in, boy. That's what my crystal ball reads."

Bob said, "I think so, too, and we may both be wrong." This last was mere offering to the gods, knocking on wood, expression of instinctive dread of *hubris*. He did not believe for a moment that they were wrong; he was convinced that they were in. In this business you learned one thing, if you learned nothing else: the trick was to be optimistic right up to the moment of failure, because, in that way, you had only one disappointment to suffer instead of days and weeks of gnawing doubt. Pessimism during the waiting period between presentation and answer could drive a man into the booby hatch. In more than one instance it had. You won your ulcers soon enough merely from the day-to-day pressure. Ulcers, or, say, persistent rectal itch; Bob knew one account executive no older than he who simply could not sit still no matter what the medicos tried.

The copy chief said, "Well, back to the salt mine. You're coming in?"

Bob had thoroughly intended to go back to the office; he had not even considered that he might, if he chose, exercising an agency Vice President's occasional prerogative, decide the hell with it, he'd had enough for one day. It was the question, innocently put, that brought the possibility to mind. The possibility, and the possible ramifications.

It was early yet, and Paul Warren, a methodical man, was never home before six at the earliest. And Joy knew all about this Barker presentation, and if, for any reason, she were to call the office, his, Bob's secretary, would have the sense to say merely that he hadn't yet come back from Newark. So? He felt a vague stirring within himself, a kind of recklessness arising not entirely from the two martinis. "No," he said, "as a matter of fact, I'm not going back. If anybody asks, tell them I dropped dead."

"Oh, to be a VP," the copy chief said, by the implication lying in his teeth. Not for the world with a pink string around it would he have accepted the responsibility that went with the title of agency Vice President. He had found his niche years ago, and he liked things just the way they were—the pleasant home in Darien, the garden, his plump, unintellectual wife, and the prospect of a retirement he expected to live to enjoy. Standing, he smiled down at Bob who was not, really, much too old to be his son. If he had ever had a son. "You did a fine job, boy. Go out and get roaring drunk. Or find yourself a good lay and then get drunk. You deserve it."

"Do I?" Bob said. And then, "Thanks." Encouragement from any source was wonderful, even if it didn't mean much.

9

IN LONDON it was nine-thirty Thursday evening. Johnny and Martin had had dinner. They sat now in

Martin's hotel room, blueprints scattered on the floor, the aircraft service manual and specifications book lying open on a table, Martin's neat, penciled notes on his lap.

Johnny Richards said, "You know, I'm a bourbon man. Always have been. And I can never get over the idea that when I'm drinking scotch I'm drinking medicine." He had a glass in his hand.

"Alcoholic therapy," Martin said. He smiled. Then, "So we've demonstrated that the big hoses are all right." He studied the figures in his notes.

"I ruined three of them on the test stand," Johnny said. "We'd better remember to get them replacements. The weakest failed at eleven thousand pounds, which is over double maximum surge pressure. And none of them failed at the fittings. The hose itself ruptured, shot out a little squirt of hydraulic fluid and the pressure dropped to zero." He paused. "Thank God we weren't dealing with air pressure. Eleven thousand pounds letting go would have torn up the pea patch." And then, "So? Do we know any more than we did?"

"Just that one little thing," Martin said. "The hoses themselves are all right."

"On a test stand," Johnny said. "Maybe on the aircraft it's something else again."

Martin said quickly, "Had the fittings failed on the two ships that had trouble?" He was thinking of harmonics, that dreadful force that sometimes crept in undetected, not even guessed at until suddenly, inexplicably, metal failed where all calculations showed that metal could not fail.

You struck a certain note on a violin and across the room a wine glass shattered—that kind of thing. If the wine glass was resonant to a particular pitch, would vibrate to it, the wine glass would inevitably shatter itself if the violin note at that pitch were prolonged.

Martin had seen it once during the war in an aircraft engine being developed for production. Every aircraft that flew with those engines came to grief—cowl panels split, starters and generators were shaken loose, even forgings failed in parts of the aircraft that had no connection with the engines. Until the source of the trouble was found—the almost imperceptible vibrations from the engine crankshaft broadcast with the persistence of the stroked violin note—no remedy was even temporarily successful.

"The jugheads," Johnny said, "replaced the hoses and everything else they could think of, checked out the whole hydraulic system and were ready to start flying again when Brookings said no, we'll call in the factory people." He spread his hands. "You're thinking of vibration?"

"I hope that's not it," Martin said. "We're in trouble if it is."

Johnny finished his drink. "It can't be. Only these two ships have had hydraulic problems. If it was vibration it would have turned up all over the place way back during first flight tests. You know that." He frowned at his empty drink, set it down. "It's not like you to borrow trouble. What goes?"

"I'm tired, I guess," Martin said. And he was trying to hurry, and he knew it, even though hurry was not possible, or safe. The knowledge irritated him.

"Then let's call it a day," Johnny said. He stood up. He grinned. "That makes it night, doesn't it? And nighttime is fun, even in London." His grin spread. "Did you ever notice that all English girls are named either Daphne or Cynthia? Just the way all English men are named Peter?"

Martin smiled faintly. "I hadn't noticed. Have fun."

Johnny stopped, his hand on the door. "I still say the design stinks. You ought to try attaching one of those hoses yourself sometime. You stand on your head and even then you can't see what you're doing, or what you've done. I'm not trying to hurt engineering's feelings, but—" He flipped his hand. "Night, night." He was gone.

Martin looked at his watch. It was quarter of ten, which meant quarter of five at home. He wondered what Madge would be doing. He wondered if George Hanks might even now be strolling up the path bent on a drink, and talk, just letting Madge know, in his offhand manner, that he was there, sort of keeping an eye out for her while Martin was away. George was like that, for all of his belligerent independence. It was not that George had a heart of gold; he did not. But he liked Madge, and Martin.

Martin gathered the blueprints, stacked them with the service manual and his notes. He began to undress. Quarter of five at home. To his own body and mind, after only this brief time, you would think that it ought to be quarter of five here, too. But it wasn't. He had a quarter-of-ten tiredness, illogical or not. Maybe in the transition in space, moving three thousand miles eastward, you also actually made the transition in time, lost the five hours out of your life, and your mind and your nerves and your muscles made the rapid adjustment. It was an amusing concept. Did you, then, gain five hours of living when you flew west? Maybe immortality awaited the first man who got into a fast jet and started west and just kept on going, around and around the earth? You could play with a thing like that almost endlessly.

He took one last look at his watch before he turned out the light. Ten o'clock; it was now five at home. He wondered what Roz Warren was doing, three thousand miles and five hours in time away. This was his last, guilty thought before sleep came.

10

MONA PETERS waited until Wally walked in the front door before she had her hysterics; she had no intention of wasting emotion on an empty stage. "Well!" she said, and there was that in her voice that widened Wally's eyes, and then narrowed them. Mona said, spacing the words for shrill emphasis, "Did you have a good walk, dear?"

Wally closed the front door. "What's wrong with you?"

Mona addressed an invisible audience. "He asks me what's wrong!"

"Well, what is?"

Mona breathed hard. She blinked rapidly, and tried hard but she was unable to produce tears. "Oh, you!" she said.

Standing there, watching her, in effect seeing through her as he had seen through her often enough before, her childish tantrums, her small selfish machinations, her gay ebullience at parties (but rarely at home) her cute helplessness that was really immature indecision—seeing all of this and finding it at the moment too much to try to bear, he said, "Your dialogue isn't very good. And you're overacting."

It was rare that he tried deliberately to hurt anyone. He was a peaceable man, preferring to bend with provocation whether physical or mental, not turn the other cheek, but move away, out of range. And it astonished him now that he should react like this, and yet he knew the cause. "If you have something to say, say it. Otherwise, what's for lunch?"

It was the casual brutality that shattered her, rather than any deep unhappy emotion of her own. She had intended to use what Mildred Pierson had told her, whether true or not, as a club, another useful weapon added to her arsenal. She had expected great things of it, a continuing effect; she had foreseen that in weeks, even months to come, mere mention of the subject would be enough to reduce Wally to pliability. His attitude now was simply unbelievable, almost frightening.

"Well," Wally said, "I asked a question. Is there anything for lunch?" It was late afternoon, but the incongruity escaped both of them.

Mona opened her mouth. A wail came out, a child's wail of sheer frustration; it rose almost to a scream. She turned and ran for the stairs, her high heels tapping like angry castanets. She flew up the stairs and down the narrow hall to the bedroom. She slammed the door, locked it. And there, at last, with no one to see or be moved, no audience at all, the tears began, and would not stop.

11

LOUELLA ACCEPTED the drink Sam mixed for her. She set it down, untasted. "How was the market today?"

Sam was not without humor, although he rarely smiled. He smiled now. "Which do you want, Dow-Jones analysis, Standard & Poor's, or the *Times* averages of fifty most active stocks? And the volume was 3,219,000 shares."

"Is it funny?" Louella said. She had been serene in her belief that she knew people, understood them; after all, she wrote about them. And for years she had watched Sam, studied Sam sometimes in the manner of an entomologist studying something impaled on a pin. It had never occurred to her to doubt that she knew Sam thoroughly, inside and out, his weaknesses which were many, his strengths which were few but the more precious for their rarity. All other emotions aside, she was puzzled now, and disappointed in herself, her lack of acuity. And, adding to the inner confusion, she was conscious of a kind of mental dichotomy —that dreadful, overused word.

One part of her mind, the part that dreamed and studied and weighed and evaluated and lived vicariously, the writer's part— this continued to function in its detached fashion, watching herself, Sam, the entire scene, storing it up in memory as something to be brought out later, set down on paper, *used!* She tried to stop it, and she could not; it was part of her and yet autonomous, and at the moment she hated it. She had read once that Goethe in the act of copulation had, upon occasion, tapped poetic rhythms with his fingers upon his mistress's back. Louella had been shocked beyond words that anyone could be so callous. And now part of her mind was behaving in the same monstrous fashion, while the rest of her—merely another segment of the peepshow—seethed and hated and suffered.

She said, calmly enough, "I repeat, is the stock market really funny to you, Sam? Is that why you're smiling? Because I thought it was the one serious thing in your life. Have I been wrong?"

His smile was gone. "There are others. Some of them even more serious to me." And he sat quiet, puzzled at the direction the conversation was taking, waiting for Louella to give him his next cue.

There was silence. It grew, stretched taut. Louella's eyes did not leave Sam's face. Sam said finally, in a kind of desperation, "Are you measuring me for a sword, Louella?" And that seemed to break the spell.

Louella dropped her eyes. She appeared to see, for the first time, the drink he had mixed for her. She picked it up, sipped it, set it down again. "No," she said then, "not exactly that, Sam. I was just—wondering."

"About what?"

Her uncompromising honesty would not be denied. And still that dreadful part of her mind watched, and listened, and remembered. She tried desperately to behave in a manner memory would not shame. "Tell me," she said, "tell me honestly, Sam. Is she good in bed? Is she—better than I am? More satisfying?" And she watched Sam's face begin to come apart, like a photograph over-enlarged, and she wanted to turn her head away, she wanted not to see, but she could not help herself. She sat quiet, watching, evaluating, remembering, and hating herself that it should be so.

12

THE MODEL, Gladys, thank God, was gone. For a brief time after Ben's appearance, and ejection, she had been subdued. She had even come out into the studio in answer to George's summons with a robe clutched tight around her as if she were Eve and had just eaten the apple of shame. It had taken a little time to get back to the impersonal artist-model relationship, and when that was accomplished her prattle began again more voluble, even, than before. By the time the light began to fade and George stopped work, he would not, for the world, have stood any more of the girl's company. He phoned for a taxi and paid the brigand his six-dollar fee to take Gladys across the bridge and put her on the train. And then, by God, he needed a drink.

He made it strong, bourbon on the rocks in a double-sized old fashioned glass. He drank a part of it before he even moved from the buffet that was his bar. Eventually, and inevitably, he returned to the easel and stood in front of it studying the work with an objective eye. He supposed he knew what he was going to see.

The face was Gladys, an idealized Gladys, the vacuousness magically softened to sweet naïveté. But it was not at the face that he looked.

The body was not Gladys. Oh, the changes there were no less subtle than in the face—a mere lifting and ripening of the breasts, a rounding of the waist, the faintest of alterations to smooth the lovely curves of hip and flank and long, clean legs. Gladys had smiled, pleased, when she saw it. Roz Warren, George thought, would have smiled, too, but for an entirely different reason. Roz would have recognized the body because it was her own, almost photographically exact, needing no idealization, no tricks to add to its allure.

George stared at the picture for a long time. The trouble was that a man carried memories in his mind's eye, and his hands, wielding charcoal and brush, played their own jokes. He had not intended the picture to come out this way. Or, had he? And if so, why?

He said aloud, at last, "The hell with it." And he went over to the buffet bar and re-built his drink and walked out of the studio. He did not bother to lock the door. In the country, who did? Carrying the drink he walked up the path to the Fuller's house. Madge, he thought, would be glad of company, Martin off on one of his trips. So, as a matter of fact, would George.

Young Johnny Fuller met him at the door with that juvenile blend of familiarity and worshipful awe that always made George uncomfortable. "Pop's not here," Johnny said.

"I know."

"And Mom's upstairs. Want me to call her? Hey, Mom! George's here!" And then, "Look. Give me your arm. I'll show you something." He seized George's wrist, held it in both hands, studied it doubtfully for a moment, and then spun around and levered the arm over his shoulder and heaved. Nothing much happened. Johnny released the wrist after a time. "It isn't fair," he said. "You're too big."

"Good God," George said.

"I'm learning Judo."

"Is that what you call it?"

"Okay," Johnny said. "The guy who teaches it, up at the Y, you ought to see him do it. He'd toss you around." He paused. "At least, I think he would." And then his eyes grew round with wonder at the idea. "Hey. Why don't you come up, tomorrow, say, and you and him—"

"No," George said.

"Why not?" Sooner or later youth always came up with a question like this to which George had no answer.

George was the first person in the county Martin and Madge had met, when they moved in a year ago. He had merely appeared, first as a large arm reaching into the station wagon and plucking out Madge's heaviest suitcase, the one Martin said must have been filled with rocks, specifically uranium ore. With the other hand George caught the hanger hooks poking through the top of one of those oversized plastic garment bags. As he lifted the bag over the tailgate he studied Martin briefly. "George Hanks," he said.

"Martin Fuller." And that was the extent of the conversation until the unloading was completed.

They stood together on the porch, the three of them, Martin, Madge and George, after the chore was done. The broad river lay flat and calm, shining. The hills rising beyond the river were still green, strange to Madge's eyes after the brown hills of California. "It even smells different," she said. Both men looked at her. "I mean," she said, "it smells the way I always thought it would just looking at pictures of New England."

"New York," Martin said, "isn't exactly New England."

Madge shook her head. "It doesn't matter. I'm going to like it here, Marty. And we do thank you, Mr.—"

"I live next door," George said. He pointed with one large hand. "You walk along that path and you come to the kitchen. I'll be in it at six o'clock. I'll feed you—"

Madge said, "That's sweet of you, Mr. Hanks, but—"

"Tired?" George Hanks said. Martin, watching, listening, smiled at the artful questioning approach.

"Well," Madge said, "yes, of course, a little." She looked tired, and hot. "But—"

Martin said, "We accept with pleasure. Thank you."

"There's Johnny," Madge said. "He's around somewhere. He's our—"

"Progeny?" George Hanks said. He looked at them both. "I draw the line there. Your progeny can't be old enough to be interesting, or even tolerable. Eighteen is the minimum. Sometimes, with young females, I shade it a few years. With males, never. Feed the boy. Lead him to the television set. Then come over and we'll be adults together."

"Now really," Madge said. "In a strange house, the first night, alone—"

"You will," George said, "be able to hear him if he screams." And he had walked down off the porch and along the path without looking back. They had arrived, Madge and Martin alone, at six o'clock. George had been quite sure they would. This had been their particular beginning.

Young Johnny, brooding now, drifted off—probably to think up more unanswerable questions, George thought, not that it mattered much. George was sitting in the big chair he always occupied, sipping on his drink, when Madge came down the stairs.

She was upset. This was the first thing George saw. Her smile lacked conviction and there was a faint tenseness around her eyes. "I don't like to drink alone," George said, which was not strictly true. "And I don't think you do." Which was true. "So." He got out of the chair, went into the kitchen. When he came back he put a glass in Madge's hand. "Drink this."

Madge said, "Am I that transparent?" And then, "I guess I am." She looked around. "Where's Johnny?"

"Out of earshot, at least," George said. He settled himself in the big chair again. He buried his nose in his glass.

Madge smiled suddenly. "You're being ponderous, George. It's unlike you." Her flashes of humor were rare, always startling. And then, "Why don't you ask? That's the usual Hanks approach." She was silent for a few moments. "Or don't you need to ask? Do you know already?"

"I dislike the role of father confessor," George said, and he got for his pains another of her rare, brilliant smiles.

"A lie," Madge said. "You love it more than almost anything else." The smile disappeared. "I'm going to see Roz Warren tomorrow. Did you know that? I called her and asked for—an appointment."

"I didn't know." He was, he had always been slow to anger. He felt the force gathering now, illogical, but not to be denied. "And Martin, of course, doesn't know, either."

"Unless you tell him," Madge said. "Or Roz does." She set the drink down. "I'm going to crawl, George. On my hands and knees, if I have to. I'm going to plead. And if that doesn't work—"

"I think," George said, "that you ought to be spanked, put over somebody's knee and paddled on your bare bottom until you scream."

She smiled faintly at that. "Your knee?"

"A delight," George said.

Madge shook her head. "Another lie." She was unsmiling again. "My bare bottom wouldn't mean a thing to you."

George looked into his glass. It was almost empty. He shook it and the ice rattled. The anger he felt was a potent force.

Madge said, "You know where the liquor is."

George set the glass down. He made no other move. "You're a waste," he said suddenly, compelled by the illogical anger, "a damned waste."

"You, too?" Madge said. "You're going to join the rest of the men in the county and tell me that I give Martin too much freedom?" And then, "I'm disappointed, George."

"I'm not going to say anything of the kind. How you handle Martin is your own business. The waste is a matter of attitude."

She was frowning now, puzzled. She shook her head.

"You underestimate yourself," George said. "I think probably you always have. If you want to put Martin on a pedestal, why, that's all right. He's what the head-shrinkers would call a superior type. But so are you, only you won't let yourself admit it. You're a big girl. Stand up and think like one. You have looks, and brains, everything a woman ought to have and rarely does—"

Madge said calmly, "You're a man, George, a bachelor and not unsusceptible." She paused. She watched him steadily. "Do I arouse any lust in you?" And then, "The question is rhetorical. I know the answer." She paused again. "Thanks for the try. Another drink?"

And it was then that young Johnny burst in. "When's dinner, huh, mom? You going to stay, George? I'll show you some more judo, and—"

"I," George said, "am going out to get drunk." He saw the faint lift at the corners of Madge's mouth, strangely infuriating, a Mona Lisa-like expression. George stumped out onto the porch, down the steps, along the path. And then, around the last turning he stopped, stared.

There was a light in his studio where he had left no light. He approached the house slowly, frowning. He let himself in, looked around. No one was there. But someone had been there. The picture that had stood on the easel was in pieces now, slashed with a knife into bits and scattered around the floor as if by a child in a temper tantrum—or by a madman.

George stared at the mess. The anger remained, but its force was dissipated, overlaid by astonishment and bafflement. For every action there was a reason—George had amused himself by expounding this Hanks theory at some length to Martin one night—but in the implied viciousness of this act of vandalism he could find no root or cause. As far as he was aware, nobody hated him this much. Nobody—

The phone rang. George glared at it. It rang again, and was probably determined to keep on ringing. George walked over to it, picked it up, said, "I'm busy," and started to put it down again.

"George. George!" Roz Warren's voice, stripped of its usual composure.

George raised the phone again. "I'm here."

Roz said quickly, the words almost running together, "Will you come over, George? Right away. Please." Utterly unlike Roz, impossibly unlike Roz.

"I'll be right there," George said. As he crossed the room heading for the door he kicked angrily at two of the pieces of the destroyed picture.

There was a car in the driveway turn-around at the pleasant white house. George parked beside it. He trotted up the steps. Roz opened the door before he could touch the bell. "I'm—sorry, George." Merely that. She held the door wide and George walked past her.

From the living room Bob Lewis said, "Well, well, the cavalry has arrived? Good old George cavalry." He was standing beside the mantel. A half-filled glass was in his hand. He set it down. "I'm not drunk. Disorderly, perhaps, but not drunk. Maybe obnoxious is the better word." His eyes touched Roz. "Truth is obnoxious, isn't it, honey-bee?"

George looked at Roz. She was a little calmer now, some of the composure regained.

Bob Lewis said, "We've been having a talk, honey-bee and I." He spoke directly to George. "Honey-bee is—outraged." He paused. "In the great tradition of rescuer, are you waiting for me to apologize to the lady? Very well. I apologize. I don't mean it, of course, but there it is. Is honor satisfied?"

George said, "I have an idea—"

"That I'd better cut out? I thought you might. I'm not in favor of it. On the other hand, I'm not damn fool enough to argue the point with you. I'll go." He looked at his watch. "Paul won't be home for fifteen minutes yet. He's always careful to be oh, so punctual, isn't he, honey-bee? I'll be gone before he gets here, which wasn't the idea at all, but your—reinforcements have convinced me." He paused. "Would you lay hands on me, friend George, if I didn't go?"

"I wouldn't like to," George said, "but I might."

Bob Lewis said, "I like you, George. I admire you, too. You're that rarest of articles—an honest man. You make no pretense in your rutting. The rest of us are—dirt." He smiled faintly. "Maybe I am a little drunk at that. *In vino veritas*." He reached for the glass, and then drew his hand back. He looked at Roz. "You're the finest lay I've ever known, the finest lay any of us has ever known." He raised his hand. "Hear me out, friend George. We're all chums together and there's no reason why things shouldn't be said aloud."

Roz said, "Can you stop him, George?"

George said slowly, "I could. I won't. Let him get it off his chest."

"You see, honey-bee?" Bob said. "There speaks the honest man, the intelligent man. Maybe if I say it all now, I won't say it later in, say, Paul's presence. Maybe." He was silent for a moment. Then, in a different voice, "It isn't worth saying, after all. We all know what the lady is. The trouble is, honey-bee, that when you withhold your—favors after being so free with them, you've got to expect reaction." He pushed himself away from the mantel. "That's as good an exit line as I can come up with at the moment. I'm leaving."

He crossed the room steadily enough. He stopped in front of Roz. "Do I get a farewell kiss? No? I thought not." He faced

George. His voice altered again. "Would you have tossed me out?"

George was silent.

"I prefer to think," Bob said, "that you wouldn't. That way I have a little self-respect left after an otherwise dismal performance." He smiled faintly. "I set my hopes too high. That's always a mistake." He turned slowly to face Roz once more. "What men carry in their gonads, honey-bee, is a potent force. Arouse it, and you can't tell what's going to happen. Women, before now, have gotten themselves dead because they didn't remember that." He walked out then. They heard his car start up with a roar. The rear wheels spun in the gravelled drive as he swung the car around and drove off.

In the silence, George said, "I'll shove along, too."

"I—haven't thanked you."

"No need." He started for the door.

"George." And then, "Please stay. Let me get you a drink. Paul will be home in a few minutes, and—"

"You don't want me here when Paul comes home."

"That's silly. We haven't—done anything."

He faced her soberly. "You're not thinking very straight, Roz. You're still off-balance."

"Am I?" And then, in a different, quiet voice, "Is what you're saying true, George? I have no—friends? I can't have any?" She smiled faintly, mocking herself. "I've made my bed, and I have to lie in it? Is that what you mean?"

"I can't help you, Roz. And I'm sorry. I wish I could."

"Will you stay?"

"If you want me to."

"I do."

George said, "It won't do any good. And it may do harm."

"I'll mix you a drink."

Paul was prompt. They heard his car turn into the drive at precisely six o'clock. Roz went to meet him at the door, to offer her lips for his kiss, to take his hat and briefcase, to take his arm and hold it tight against herself as she led him into the living room. "George is here. He just stopped by a few minutes ago and I persuaded him to stay for a drink." She was overplaying it, and she knew it, and was unable to stop. "He came to welcome me home, and to see Paula."

"Very decent of him," Paul said. He was a tallish man, and not unhandsome. His dark hair was streaked with gray, and had been so since his junior year at college, and it was George Hanks's theory that the premature graying had, at least in part, molded Paul's personality.

"The head-shrinkers," George had told Martin once, "would probably shudder at my terminology and my analysis, but, then, I shudder when I listen to theirs. What I mean about Paul is this: he started living up to that gray hair a long time ago when he was really too young to know the difference between stiffness and dignity. You know how it is with college kids, they're great for nicknames. They probably started calling him Pop because of the gray hair. First thing you know, they're thinking of him as Pop, too, and so is he. He holds himself aloof from childish foolishness, studies to achieve dignity, sets his pattern of behavior at an age when he should have been still trying on all manner of roles for size. The stiffness is habitual now. I've never seen even a crack in the veneer. Maybe Roz has. I've never asked her. And all because his hair follicles got their pigmentation fouled up too soon. At least that is the Hanks theory on Paul. I have spoken."

George, now, standing broad, solid, wary without nervousness, said, "Congratulations, Paul. You're passing out cigars?"

"I hadn't thought of it that way," Paul said. He looked at Roz.

Roz said, "I'll get you a drink, dear."

George sat down again. He sipped at his drink. It had been a mistake to stay, and yet what could he have done? "What of the publishing business?" he said. "It marches?"

"Satisfactorily."

"Louella," George said, "has taken to brooding and striding up and down the river road—I gather those are good signs?"

"Louella is working again."

67

"And there is rejoicing at Warren & Co." George nodded. "I don't blame you a bit." He made a broad gesture with one large hand. "The house Louella's best-sellers built."

Paul's lips were a thin straight line. "I don't find that humorous, George."

"My inclination," George said slowly, "is to say, 'Oh, come off it, Paul.' But it wouldn't do any good, would it? The world cries for a little lightness of touch, but most people walk around looking like pall-bearers and resenting anyone else who doesn't. As a publisher that fact ought to interest you."

Roz had returned, handed Paul a drink, sat down. She was silent, almost subdued. Paul said, "Some things are too serious for levity."

"A truism. And like most of them a little specious."

Paul said, "Do you enjoy baiting me, George?"

And Roz said quickly, "Paul. George isn't baiting you. He's laughing at himself. He always is. You don't—"

"Granted," Paul said, "that your knowledge of George is— deeper than mine, I still reserve my own opinion."

George sighed. "You might as well say it, Paul." He grinned. "I'm irreverent—"

"Among other things," Paul said. And still the veneer showed no faintest crack. "I don't pretend to understand you, or people like you."

"Most people," George said, "like to consider themselves unique. No matter. Go on."

"I have never liked you," Paul said, "or your kind. You laugh at conventions, standards most decent people live by—"

Roz said, "Paul—"

George waved one hand, and Roz was silent. "Go on," George said.

"I intend to. I find you uncouth—"

"There's a word."

"—untrustworthy and rather thoroughly obnoxious." Paul paused. "I don't think what I'm saying has any effect on you.

I don't believe there are any sensibilities at all in that monstrous body of yours, only appetites."

Roz said, "You're being childish, Paul."

"Am I?"

"And not very intelligent." She stood up, all in one smooth movement. "I apologize for my husband, George."

"No importa."

"George," Paul said, "has undoubtedly been insulted by experts, my dear. His kind would be."

George finished his drink. He stood up. Looking down he said. "Do you feel better now, Paul? I hope you do." And then, "Good night." There was no answer; he had expected none. He walked to the door. Roz followed him. George said, "My idea of stopping by wasn't a very good one. I'm sorry, Roz."

"George—"

"Goodnight," George said. He walked out, closed the door quickly behind him. She was angry, and in her anger had been on the verge of saying aloud precisely why he, George, had come to the house. At least he had prevented that. It would, he thought, have kicked off a lovely scene.

He got into his car, drove slowly down the long driveway. He thought of Madge, of the slashed picture in his studio, of Bob Lewis and now of Paul—if this much showed on the surface, there was bound to be seething in the depths. And it was strange that he could find no amusement in the knowledge that sooner or later the pot would boil over. Usually he enjoyed watching a squabble as much as the next man. But not this time, and he could not have said why.

The hell with it. There was that nice little bar down in New Jersey where a man could drink his fill in peace, with no eighteen year old kids around, as there were likely to be in New York State bars, to absorb a snootful and start looking for the biggest man in the house to demonstrate how tough their liquor had made them. Although right at the moment, the way he felt about the day as a whole, he would not mind it at all if somebody insisted on starting a frolic. A little exercise would be a relief. But no kids. Kids got hurt too easily. The New Jersey bar it was. He paid no attention to the car that followed him. The roads were open to all.

The parking lot of the bar was almost empty, and the daylight was beginning to fade. George got out of his car and started around to the front entrance. He heard the skidding sounds as the car that had followed him turned in, slammed to a stop. He heard the car door open and footsteps running, and he spun around automatically, completely unprepared for the apparition he faced.

"It was funny," he told Martin the following Monday. "Comical, I mean. But it was pitiful, too. And, I confess it, frightening. Can you picture a mad sheep? A rabbit gone berserk? That was Ben Pierson."

Ben was all knees and elbows and waving arms. That fine deep voice screamed in falsetto, sounds, not words. He was upon George in a rush, clawing, scratching, mouthing. George gave him a hard shoulder that flipped him into the air. Ben landed heavily on his back. He was up again like an elongated rubber toy to launch the second attack, as violent, as vociferous, as the first.

"It must," George told Martin, "have been quite a spectacle. Pity there wasn't anyone to see."

George caught one of the long, flailing arms. He moved in and tied Ben into a neat squirming package, held him tight. The screaming had stopped, but the sounds that emerged were still not recognizable as words. Ben's breath had a sour sickly smell, and spittle flew with his heaving. George said, "Just what in hell is this?"

The struggles did not cease; the long arms and legs were all angles and unexpected joints. George applied pressure until the package was helplessly quiescent. Ben's eyes, round and somehow glazed, glared at him like an animal's.

"Simmer down," George said. The struggles began again with surprising strength. George applied more pressure. "We can keep this up indefinitely," George said. "I think you'll get tired first."

"Lecher!" It was the first recognizable word. And then, "Idolator!"

"This is my day to be called names," George said. There was disgust in his voice, in his mind. "Beat it, Ben. Get lost." He loosed his hold and shoved with his full strength. Ben flew across the parking lot, brought up short against the side of his own car.

He hung there for a moment, bent over fender and hood. And then slowly he straightened, walked calmly enough back along the car, opened the door.

George said, "Don't ever try that or anything like it again, whatever provocation you think you—" He stopped there. "Ben!" In a tone of command.

Ben faced him. He held a steel jack handle in his right hand, and his eyes had not lost their glazed stare. He moved forward slowly, a man in a dream, a nightmare.

George said sharply, "Ben! You damned fool! Ben!"

The moist lips were moving, but no sound emerged. A string of saliva rolled down the chin, unheeded. The jack handle was raised, the long arm tensed. The footsteps on the gravel were the only sound.

"Oh, God," George said. He moved then, with that incredible quickness and force, straight ahead, ducking beneath the jack handle. He felt it strike on the broad of his back, but the blow was off-balance and weak, ineffectual. He seized the arm, locked it, shook the handle free. And then he stepped back only half a pace. "God help us both." It was a whisper, no more. He hammered one large fist into Ben's belly, struck again without mercy. Ben folded, unhinged. George clubbed his fist against the side of Ben's neck, drove him down to the gravel, where he lay, sprawled, unmoving.

George stepped back, watching. He wiped his wrist across his forehead. It came away wet. Slowly he bent down, picked up the jack handle, stared at it. And then, in sudden fury, he threw it as far as he could off into the gathering darkness. "Ben," he said.

There was neither sound nor movement.

George bent down again. He hoisted the long thin body onto his shoulder. It hung limp. He carried it over to Ben's car, put it inside, closed the door. And then he walked around and got in under the wheel.

Mildred Pierson answered the ring. Her mouth opened and her eyes started to roll in her head. "For God's sake," George said, "no more histrionics. Wait till I've gone before you start emoting." He walked past her, into the living room, undraped Ben from his shoulder and straightened him out on the sofa. "I don't think he's hurt much," he said. "He's breathing all right. But if it will make you feel any better, call a doctor. Tell him Ben got into a fight." He faced Mildred, by his tone held her reasonably calm. "You might tell him too that Ben went completely off his rocker. He tried to kill me. You can ask him why."

He walked out then, without looking back. His car was down at the New Jersey bar—the hell with it, for now. Tomorrow he'd go down and get it. Tomorrow, too, he'd have to get Gladys out here again and start the picture all over. Tomorrow, tomorrow, tomorrow.

He walked home from the Pierson's house, mixed himself one more drink and carried it to the bedroom, not even bothering to clean up the mess of hacked picture scraps on the floor. He finished the drink as he undressed and got into bed. He turned off the light. For George Thursday was over at last. Thank God.

13

THURSDAY WAS NOT QUITE OVER for Bob and Joy Lewis. Bob was in pajamas, sitting on the edge of his bed. The effect of the drinks had worn off now and the hangover reaction was both physical and mental, debilitating and depressing. "And so," he said, "I lost my temper and made a star-spangled fool of myself, and George Hanks would have been perfectly justified in clobbering me, but he didn't, God knows why."

Joy was in her own bed, propped against pillow and headboard, staring fixedly at the far wall. She said nothing. She had said nothing during the entire recital, nor had she even looked at Bob.

Bob said, "Why am I telling you all this? Probably because I'm feeling sorry for myself, which makes me a fine spectacle, doesn't it? Don't answer that." He stood up, crossed the room, switched on the window air conditioner. The hum of fan and compressor was soothing after the silence. He went back to his bed, got in, turned out the light. Lying there, feeling the hangover and the sense of depression, the loneliness, he said, "No comment?"

Joy had not moved. Her eyes were still open, unseeing in the darkness. She said slowly, "I could kill that woman."

"Why," Bob said, "why, so could I, baby." Relief was a warm flood in his mind, washing away the hangover, the loneliness. "It's going to be all right, then?" Like a little boy, and aware of it, but beyond caring.

"Goodnight," Joy said, and that was all.

14
•••••••

LOUELLA WAS FRESH from her bath, and wearing the white Bergdorf nightie that showed her off, all of her, far more provocatively than if she were naked. She lay down on top of her bed to wait. The clock radio on the bedside table was tuned low on WQXR, the station of the New York Times—the music was Handel, the *Water Music,* which Louella loved. Usually each night in bed she read for a little time, but reading meant wearing her glasses, and so tonight she did not read. The door to Sam's dressing room-study was ajar. Light showed, enough light.

Sam's voice said, "You're not going to read?"

"No."

"Then I'll close the door," Sam said, "so the light won't disturb you." Louella heard him push back his desk chair, cross the room. She held her breath.

"Goodnight," Sam said. He did not even look in. The door closed, and there was only the darkness.

Louella wept.

15
● · · · · ●

MILDRED PIERSON got Ben upstairs after a time, and, by dint of clumsy struggles, out of his clothes and into bed. In the fine deep voice Ben said that he was all right, maybe a rib or two broken, but nothing to worry about, nothing at all. The scene could have been *Camille,* roles reversed.

"Sleep," Mildred said, giving the word its full measure of emotion. "Rest."

"Yes." Ben's voice was faint, but resonant.

"Gather your strength."

"Yes." Fainter than before.

"Sleep well, love," Mildred said. It was the curtain line. She switched off the light.

16
● · · · · ●

ROZ HAD A LAST LOOK at the baby. All was well; the baby slept peacefully, one tiny fist clenched. On the way to the bedroom, Roz passed Paul's study where he sat, manuscript in hand. "Goodnight," she said

Paul looked up then. "Roz."

"Yes?"

He raised a page of the manuscript. "This—isn't very good.

It can wait. I can read it tomorrow. Or over the weekend."

"It may get better as you go along," Roz said. "Read it and find out." And then, again and with finality, "Goodnight." She walked on, into the bedroom. She closed the door, and then remembered, and opened it again, because—and this was her only thought—the baby might cry in the night.

17
•••••••

WALLY PETERS SAID, "Will you open this goddamned door?" There was no answer, but there were sounds indicating that the door was at last to be unbarred. It was. Wally walked through without a glance at Mona. He opened his closet. "I want my pajamas." He got them. He walked back out of the room and down the stairs. He had slept on the sofa before, but never of his own choice. He felt rather exhilarated by the strength of the decision, almost heroic, like one of the characters in his books. The only trouble was that he had forgotten how uncomfortable the sofa could be. No matter, his mind was made up.

18
•••••••

MADGE LAY IN THE DARKNESS and watched the luminous hands of the alarm clock creep. Midnight—five o'clock in the morning in London. And sixteen hours left before she went to see Roz.

She closed her eyes and tried to relax, but sleep just would not come. She waited an eternity before she opened her eyes again. The clock hands now read ten minutes past midnight. Thursday was officially over.

Friday

1

"SOMETIMES," George Hanks had told Martin once, "we tend to forget that we aren't the only people in the county. We're quite sure, of course, that we're the only ones who count, but that isn't the same thing at all. In a sense, we're merely the frosting on the cake, or, better yet, the candles stuck in strictly for display, no good at all to eat. I suppose sooner or later everybody gets so wrapped up in himself and his own little circle that he thinks the rest of the world is pure stage setting, unreal. But we seem to do it more often, and more thoroughly, and with a kind of unconscious arrogance. You'll see what I mean when you've been here a little time."

And it was true. The hamlets and the incorporated villages, the towns within the county and the county itself had all existed for a long time before the kind of people George spoke of had ever discovered the place and begun to dribble in. But they were the articulate ones, versed in the tricks of modern civilization; they were the ones whose voices, once raised, were heard; and so their impact upon the county was out of all proportion to their numbers.

"Actually," George said, "we're a bunch of saber-toothed mice. I'm sorry you weren't here, for example, when the bridge was being built. There was more breast-beating and wailing and scurrying around than you'd be prepared to believe. Delegations invaded Albany, were repulsed, attacked again. Louella Bloom had a piece in the *New York Times Magazine* on the subject of desecration of historic countryside. Her by-line, of course, because of the weight her name carries, but actually it was Wally Peters who researched the piece and wrote it—the only time on record when Wally and Louella played in the same league. And then when the governor came down to open the bridge we staged a sort of parade of protest. I did some fine placards, and Ben Pierson directed the show, the local pulchritude, plus a couple of ringers I got in from a model agency marching back and forth behind Mildred Pierson, who was Cassandra to the hilt in a mink coat and pasty make-up carrying a sign that read, 'SAVE OUR VILLAGES.' It was great. We all agreed that it was great. The *Times,* the *Trib, and* the *Daily News* all covered it. Bob Lewis even wangled a TV spot."

"And?" Martin said.

"Nobody took the bridge away," George said. "Or the approaches to it. We had raised our fuss, and accomplished nothing, and things settled down, and everybody forgot all about it. We're about due for a new diversion of some kind. God knows what form it will take. But the whole county, the people we keep forgetting even exist, will sit up and take notice when it happens. Some of them may even manage to get themselves involved, although they'll be smarter if they don't."

2

LOUELLA DID not come downstairs for breakfast that Friday morning. Sam ate alone, his inevitable fruit juice, toast and imported marmalade, and black coffee served on the gleaming, and overlarge, dining room table. When he had finished and it was time to leave he debated briefly with himself the advisability of going upstairs to say goodbye to Louella and decided against it. He was being punished, and he would not for the world have interrupted the process.

Sam was, basically, afraid of Louella. He was vaguely aware that she was far more intelligent than he, a fact he could not understand at all because he had been brought up to believe that men were always, and in all ways, superior.

Sam earned a very solid living on Wall Street, but Louella's earnings far surpassed his, and this, too, tended to rob him of confidence even though money received for the writing of books did not seem to him money earned, but merely a kind of manna from Heaven, inexplicable, outrageous and bordering on the unbelievable. Sam could, and did, comprehend the vast sums that represented corporate earnings. But when a movie company paid *four hundred thousand dollars*—spread over five years, of course, in order to reduce taxes—for one of Louella's novels, the transaction seemed strictly in the realm of fantasy.

Even in their personal lives there was to Sam a kind of unreality about Louella. She was as American as he—more so, in fact, if one went into genealogy, as Sam had done once upon a time, confident what the research would show and aghast that it did not. And yet Louella was not American in Sam's understanding of the word, which was somewhat limited by mores, attitudes, behavior and appearance customarily found amongst the eastern seaboard upper classes—a phrase now unfortunately gone out of usage probably because of that fellow Roosevelt.

There was about Louella a kind of exoticism, an almost oriental opulence of body, and of mind, that both baffled and delighted Sam. He and Louella once had stayed at the Parador de San Francisco in Granada, and in the early evening had strolled on the hill of the Alhambra. In Louella's presence the Moorish ruins had moved him strangely. "You belong here," he had told her. "It's in this kind of setting that you fit, amongst sunken baths and eunuch slaves and string music and woman attendants to prepare you for the Sultan." He had felt a trifle foolish saying such things aloud even if they were true.

And Louella had said, "That's nice, Sam. Nice that you should say it, even better that you should feel it." And then, "Let's go back to the hotel now. Let's—hurry back."

There were times when Sam told himself that he did not deserve Louella, and almost, but not quite, believed it. He had never had the imagination to think of life without Louella, probably because there had never been sufficient stimulus to stir him to such imaginings. But he thought of it now, and had been thinking of it ever since that scene before dinner last night. And the prospect of life without Louella was frightening.

He did not know what to do to forestall the possibility, and this was frightening, too. Measured reasoning, pleas, cajolery, even argument—he had considered and rejected them all. He was helpless. He could merely wait, in dread, for whatever judgment Louella, in her exoticism, chose to deliver. And the oriental mind was capable of cruelty almost beyond belief. Everyone knew that. Sam suffered agonies of apprehension. And all because of that one woman, Roz Warren.

Sam had been brought up to believe that no gentleman should be impolite to a woman even in his thoughts. But there was no escaping the fact that Roz Warren was a bitch; worse, an adulterous slut. The world, Sam decided, would be far better off without Roz Warren. The decision gave him a little, but not much, satisfaction.

3

STANDING AT her bedroom window, still in the Bergdorf nightie, Louella watched Sam's car drive off. Her tears were finished. What remained now was anger and sense of insult.

Sam—in her honesty she understood that her anger was not directed at Sam. He was a man, hence susceptible; and Louella had no illusions that the lure of stolen fruit was less than commonly believed. Roz Warren was a beautiful woman; there was no denying that, either. Worse, Roz Warren was a beautiful woman thoroughly cognizant of her beauty, of her attraction to men. Louella imagined that Sam had been, in a sense, a small mouse venturing within a tigress's reach, as helpless, as ineffectual as that.

Sam—Sam could be forgiven eventually. But someone had to be made to suffer. Sam's evaluation had been more accurate than he knew; Louella's mind did, at times, work in a tortuous, and torturous, fashion.

She walked into Sam's dressing room-study, picked up the phone. She dialed the number and waited while it rang. The incongruity between the Bergdorf nightie and the vicious anger in her mind did not even occur to her; nor, if it had, would she have found it overly strange. One of the intriguing qualities of Louella's heroines was their ability to shift from helpless compliance to decisive, and sometimes almost sadistic, action without hesitation, or regret.

It was Roz Warren who answered the phone. Louella said, "Louella here, Roz. May I speak to Paul, please?" Her voice was calm, entirely natural.

And when Paul came on the phone, "I'm coming in to town today," Louella said. "I'd like to talk to you."

"But, of course," Paul said. "Lunch—I have an engagement, but I'll cancel it, of course—"

"No," Louella said. "Not lunch. In your office, Paul. And alone."

"Whatever you like," Paul said. And he hesitated. "Is it—something about the new book, Louella?"

"Eleven o'clock," Louella said. "I'll tell you then." She hung up.

Standing there, she looked around the room, Sam's room, his imprint plain upon it, his imprint made possible by her money—the expensive, unostentatious and unimaginative furniture suitably masculine almost to the point of monasticism, the rack of pipes Sam seldom smoked; the financial papers, books; the college anniversary reports wherein his classmates, in juvenile prose for the most part, kept one another informed of their progress through life; Sam's dressing gown, slippers and fine broadcloth pajamas—all Louella's purchases—laid neatly over a chair for the maid to put away; on the chest-on-chest a silver-framed picture of Louella taken, by a *Life* photographer, at the chalet she and Sam had rented near St. Moritz one spring. Sam's imprint, and hers, too. Yes, someone had to suffer for the—effrontery.

4

THEY HAD checked out the landing gear on both aircraft and found them operating perfectly. Still the fact remained that they had not operated perfectly in flight, and only emergency procedure had managed, in one instance, to avert calamity. "So now, what?" Johnny Richards said.

It was like a puzzle, a mystery to be solved. One by one you eliminated the possibilities. What remained should supply the answer. It was as simple, and as complicated, as that; complicated, because the possibilities could be almost infinite if they were considered, as they had to be, in pairs and multiple combinations. Still— "You don't like the way the big hoses attach," Martin said. "Tell me why."

"Because they're hard to get to," Johnny said. And then, "I know, I know—" He was grinning. "I sound the way every mechanic sounds when he's talking about how the engineers design the flying machine." He shook his head. "This is different. There's a bend in the hose—"

"Not enough of a bend to cause trouble," Martin said. "That's been checked and checked again."

"Not trouble in function," Johnny said. "I know that. I'm talking about installation. Here." He picked up one of the hoses, held it out. It was four feet long, of black neoprene, perhaps three inches in diameter, with heavy female fittings at the ends. Within the hose body were three separate layers of steel mesh for strength, the whole bonded into a solid unit. These hoses were the connection between the hydraulic pumps driven by the engines and the thousands of feet of hydraulic piping within the body of the aircraft. Hydraulic fluid pumped through these hoses at pressures as high as four thousand pounds to the square inch operated the aircraft's landing gear and flaps, supplied most of the motive force for control surfaces, opened and closed landing gear doors, mandatory functions. "Bend it," Johnny said.

The hose was, to an extent, flexible. Being the connection between engine and airframe, it had to be. But it did not bend easily. "So?" Martin said.

"You've got to bend it," Johnny said, "in order to attach it. It isn't easy—"

"But it can be done," Martin said. "Obviously it can be done." He was impatient, the fact of time beating at him, and he knew that he should not be impatient. But what Johnny said, and had kept on saying, made no sense. And yet Johnny was not a person to deal in nonsense. Long ago, years ago, Martin had put aside the conceit that an engineering degree raised a man to a level where he had nothing to learn from the shop, from the men who worked with their hands. He had no patience for engineers, and there were many of them, too many, who had not put aside that conceit. "I don't get it, Johnny." And that was the wrong reaction, too. Damn this consciousness of time running past. He, Martin, had a job to do here, and a job was a sacred thing, and had to be done right, and would the Heavens fall if he could not get home for that silly Saturday party? Well, would they? And unless he settled down and got himself and his thoughts in hand he wouldn't have a chance of getting home anyway. Why hadn't he thought of it this way before? It was as if a door had opened in his mind.

"Maybe I'm not making any sense," Johnny said. "Hell, I don't know."

"Maybe you are making sense," Martin said then. It was funny, all at once his mind was loose, easy, the impatience all gone. No matter why, or how; the fact of the ease and the looseness and the confidence was all that mattered. "Let's find out," he said. "We'll jerk one of the hoses off, and you'll put it back on and I'll watch you do it."

"Me and my big mouth," Johnny said. And then, "Okay. Let's go. I'll borrow tools from one of these jugheads, and see if I remember how to use them."

5

GLADYS, naked on the low dais, said, "I don't understand. Not that I'm complaining." She giggled. "But I thought the picture was fine. Why—?"

"Mice ate it," George said. "We have big mice out here. Hold still, woman. Suck your belly in and stick those things out. This isn't a flat-chested fashion sketch for *Vogue*."

It was Ben, of course, who had committed the vandalism, and, in a vague way, George thought that he could comprehend the motive. Pure conjecture, and yet it added up. The two coherent words Ben had uttered provided the clues.

Lecher. Ben's eyes, somehow, had been opened to the fact that he was not alone in his extra-marital possession of Roz; that George, too, was, as it were, a member of the club. Hence Ben's bursting into the studio yesterday afternoon—to find a naked Gladys sipping sherry, and what would that indicate to Ben's already outraged circuit-rider mind except that George took his fun wherever he could find it? And would not this be considered by Ben as an insult, a further soiling of the idol, Roz? Hence the second word—*Idolator*.

And so Ben, fuming, had returned to the studio after a period of self build-up. And the picture itself, Roz's naked loveliness —Roz's!—further sacrilege, had touched off the explosion.

George was satisfied that this was the explanation, and at first it had angered him, and then the anger had slipped away into a kind of pity. "We all have worms," he had told Martin once, "or we wouldn't be doing the kinds of things we do, writing fiction, painting pictures, acting. Everybody has a desire for recognition and goes about gaining that recognition in the best way he can. Some people, yourself, for example, do it in a quiet way by being good at engineering, or business, or the practice of law. Some men build themselves up by beating their wives. Some of us, whose worms are active little rascals, crave a larger stage to perform on, a greater audience to impress. So we write or paint or act—"

And Martin, smiling, had said, "Or go into politics?"

"Interesting thought," George had said. "From their behavior I think a good case could be made that some politicians do not play with a full deck of cards."

George knew (as who did not in this day and age?) the arbitrary psychiatric classifications—neurotic, psychotic, psychopathic, in descending or ascending order, depending on which way you looked at them. "Actually," he had said once, "I think it takes a mild neurosis to make anybody interesting. Can you imagine how dull, how completely predictable a thoroughly integrated character would be? His thoughts would be gray, no blacks and whites, certainly no bursts of color. He'd bore you to tears. Give me the neurotics. And I have an idea that some of the people out here, the tranquilizer-sleeping-pill-benzedrine set, have already won their junior psychotic rating. I don't think we have any psychopaths walking around loose. On the other hand, I wouldn't place a large bet on it."

Thinking of Ben now as he worked, George wondered what the head-shrinkers would make of last night's performance if somebody were to tell them. Would they give Ben his letter in psychopathology and lead him away? Or would they, in their wisdom, explain that a temper tantrum could happen to anybody and did not represent cause for alarm? George did not know the answer. He was prepared to forget the entire episode, and he hoped that Ben was too. After all, nobody had really been skinned up, although Ben probably had a sore belly this morning. Let it go, the whole stupid affair.

"Honey," George said, "if you have to go to the john, go. Don't stand there and wiggle."

6

THE COPY CHIEF said, "Did you tie one on last night, boy? Your eyes do look a little beady."

"No comment," Bob Lewis said. The physical hangover was gone, washed away by the night's sleep. But shame remained, shame at his behavior at Roz's house, shame at his childish confession to Joy. Of the two, the second was the deeper shame. It was also cause for worry.

Only Roz and George Hanks had witnessed his actual performance. As of now Bob hated them both for having seen him so far off-balance. But, hate or not, he was confident that neither of them would talk, put the story into the county grapevine to be told, retold and embellished over countless cups of coffee and early afternoon martinis; to be brought to mind for months to come by knowing smiles at parties, on the street, anywhere and everywhere. Whatever else they might be, Roz and George Hanks were not talkers in that sense. They watched, they enjoyed spectacle, but they kept their amusement quiet, locked up. Still he hated them, both of them, but Roz the more. She was the cause of his shame, and of his confession to Joy, and yet she, Roz, would not suffer at all, she would go scot-free, and only he, Bob, would suffer the punishment of indignity, and worse.

Because he still had no idea what Joy's reaction would be. There was, there had always been in Joy, a kind of still-waters-run-deep quality that baffled all attempts at understanding. Her surface moods were rare; there was a consistency to Joy that was sometimes maddening, and sometimes, like now, almost frightening. Bob thought often, and unhappily, of the night their first child, Vicky, was born.

Everything had gone wrong; it was one of those times. When Joy awakened him and said in her calm voice that she thought they had better get to the hospital he had tried desperately to react in a sensible manner, without panic. But he had trouble finding his clothes, even deciding what it was he was going to wear if he could find it—considering the lateness of the hour and the fact that he'd probably be sitting, and be seen, in the city hospital, and there were, after all, certain conventions of dress. He had even wondered if he should take time to shave.

And then the car wouldn't start, the goddamned car. The carburetor flooded easily, of course, but why did it have to pick this time? It was Joy who said that they'd better wait, hadn't they, until the surplus gasoline evaporated, and then try starting the car again? Joy, sitting there like a swollen statue, feeling God only knew what agonizing pains, but uttering no single word or even sound of complaint.

At the bridge toll station Bob found that he had no money in his pocket, none. Joy had, of course. And in addition to the toll she handed him a ten dollar bill without a word of recrimination.

Across the bridge Bob took the wrong turn and got all fouled up in one-way streets going the wrong way, ended up at last at the ambulance entrance of the hospital instead of the front. Under the circumstances it was probably just as well, but he hadn't intended it that way. Joy got out of the car calm as you please and walked in carrying her overnight case and said conversationally to the first person in white she saw that she was about to have a baby and where would be the best place?

In the confusion that followed Bob was completely, and deprecatingly ignored. People walked around him as if he were not there. Joy bore the child there in the emergency room and there was not even the drama of screams and struggles Bob had been led to expect, and thought he was prepared for, but the spectacle had upset him anyway and the only place he could find to vomit was out on the street, near his car which had already managed to acquire a traffic ticket for illegal parking.

He returned to the hospital later that morning, loaded with flowers and candy and books and magazines. Joy gave him that enigmatic smile and said that she felt fine, a little tired, but that was all, and it was sweet of him to come.

The candy turned out to be dreadful stuff, all gooey fruit inside the sculptured chocolate. The flowers were nice—white roses—but maybe they had been sitting in the florist shop too long because they started, at once and with determination, to shed their petals all over the floor. "Did you ever sit and listen to rose petals bounce?" Bob asked afterwards when he told the story, or most of it anyway, by humorous self-deprecation compensating at least in part for his shame.

As far as he knew Joy never even opened the books, and neither did Bob. He hadn't paid much attention when he grabbed them from Scribner's bookstore shelves, and *The Power of Positive Thinking* and a novel by an angry young man remained, as far as Bob knew, somewhere buried in the hospital library.

Joy did take pleasure in the copy of *Vogue*. But she had never much liked *Playboy*, and *True* merely brought back that enigmatic smile. Oh, it was a fine performance all around, and although, later, Bob tried many times to find out what Joy thought, what she really thought about the whole thing, he was never able to plumb Joy's depths, reach her secret places—in that, or in anything else.

Joy did nothing in haste, and nothing without thought. In all things she took time for judgment, and then acted, and it was this controlled patience of hers, the quiet strength it demonstrated, that was the most disconcerting trait of all. The trouble was, you never never knew what she was thinking, and so you were always completely unprepared for what she did. Bob's feeling on this morning was that of a small boy cowering in his room, while downstairs, in quiet, measured tones, his punishment was being discussed.

The copy chief said, "I can offer you a cure for your hangover."

"I don't want anything," Bob said. "Not a thing."

"You'll want this, boy. Old Man Barker himself called yesterday afternoon late. I talked to him, said you were out of the office on a business call. They're buying the presentation, lock, stock and barrel, just the way you lined it out for them. Seems the old man always has thought his cousin the sales manager was a horse's ass and he liked the way you made everybody else see it too. We're in, boy."

Bob spread his hands on the top of his desk. He studied them. He said finally, "Great."

The copy chief smiled. "Crazy, is what you mean."

Bob looked up then. Slowly he nodded. "Yes," he said, "I guess I do. Plain crazy."

7
•••••

FOR LOUELLA there was no waiting in a publisher's outside office. She was shown swiftly into Paul's inner lair, and Paul came to meet her at the door, both hands outstretched. "Stunning, Louella. Even on the hottest day you always manage to look fresh." He closed the door. "Sit down, do. Cigarette?"

"Thank you, no," Louella said.

"Now what can I do for you? Name it."

"The new book is going well," Louella said.

"Wonderful. I've been wanting to ask, but I didn't dare disturb you. Not when you're creating." It was Paul's erroneous belief that all authors loved that word. He used it frequently, as a kind of accolade.

"I'm not creating," Louella said. "I'm not an angry young man, Paul, who needs to build himself up with words like that. Nor am I God. I'm simply working, writing a book."

"It was just a figure of speech." Paul felt a trifle off-balance.

"And," Louella said, "I think it's going to be the best book I've done."

This was better, safer ground. "I'm sure of it. Each one of yours has shown more depth, more perception, greater power than the last." And larger sales, although he left this unsaid—larger, more wonderful sales.

"And," Louella said, "you're not going to be the one to publish it, Paul." She let the sentence hang in the air, reverberate gently from the paneled walls, echo and shimmer until its full effect had been gained. Then, "Shall I tell you why?"

Slowly, distinctly, in lucid sentences, she told him why.

8

FOR MONA PETERS Friday was a day of mounting hysteria. There were simply thousands of things that had to be done in preparation for the party—food and liquor and some kind of flower decorations, and, of course, the house was simply a mess and had to be gone over thoroughly. The enormity of the project reduced Mona to impotent panic.

In the normal course of events, Wally would have been coerced from his typewriter, handed the problem entire, and told to cope, although, of course, if the party was a success, and Mona's parties always were, the credit for the preparations would go to her—and why not? She had planned the whole thing, hadn't she?

But on this morning Mona would not, she simply would not ask Wally for a thing. The very idea of his sleeping on the sofa—how childish, and how insulting, could a man be? She was not speaking to Wally. As a matter of fact, Wally was not speaking to her, either, a stand-off. And so Mona, face to face with the decision of what kind of casserole to serve, completely, utterly unable to make up her mind, did the next best thing. She telephoned Madge Fuller and asked her to come help. And then, for good measure, she telephoned Mildred Pierson too, although if the emergency had not been grave, Mona would have thought twice before she called Mildred, because even though it was very good of Mildred to say what she had said about Wally and Roz

Warren, bringing to Mona's attention what Mona certainly ought to know, still, well, Mona wasn't sure that she liked being told, particularly in view of Wally's reaction. But crisis demanded extraordinary measures, and so she did call Mildred as soon as she had finished talking to Madge.

They came. One of the verities of the county was that whoever was summoned always did drop whatever he or she was doing and rally around, because Mona was so helpless, and so sweet, so gay. Everybody, that is, except George Hanks. Mona had made the mistake of calling him once when he was at work.

"Wally's in town with the car," Mona had said, "And I simply have to get up to the village. I have an appointment with the hairdresser and all kinds of errands, and I wondered if you would mind driving me—"

"For Christ's sake!" George had said, and had hung up the phone. (But, of course, George was a character, and you simply had to put up with him.)

Madge arrived first. Over a cup of coffee, and lists, she said, yes, Martin was still in London, but she hoped he would be back in time for the party.

"He likes London, doesn't he?" Mona said. "I mean, he's been there before—"

"Several times," Madge said.

"Have you?" Mona's face was bright, interested. Her panic was gone now that reinforcements had arrived.

"No," Madge said, "I've never been outside of the country."

"Funny," Mona said, "isn't it? That he goes, I mean, and never takes you? Does he have—friends in London?"

You couldn't take offense at Mona, because she never intended to give offense. It was just that sometimes she said things without thinking. Madge said, "I think the beef pilau is best. You do it so well and everybody likes it."

"Well," Mona said. And then, "If you really think so."

"Get the recipe," Madge said, "and we'll make a shopping list."

"Oh, I don't have a recipe. I just—put it together according to my mood." She made fluttering gestures with both hands. "You know."

"Well," Madge said, "there's beef, of course—is it stew beef? And rice. And mushroom caps—"

"Oh," Mona said, "there are lots of things, simply lots." Madge waited, pencil poised. "I mean," Mona said, "they're all at the store. I just go, and look, and pick them out."

"I see," Madge said.

Mildred rang the doorbell. Upstairs Wally's chair scraped hard on the floor in protest. "That boy!" Mona said. "Honestly!" She went to let Mildred in.

Mildred said, "I could stand a cup of coffee, several cups, as a matter of fact." She made her entrance, smiled heroically at Madge, sat down. She raised her voice to Mona, busy with coffee-pot and cup. "Is George Hanks coming tomorrow night?"

Madge's eyebrows rose at Mildred's tone. Mona appeared in the kitchen doorway. "George is coming, of course," Mona said. And then, "Why, dear?"

Mildred produced a cigarette. She snapped her lighter viciously. Smoke trailed from her nostrils. "That—hairy ape! Did you know that last night he deliberately led poor Ben down to a bar in New Jersey—"

Mona said, "No!"

Madge was silent.

Mildred said, "Yes. And then, in the parking lot he deliberately attacked him and beat him mercilessly. To a pulp!"

Mona said, "Oh!" In the single word she managed horror, incredulity, and delight. "He didn't!"

Madge said quietly, "I don't believe it, Mildred. I think you're twisting it some way."

"Well!" Mildred said. And then, "I always knew there was something—monstrous about George Hanks. Something—unbalanced. He—"

Madge said, "Have you gone to the police? If it's true, I think you should."

Mona nodded eagerly.

Mildred sat erect. "Why, in the world," she said, "would I go to the police? What could they do for poor Ben?" There was silence.

"Honestly!" Mona said. "Led him down there and then attacked him!" She wanted desperately to run upstairs, because Wally simply had to be told, a thing like this. She could excuse herself from Madge and Mildred by saying she was going to the bathroom, and it would only take a minute— And then, unhappily, she remembered. She was not speaking to Wally. It was—maddening.

Madge said, "Let's get on with the lists." She gathered both women with her eyes. "That's what we're here for, isn't it?"

9

THEY HAD removed one of the big hoses, bright red hydraulic fluid dripping messily. Johnny Richards labored to re-attach it. Martin watched as best he could. Johnny said finally, "There. The son of a bitch is home." He emerged from the engine nacelle. "Now do you see what I mean?"

Martin said thoughtfully, "I see." And then, "You attached the engine end first. Why, Johnny? Or doesn't it make any difference?"

"It makes one hell of a difference," Johnny said. "With that goddamned bend, you've got to attach the engine end first, or you can't get it threaded straight—" He stopped, his eyes round in wonder. "Jesus!"

"Yes," Martin said. "And the service manual says nothing about it."

"And you can't get in to see," Johnny said slowly. "You have to do the whole thing by feel—"

"Let's take it from the beginning," Martin said. He paused,

setting his thoughts in order, his mind still loose, easy, confident. "If a mechanic attaches the wrong end first—"

"Then," Johnny said, "he's fouled it up for fair. He can't get the engine end threaded straight. He may think he has, but he hasn't, or at least he may not have, which is just as bad. If he could see, he'd know. But he can't see, and so he feels, and his fingers may tell him wrong." He was silent.

"And the gear and flaps and controls," Martin said, "may operate on test satisfactorily. But in flight, when you get surge pressures you may develop a leak—"

"And then you've got no pressure at all," Johnny said, "and you're up you-know-what creek without a paddle. That has to be it, the whole goddamned trouble—which end of the hose you attach first." He spread his hands. "I never even thought about it. I mean, I suppose I assumed that any mechanic would figure it out for himself. But you get a jughead, and maybe he's in a hurry, or thinking about his girl, or—" He stopped. He picked up a bunch of waste and rubbed idly at his large hands. His smile was rueful. "I guess you slide-rule characters have your uses after all. Some, anyway, the good ones like you."

There was satisfaction in accomplishment that never, never grew old, or worn. Martin supposed that this was what George Hanks had meant when he said that everybody had a desire for recognition and went about achieving that recognition in his own way. Maybe it was strange that he should experience a little thrill of pride merely because a first rate mechanic wiping his oily hands said that he, Martin, was good at his job. Maybe it was even a little silly, that feeling of pride. But it was real, and that was a fact that could not be ignored.

"Suppose—" Johnny began.

"That we cut a small inspection door?" Martin said. He nodded. "So you can see whether the attachment is solid or not. We'll do just that."

"Yeah," Johnny said, again with that rueful grin. "You're way ahead of me, as usual."

10

IT WAS twenty minutes of four. Except for last minute matters, which somebody, probably Madge, would come early to attend to, Mona's party was ready for launching—the beef pilau casserole finally assembled and cooked, needing only re-heating tomorrow night; salad greens washed, wrapped in layers of paper towels to dry and crisp; three different kinds of canape spreads mixed and covered with aluminum foil; the house cleaned and polished; liquor, glasses, jigger, ice breaker, and ice bucket arranged on one side of the kitchen sink; wine glasses assembled, with wine and corkscrew in handy juxtaposition; plates, silverware and napkins counted and ready; mints for dessert sitting cheek by jowl with demi-tasse cups; and, oh, yes, two different flower arrangements on opposite sides of the living room. Mona had arranged the flowers.

At about one o'clock, Wally had come downstairs, made himself a peanut butter sandwich and poured a glass of milk, and with these in hand returned to his tiny study without a word, his ears closed to the female cacaphony. The heavens could fall, or open up into brilliance; Wally worked at his typewriter—or he, and Mona, didn't eat. It was as simple, as inexorable as that. His back was a little stiff from that damned sofa. But it had been worth it. The story was back on the rails again.

"Well," Mona said, "I guess we've done simply everything. I'm so grateful for the help." Nobody, and certainly not Mona, remarked the understatement in the word *help*. Mona had arranged the flowers, period. "Now let's all have a drink. We deserve one."

"I am ready," Mildred said.

"I have to go," Madge said. "I'm sorry. I have an—appointment." And she was conscious that both women watched her and waited for further explanation, but all she said was, "Goodbye. Until tomorrow night." She was gone.

11

MONA SAID, "It's not like Madge to be so mysterious."

Mildred said, "Never mind, darling. That drink you mentioned." And then, memory of Madge's rejection of the George Hanks story still rankling, "There could be a perfectly simple explanation. If she had an appointment with a doctor, for example—"

"But," Mona said, "I'm never ashamed when I'm going to a doctor." She giggled. "Everyone does. Why should she be?"

Mildred smiled wickedly. "Suppose Madge thought she was pregnant, but didn't want to talk about it until she was sure?"

"Oh!" Mona said. And then, again, "Oh! Do you think that's it?" There was hope in her voice. Such a lovely exciting day, so many things happening. "Do you, Mildred?"

"Why," Mildred said, "I wouldn't know, darling. How on earth could I know?" And she smiled again, pure malice. "Maybe George Hanks knows."

12

MADGE DROVE slowly on the pleasant winding road. She had thought that the time would never pass, but it had, and now, with the moment at hand, she was a little frightened at what she was going to do, what she was going to say to Roz Warren. She was going to make a fool of herself, that much was sure. So? "All right." She said it aloud, throwing the phrase at herself, her reluctance, flaying herself with it. "All right!" And she drove on steadily, turned without hesitation into the long drive that led to the pleasant white house.

It was strange, she thought as she got out of the car, everything seemed so sharp, so preternaturally bright, the two enormous white pines etched against the sky, the house itself every clapboard underlined, the green of the grass, the white of a single summer cumulus cloud, everything. It was as if her eyes of their own volition had opened wider than they had ever opened before. "And maybe they have," she whispered to herself. "Because I'm scared."

Roz answered the door, Roz in a sleeveless white dress and sandals, her arms and legs bare, golden-tanned. She wore the faintest of smiles, neither friendly nor mocking; and Madge, facing her, taking all of her in with this sudden new clarity of vision, thought that she had never seen a more beautiful woman, face, body, everything—the calm eyes glowing with intelligence, the faintly smiling lips red and ripe, the rounded shoulders and arms, the subtle high cleavage of full breasts peeping shyly above the dress top, the waist slim as a young girl's but without the juvenile angularity, the hips, the long, straight, clean legs—
"I can't compete with you," Madge said, and was never afterwards sure whether she had said it aloud or merely within her own thoughts, because nothing changed in Roz's face, nothing at all.

"Come in," Roz said. "You're punctual. I appreciate that. Someone said once that punctuality is the politeness of kings, and I've always remembered it even though I don't know who said it. Maybe you know?"

"No," Madge said, "I don't know. Martin probably would." And she could have bitten off her tongue for adding that, but it was all right, perfectly all right.

"Yes," Roz said, "I think Martin might." Merely that. And then, "Would you like to see the baby before we—talk?"

Madge had not thought that it would be like this; and she told herself with some asperity that she had had no idea how it would be, and so surprise, astonishment or any other reactions were silly, weren't they? How could she have known? What experience did any woman have in this kind of—mission?

They admired the baby; in their way discovered a kind of kinship between them as they bent over the crib. Roz said, "They don't really look like much at this age, do they?"

And Madge said, without hesitation, "No, they don't. It's—disappointing. You think that your child is going to. To you, anyway."

"Disappointment," Roz said. "Yes." And then, "I like you for saying that." She turned. "Shall we go downstairs?"

A shining tea service was set out on the table by the sofa. Roz brought the tea, poured it. "Sugar? Cream? Lemon? No?" And then she settled back, her own cup in her hand, and she said, calmly enough, "You want to talk about Martin, don't you? And about me." Her eyes studied Madge's face without over-boldness or resentment or shame. "I could say I'm sorry," Roz said then, "but I wouldn't mean it. I like Martin very much."

Madge said, "You're not being cruel, at least not intentionally. I know that." She was silent for a few moments. She said at last, "I'm not going to embarrass us by crying. I detest women who do that."

"So do I," Roz said. She studied Madge. "Does Martin know that you know about us, him and me?"

"No."

"I thought not."

"You went away," Madge said. "No one knew where—"

"I went," Roz said, "and told no one except Paul because I didn't want to be leered at, or even thought of, swollen and ugly. Does that shock you?"

"I think," Madge said, "that a lot of women would do the same thing if they could. I would have. Instead I stayed in the apartment Martin and I had then in California, and watched my belly get bigger and bigger, and my breasts distort, and watched Martin try his best to ignore it, and I loathed the entire process. Bearing Johnny, pain and all, was almost a relief. If that's not the way it's supposed to be, then there's something wrong with me. If it's immoral to feel that way, then I'm immoral. Does that answer your question?"

The faint slow smile appeared. "I want to dislike you," Roz said. "Because your purpose in coming here was to tell me in effect that I'm a bad woman—"

"No."

"Yes," Roz said. "Implicitly or explicitly, that was the reason. I've gone to bed with your husband. Adultery is bad. Therefore, I'm a bad woman, and no woman wants to be told that, or even thought of in that way." The smile returned. "The trouble is, it isn't easy to dislike you. You're honest with yourself. That's a rare quality. You set what you want, Martin, against the cost of trying to keep him, which meant coming to me—"

Madge said, "I'll plead, if you want me to. I'll crawl."

Roz nodded. "I know you would. And I like that about you, too. I don't want you to plead, or crawl. It isn't necessary."

"Will you leave him alone?" Madge said.

There was a silence. Then, "That doesn't put Martin in a very manly role. The male is supposed to be the pursuer."

"Do you believe that?"

"Not always," Roz said. "Not really. Not infrequently it's the other way around." She was silent, thoughtful. She looked up at last. "What kind of answer can I give you?"

And Madge said, "I guess you've already given it." She sipped her tea. When she spoke her voice was entirely steady. "What shall we talk about now?"

It was twenty minutes of five when Madge left, only forty minutes, time enough to lose a world, but not to gain one. She stood at the door, stopped there for one final word, a question. "I mean no offense," she said. "But tell me, what do you think about when you're alone? Lying awake at night, perhaps?" And the silence held so long that she thought there would be no answer. But there was.

Roz said, "You know the Faust myth?"

"More or less," Madge said.

Roz nodded then. "It should have been told about a woman, not a man. That's what I think about." She held out her hand. It was cool, firm, steady. "Thank you for coming. I know you better now." And, with the same faint smile she had worn at the beginning, "Goodbye."

Madge drove straight home. She wanted to see no one, be seen by no one. She sat down in front of the picture window and stared at the evil river. When the phone rang she wanted to ignore it, and dared not, because a ringing telephone could mean many things, so many terrible, sometimes wonderful things. It was young Johnny, in his usual breathless state.

"Hey, mom. Look. I'm down at Jimmy's. And we're going out in their boat—Jimmy's father's going to take us, and we'll eat on the boat and come back late and they say I can stay here tonight, can I, huh, can I, Mom?" And then, "Just a minute."

And the mature, male voice of Jimmy's father said, "Mrs. Fuller? I've invited the boy to come with us, if he has your permission. I promise you that he'll be well looked after. Short notice, I know, is an imposition—"

Madge said, "You can't know how grateful I am. Of course he can go."

Johnny's voice on the phone again said, "Gee, thanks, Mom." And, "Ripsey-doo and skippety-witchet." His current phrase, etymology unknown.

Madge was smiling faintly as she returned to her chair, and her thoughts in which there was nothing at all to smile about. Afterwards she was never sure how long she sat there lost in her helplessness before George Hanks came walking up the path, drink in hand, and there was nothing to do but let him in.

He took one look at her and then put his own drink in her hand. "You need it more than I do. Suck on it while I mix another." With his almost feminine sensitivity he remained in the kitchen for some minutes, making large fuss with ice and glass and bottle, giving Madge ample time for composure.

When at last he returned and sat down he said merely, "So you swung and you missed. It happens to the best of us." And, as last night, he felt the illogical anger begin, although he allowed none of it to show in his voice, or his manner. "Do you want to tell?"

To George she could talk. She did not understand why, or how it had come about, but there it was, no need for sham or pretense—and this, Madge supposed, was merely further proof that she was insufficiently a woman. "I can't compete with her," she said. "I'm completely outclassed."

George stared into his drink.

"I never quite realized it before," Madge said. "The difference, I mean, between someone like me and someone like her. She has—devoted her life to herself, like an actress. She knows precisely what she's doing every moment, what to say, what not to say, what clothes to wear, and, probably, what clothes not to wear. To be unladylike about it, I've never seen her naked, as you have, as Martin has. But I can imagine what she must be like. If I were a man—"

"That, goddamn it," George said, "is just the point. You aren't a man. You're looking with the wrong eyes, and in the wrong direction. You're—"

It was then that the phone rang, and they both stared at it until it rang again. Madge went to answer it. "This is Mrs. Fuller," she said. And then, after a pause, "Thank you." She hung up and merely stood there for a little time, her back to the room. "A cable from Martin," she said at last. "He gets in tomorrow afternoon. In time for the party."

In the silence, George glowered into his drink. The anger was stronger now, and directed at no person but merely at a concept he loathed—waste, the frittering away of talent of any sort and for any reason whether it was sheer laziness or mere ignorance that was the cause. Some people knew they had talent and deliberately threw it away in dilettantism. But some people were not even aware of what they had, what they were, what they could be, and if the fault of the waste was not really their own because they knew not what they did, the result was still the same. Here was the root of the anger.

He stood up suddenly. "Then," he said, "we don't have much time, do we?" He watched her turn, face him, puzzled. "Come on," George said. "As Johnny would say, I want to show you somep'n. Bring your drink."

The light in the studio was not good, faded, uneven. George drew the drapes across the great north window, switched on the studio lights. "Not as good as the real thing," he said, "but it will do." He gestured towards the easel where the new picture stood, the idealized Gladys face on the Roz Warren body. "That's what you're talking about," George said. "Take a good look at it."

He watched Madge, studied her as she stood in front of the picture. She said at last, "Yes. She's the way I imagined her." And then, "So?"

George took the picture out of the easel clamps. He set it against the wall. Then he walked to the front door and shot the bolt. "Just so we won't have any interruptions," he said.

Madge was frowning at him.

"I'm not making a pass," George said. "It wouldn't work. I know my limitations, some of them, anyway."

"Then?"

His broad back was to her. He picked up a blank canvas already stretched, prepared. "Get up on the dais," he said. "Take your clothes off. All of them. I'm going to show you what you look like, Toots, seen through the right eyes in the right direction. Maybe it'll help you think of yourself as a big girl."

There was silence. Then, "You're joking, of course," Madge said.

"No joke." He walked past her, began to set up the fresh canvas in the easel.

"George."

"Say it." His hands worked on, unperturbed.

"Why, it's ridiculous," Madge said, "perfectly ridiculous. I'm not—insulted, that isn't what I mean, but—"

"Just what do you mean?" George said. He had finished with the canvas. He faced her now.

"I'm not a prude," Madge said. "I don't mean that, either." She was close to laughter, or to tears, and she did not know which. "I—couldn't do that, George. I mean—flaunting myself in cold blood. I'd—I'd giggle!"

His face softened. His smile was gentle. And his voice. "Go ahead and giggle." And he turned the broad back on her again, busied himself with little tubes and pots and things as if Madge no longer existed.

She stared at his back. She stared at the dais in a kind of fascination. "George."

There was no answer.

"It's—ridiculous," Madge said. "Isn't it ridiculous?"

Still no answer. It was almost as if she were alone in the studio. She walked over to the dais. Her heels made impossibly loud sounds on the floor. She turned to look again at George's back. "No," she said. "Of course not. It's silly, George. I know what I look like. I have a mirror."

"And the wrong eyes," George said. "I'll show you what mine see. What Martin's see, or would see if you made him look." And then, "Take the step, Toots. The rest is easy." He had not turned; it was still only his back that she faced.

Madge set her drink on the edge of the dais. She stepped up. He was wrong, the rest was not easy, it was—impossible, ridiculous, as she had said, and silly, and all the other things words or thoughts, could conjure up. She was astonished to find her hands undoing the belt of her dress, her fingers working clumsily on the zipper. She took a deep breath and peeled the dress over her head, shook her hair back into a semblance of order. There was a chair, and she tossed the dress on it, and then her bra, and then her panties. She stood there, uncertain still, not knowing what to do with her hands, her arms, with any part of her. "I guess I'm —ready." It was not her voice; it belonged to someone else, someone she really didn't even know, someone maybe she should have striven to know a long time ago.

George turned then. He looked at her for a long time in silence, an eternity. And then, at last he nodded. "You don't disappoint me. You won't be disappointed, either. I promise you." He walked to the dais, stepped up to her. "Let's get to work. Your leg so." His hand on the bare flesh of her thigh was strong, sure, and alive. "Good. Now this arm so, shoulder back, we want your breasts out. Good. The other hand on the chair back. That's it." His hand moved her chin, tilted it. For a moment he studied her, and then, satisfied, he stepped down from the dais and walked back to the easel.

"George."

"Keep your chest out. But don't exaggerate it. You have plenty." And then, "Can you smile?"

"I feel so—so naked!" And the giggles began at last, impossible to stifle, or control, the near-hysteria of the entire day coming into focus on this ultimate senselessness. "It's no wonder, is it?" she said then, and the giggles simply would not stop. "Because I am naked!" The ultimate, devastating joke.

"Just keep on giggling," George said, "and we've got it made."

13

BEN PIERSON NURSED his wounds which, disappointingly, did not show at all in clothes, and not very spectacularly without them—two vaguely purple patches on his middle where George's fists had landed with that unbelievably devastating impact. Ben's stomach was sore, good and sore. And so was his neck, although he had no idea why; the final blow had been beyond Ben's power to feel.

But the real hurts were inside his mind where they could not be displayed, and from which secret place he would not have plucked them even if he could. He retained still his sense of outrage, begun by Roz's treatment of him yesterday, compounded by the sight of that naked hussy in George's studio caught outright in what should have been her shame and was not, boosted into something incoherent and uncontrollable by the sight of Roz's loveliness in a picture destined to be seen by millions of leering magazine readers.

Because of the outrage he, Ben, had lost his temper, and suffered indignity, which was not really unpleasant, cradled there in the secrecy of his thoughts, a kind of martyrdom carrying its own sense of healing as by fire, cauterization.

He was free of Roz now, the incubus, no, the succubus exorcised. He felt cleansed, refreshed, a whole man again. Still the sense of outrage remained and had to be satisfied, as it had not been last night. Last night, too, because of his blind temper, he had sought that satisfaction in the wrong direction. He saw this now. It was not against George that he should have directed his rage. The Georges of the world, the lechers, the idolators, were legion, and not really important. Also, they were formidable. The root and the core of the matter was not George, but Roz; in his new-won freedom Ben saw this clearly now. Roz should be punished, made to suffer as he himself had suffered. Martyrdom would benefit Roz.

And so Ben puttered away the afternoon and early evening amongst his roses, brooding, and destroying aphids, beetles and a single slug with a kind of Godlike impersonality. He wore dark glasses, and continued to wear them even after the light had faded—simple, effective make-up to indicate his physical and mental suffering; passers-by, seeing Ben, and the dark glasses, could only be touched by the depth of his anguish. And as he puttered, and brooded, and destroyed with Godlike impersonality, and suffered, he turned over and over in his mind the various methods by which martyrdom could be brought to benefit Roz. His imagination was not vast. He could think of only one or two methods that would suffice. But in their contemplation he found further therapy and a deeper sense of healing.

14

BOB LEWIS STOPPED at the village florist on his way home that evening. He was not knowledgeable about flowers; he had difficulty remembering the names of even the more common ones—jonquils and daffodils and narcissi, for example, were a perpetual source of confusion in his mind simply because he was not, and had never been, much interested in gardening.

Oh, the first summer in the county he had bought seed packets and tomato plants and sent away for onion sets, that kind of thing that everybody did. But it was too wet that summer, or too dry, something; and for every kind of plant there were at least a dozen enemies that crept or flew or oozed or simply existed, and a man could spend his life energy defending a meagre stand of corn and what did he have when he was done? Particularly in view of the fact that there were farms nearby where, for some reason, the plant enemies were non-aggressive and the corn grew high and sweet, and the tomatoes luscious, and tiny onion sets became, miraculously, full sized onions instead of disappearing early without a trace. And if you wanted flowers you could buy them, too, or get them merely for the asking from Ben Pierson, so what the hell? The second year Bob had the flower and vegetable garden planted to lawn and that was that. His talents lay in other directions than horticulture.

But flowers were good things, as opposed to bad things. Women loved flowers, were touched by them, and in his penitent mood flowers seemed like a fine idea.

He looked around the florist shop, confused by the superfluity. There were big flowers and little flowers, smooth and shaggy, and they came in pots and in vases or put together in wreathes and corsages and some of them had fragrance and some, apparently, did not, and he couldn't say right out that what he wanted was a peace offering, but he had an idea that the young lady florist knew that already, which made him even more uncomfortable.

"Anything but roses," he said, remembering the petals bouncing on the hospital floor. And then he pointed at some rather fancy red-and-white blossoms standing erect on their stems, looking stout and healthy. "Those."

The florist smiled. "Peonies. They are lovely, aren't they?"

Once bitten, twice shy. "Are they fresh?" Bob said. "I mean, good and fresh? They won't start coming apart as soon as I get them in the car?" He was assured that they were quite fresh. "Wrap them up," Bob said then, "or put them in a box, or whatever you do." He had a male dislike of dawdling in a store. You saw what you wanted and you bought it, and why women had to fuss and fumble and look at the same thing in half a dozen different places was more than he had ever been able to understand.

"Would you like to enclose a card?"

"No card. I'll make my own presentation." Presentations were something he understood and knew how to handle. You thought the whole thing through, arranged items in their proper dramatic order, laid out ahead of time what you were going to say and how you were going to say it—not the exact words, of course, because you wanted spontaneity and you weren't, after all, peddling Fuller brushes or vacuum cleaners, and, God knew, if there was one thing Bob could do it was talk off the cuff.

And so, actually, he felt fairly good driving home, the flowers on the seat beside him. His ingrained sense of optimism was at work. First the flowers placed in Joy's hands, a gift bestowed rather shyly, almost with juvenile embarrassment and not too many words because glibness would spoil the effect.

And then, when the flowers were in a vase—Joy would want to do that right away, of course, and he would be patient during the process—then, maybe over a martini because it was, after all, Friday, he would shift to the second, more dramatic point, which was the success of the Barker Manufacturing Company presentation, a new account brought into the agency which wouldn't do him, Bob Lewis, any harm at all. He would explain that the new account would mean more work for him, of course, which was perfectly true, but that it was worth it, certainly worth it—and the impression would be left that no labor was too great if it brought added return to wife, home and family. All in all, he thought, it was rather a neat package he had to present.

Joy was in the kitchen. Bob kissed the back of her neck.

"TGIF," he said, "Thank God It's Friday." And then, "I—brought these for you."

Joy looked at him in her quiet way, wearing that enigmatic smile. "You're sweet, Bob." She opened the box. She was silent for a moment looking at the flowers. "Peonies," she said. "They're —beautiful."

It was going to be all right. It was going to be fine. "I'll mix us a drink," Bob said, "while you stick them in water." And when Joy seemed to hesitate, he added, puzzled, "They do go in water, don't they? I mean to keep from shriveling up or something?"

"Yes," Joy said. "They should."

"Then you do it while I mix us a drink. God, how I need one. It was a madhouse today. I'll tell you about it. You may be interested."

He carried the martini pitcher and lemon peel and two glasses out into the living room. He sat down to wait, stirring the martini mixture carefully because there was something about bruising the vermouth if you stirred too hard, or maybe it was the gin; and although he had never been able to taste any difference even if martinis were shaken until they clouded with tiny air bubbles, there was a right way and a wrong way to do almost anything, and careful stirring was the right way to make a martini. He looked up as Joy appeared in the doorway. He said, "Hey, how about the whatever-they-are flowers?" And he added, almost shyly, "Don't you like them?"

She was gone without a word. She returned with a vase filled with the peonies. She set it on a table.

"They look swell," Bob said. "I mean, the way you arranged them." He poured the two drinks, squeezed lemon peel carefully over each glass. "Here. A little celebration." Extending the bait, waiting confidently for it to be taken.

Joy said, "Celebrashud?" It sounded approximately like that.

"I got the Baker—" He stopped there. "What's with you? You're catching a cold or something?"

Joy shook her head. Her eyes were pools of misery. She sniffed, sniffed again. She sneezed.

"Oh, my God!" Bob said. "What set you off this time?" And

then, "Well, don't just sit there. Go take one of your pills." And when she made no move, "Dammit," Bob said, "when these things start they have to be stopped. I mean do you want to swell up like a poisoned pup the way you did in New York that night when we ended up at St. Vincent's, the emergency ward, for God's sake? Go take a pill. Take two, if you have to."

"I'b sorry," Joy said. Merely that.

"Beat it," Bob said. "And stop apologizing." And when she was gone up the stairs, he sat for a few moments staring into his martini in disgust. He raised the glass finally and drank the whole thing almost at one gulp. Then he got up and walked over to the table, picked up the vase of peonies, carried it into the kitchen and through, across the back lawn into the woods where he dumped the flowers on the ground. "Nice try, buster," he said. "A real fine college try."

Walking back to the house he thought that that goddamned Roz Warren must be a witch or something the way she managed to put a hex on everything he tried to do. And they burned witches, didn't they, or hanged them, or just plain wrung their necks? There had to be something somebody could do before he, and probably the whole county, went nuts.

15
●●●●●●

MONA WAS in an agony of indecision, sitting alone over a drink, her second, after Mildred had gone. There was that simply fascinating thing about George Hanks almost killing poor Ben Pierson. There was also that thought— it was now, in Mona's mind, probability, no longer idle conjecture—that Madge Fuller was afraid she was pregnant. Madge, of all people, but, then, you never really knew. And George Hanks, who lived only next door to the Fullers—obviously Mildred had it right; George and the Fullers were so close, everybody knew that; who else could it possibly be but George Hanks?

Mona simply had to tell somebody, talk over the ramifications of everything. But she had called Joy Lewis as soon as Mildred's car was out of the drive, and Bob had answered and said merely that Joy was busy and couldn't come to the phone, which was, of course, simply ridiculous, but what was there to do?

Mona had even thought of calling Louella, but, well, Louella was funny sometimes, especially when she was working, and you never knew how she was going to react when somebody was simply being neighborly and telling her what she, as a county resident, certainly ought to know. So, reluctantly, Mona had refrained from calling Louella.

And who did that leave? Or was it whom? She wouldn't for the world speak first to Wally. Wally—that boy!—had to apologize before Mona would give him a single word. Honestly. He and that Roz Warren. But who was there to talk to? Mona sipped her drink.

She heard Wally push back his chair. She heard him unlock and open his study door. Maybe he was only going to the bathroom. There was, Mona was sure, something wrong with Wally's kidneys the way he went to the bathroom all the time when he was working. Maybe he drank too much. There was something.

He did not go to the bathroom. He came down the stairs. In the kitchen, in complete verbal silence, he mixed himself a drink. And then, of all things, he actually started back up the stairs. It was too much, simply too much. "Well!" Mona said. And then, again, "Well!"

Wally's footsteps returned, came through the kitchen. Drink in hand he stood in the doorway. "You spoke?"

"I certainly did," Mona said. "You simply can't treat me that way. I won't stand for it."

"Oh?"

"Honestly," Mona said. "After carrying on with Roz Warren, sneaking over there behind my back!" Her voice became nasal. "'I'm going for a walk. I've got some thinking to do.'" Her voice turned normal again. "With that woman!"

"You don't seem to like Roz," Wally said.

"I hate her! I always have!"

"You invited her to the party. As a matter of fact she's the reason you're giving it, isn't she?"

Mona breathed hard. "Will you tell me what that has to do with it? Do I have to like somebody just because I invite her to my house?"

"*Your* house," Wally said slowly. And then, "You confuse me. I'm beginning to think you always have." He turned back into the kitchen.

"Where are you going?"

"Back to work. I've got some editing to do." His footsteps climbed the stairs. The study door closed. The bolt shot home.

Mona could have screamed. He hadn't even stayed to listen to all the fascinating things she had to tell him.

16

SAM AND LOUELLA had their cocktails together before dinner like two civilized people. They talked of non-essentials. From Paul Warren's office, after detonating her explosion, Louella had gone shopping, and she told Sam what she had bought—a new swim suit; a new fall dress, bag, shoes, gloves and hat, just in case the weather turned unseasonably cool. "It does sometimes," Louella said.

Sam agreed that it did, although tomorrow was supposed to be hot. He had had all day to suffer, and he wished Louella would say something right out and get it over with. Almost anything would be better than waiting in dread, wondering what direction Louella's exotic mind might take. Still, he was completely unprepared for, and stunned by, her question, coming, as it did, without warning or preamble.

"Is it your baby, Sam? Roz Warren's, I mean?" Louella's voice was entirely calm.

"Of course it isn't," Sam said. And then, "I mean, it can't be."

"Did you take precautions?" Louella's eyes watched him steadily.

Sam said, "People don't talk like that, Louella. I mean, it's not—decent."

Louella smiled faintly. "It's all right to go to bed with a woman, but not to talk about it? I'm familiar with that concept, Sam. I'm the one who's acquainted with history, not you. And that gentleman's code was buried with Queen Victoria. I repeat, did you take precautions?"

In his wildest dread he had not pictured this exquisite agony of embarrassment. "Well, I mean to say, she did. I guess. I—hope she did. I—don't know, Louella." And then, "Please."

Louella said, "You're not very experienced, are you, Sam? At wenching, I mean."

"No, I'm not. You know I'm not. Now—"

"Let's talk about something else?" Louella said. "No, Sam." The faint smile was gone. Louella's face was thoughtful. "It could be your child then, couldn't it?"

Sam set his glass down. "That's ridiculous. You and I—"

"There was never the slightest chance," Louella said. "I've never given you the opportunity to find out whether you're fertile or not. Since you bring the point up."

"I'm—shocked," Sam said.

Louella shook her head. "I don't think you are. I don't think you wanted a baby any more than I did. You wanted a mother. I wanted you, maybe for the same reason in reverse." She was silent for a few moments. "It didn't work out badly, Sam. Do you think it did?" She smiled again. "You don't need to answer. I know you think it did."

There was a long silence. Then, "Tomorrow night," Sam said. "Do you really want to go to the Peters's?"

"Yes."

"She—Roz will be there."

"That," Louella said, "is the main reason I want to go. Does that shock you, too?"

"Sometimes," Sam said, "You're frightening, Louella." And he added, quite truthfully, "Now is one of those times."

17

IT WAS quite late. George had worked steadily, and Madge had stood, holding her pose as best she could until she ached all over, the giggles long since gone, and the first embarrassment; and all that remained now was a sense of the ridiculousness and a growing annoyance with herself, and with George, that this senseless charade had ever been allowed to begin. She must have been mad, completely, utterly mad.

And she had tried, and failed to find an excuse to break it off, to stop this foolishness; but stopping without an excuse would have been somehow worse than allowing the whole thing to go on. Stopping without an excuse, a logical excuse, would have been tantamount to admitting that she had stripped herself for his inspection, flaunted her nakedness, without reason; and if the alleged reason no longer seemed even faintly valid now that the madness had worn away, at least she could do nothing less than continue the pretense.

Why on earth, she thought, did it have to be this night that Johnny was taken off her hands, out of her responsibility? He would have been the logical, irrefutable excuse. Now there was none. Now there was only the sense of ridiculousness, the growing annoyance that was turning to anger as her muscles and nerves ached and complained. They had taken breaks. She had no clear idea how many. But despite them, she was close to exhaustion. "George."

"Getting tired?" George said. He nodded. "I know. So am I." He studied the canvas. He sighed. He said slowly, at last, "The best I can do, Madge." It was the first time he had spoken her name. He seemed subdued, almost embarrassed. Picture George Hanks embarrassed. "You can come down now," he said. "It's not finished, of course, but you'll get the idea." He turned away suddenly. "I think we both need a drink."

He was gone a long time. When he returned, drinks in hand, Madge was still standing in front of the picture, staring at it, in oblivious unbelief.

George said gently, "Better put your clothes on, Toots. The show's over."

She shook her head, not in negation, merely in unconscious bewilderment. She said slowly, wonderingly, "Do I really look like that, George? Is that what your eyes see?"

"And Martin's," George said. He set the glasses down. He walked to the wall and returned with the Gladys-Roz portrait, held it up. "Well?"

She looked at it. She looked at her own picture. She said, "Oh, God, George." And then, at last, she looked down at herself, her nakedness. "I—don't have any shame at all, do I?" And she walked quickly to the dais, reached for her clothes. George turned his broad back.

She came down slowly from the dais, dressed again. She accepted the drink, held it in both hands because her fingers were not quite steady. She was unable to take her eyes from the two pictures. (Of the one of herself, someone was to say later, and mean, "There's only one way to describe it. It's a soul, painted into the likeness of a woman.") She said, "What do I say, George?"

"You've said it."

She turned to him then. "How do I—thank you?"

"That I can answer. By going home. Now. Before I forget that I'm just the artist, not a man who's been looking at you."

She gave him one of her rare, brilliant smiles touched only faintly with shyness. "More therapy, George? It isn't necessary. Not now."

"Beat it," George said. He pointed at the picture. "Just keep that in mind and start behaving like a big girl."

Madge was at the door. She stopped, turned. "I promise."

This was Friday.

Saturday

1
●●●●●●

LATER, when it became necessary, even mandatory that Saturday's pursuits and activities be sorted out, the task proved to be almost impossible. The difficulty arose from the fact that a weekend in the county, particularly a summer weekend, was always less ordered than, and qualitatively different from, the run-of-the-mill week itself. In a way, this was strange, but it was so.

Oh, there were those in the county to whom Saturday and Sunday were a complete break in routine. Sam Barnes, for example, never went into the city on Saturday; the Stock Exchange was closed. Bob Lewis rarely went in; Paul Warren almost never. But to Wally Peters and George Hanks and Ben Pierson, and to all of the wives, there was, really, nothing to mark a change.

Wally's typewriter was there, waiting, beckoning whatever day it was; and George's easel; and, of course, Ben's garden or woodpile and always the possibility of a phone call offering a TV part. And to the wives it was, or should have been the same on a Saturday morning as on any other morning—in summer there was not even the fact that children stayed home from school to break the routine. And yet weekends were different, for everybody, a fact that was difficult to explain.

"It is, I think, a national phenomenon," George had said once, "although maybe that's the chauvinist in me speaking. Have you ever considered, friend Martin, how deeply rooted a sense of chauvinism is in everybody? I'll expand that another time. The point is that Saturday morning is a thing apart. It's Christmas-once-a-week. It may be raining or snowing or gray and miserable or a lovely day. The result, no, the fact is unaltered, unalterable—it is Saturday, and you can feel it the moment you open your eyes. There is something in the air."

And Martin, smiling, had pointed out that not so long ago even banks had opened on Saturday morning.

"My point, exactly," George said. "Or, close enough. Back then the witching hour was noon, not daybreak. When twelve o'clock struck, everybody said to himself, 'Thank God,' and he relaxed. The point in time has been altered by custom, but the phenomenon remains. You simply do not do on Saturday what you do the rest of the week. You may think you're going through the same motions, but your attitude is different, and so, inevitably, your activities are different, too. Try sometime to remember exactly what you did on a Saturday, every single thing. I doubt if you can, because it's a day unique, with a different feel all its own and you have no real reference of routine against which to remember all that you did. Think about it."

2

FOR MARTIN, in London, there was no question that Saturday was different. By Friday night he had drawn up a sketch, dimensioned it, set forth in meticulous detail the requirements of piano hinge, spot welds, stiffeners and Dzus fasteners that went to make up the small inspection doors cut in the engine nacelles in order that the attachment of the big hydraulic hoses might be seen, visually inspected, and not merely felt by a blind hand. He had also, with Johnny Richards's help, written out in step-by-step detail a procedure for attaching the hoses—engine-end first. He had overseen the work of cutting the inspection doors on the two grounded aircraft, and had been assured that all others, as they came in for top, or for major, overhaul, would be treated in the same manner. He had talked with Brookings, and Brookings was satisfied, and pleased, that the difficulty had been found, and eliminated. Full information, complete with sketch copy and attachment procedure, was already on its way by airmail to the home factory in California, where tracings would be drawn from the vault and altered accordingly, new part numbers established, new blueprints issued, and the entire change, together with its reason, sent all over the world, to every point where Coast aircraft flew, or were serviced on the ground in order that this particular malfunction might never again occur. His job was done, satisfactorily done, and so for Martin Saturday was a day apart, and it was true what George Hanks had said that there was a different feel in the air.

It was raining in London when he awakened. He had breakfast downstairs in the hotel with Johnny Richards; and afterwards phoned the airline office at Croydon and was assured in measured British tones that his flight would take off on schedule (not skedule) that the wind patterns over the Atlantic were favorable, and the weather on the Atlantic Coast of North America offered no hindrance whatsoever to arrival also on schedule (not skedule).

Which left a few free hours before early afternoon (Greenwich Time) departure. Martin went shopping, bought a Liberty silk scarf for Madge, a Sheffield steel pocket knife for Johnny, and then, extravagantly in a surge of affection, a cashmere sweater of frosty beige in what he hoped, even prayed, was Madge's size. He had the sweater tried on by not one, but three different female clerks before he was satisfied, or as close to satisfaction as he could come.

It had never occurred to him before, but the question popped unbidden into his mind now and stunned him by its obviousness —why in Heaven's name did he not, perhaps next time, arrange to bring Madge with him on one of these trips to try on sweaters for herself? Or whatever else caught her fancy? And why had he never thought of it before? "Why, she's never even been out of the States." He said it aloud in wonderment. And then, conscious that female clerk number three was looking at him in a strange way, "My wife, I mean," he explained.

The clerk said, "Really?" ("Rahly?") And her tone expressed pity for anyone, even an unknown, so benighted as never to have visited England.

His flight did, indeed, take off from Croydon on schedule (not skedule). And the wind patterns over the Atlantic were favorable. And New York City, as they circled for a friendly view, lay bright and shining in the summer sun. Nor were they stacked up over Idlewild, and so the landing and debarkation, and even Customs, took practically no time at all.

What no one, particularly the Croydon airport people, had thought of was the fact of weekend vehicular traffic. The traffic was appalling.

3

GEORGE HANKS breakfasted on his patio wearing paint-stained denim shorts and sandals, his enormous torso and solid legs bared to the warm sun. He ate slowly and with relish his eggs Benedict—George's *sauce Hollandaise* was the envy, and the despair, of the county wives who fancied themselves as cooks—three cups of the coffee he had especially blended for him at that place on Madison; and, afterwards, a beer.

He, too, felt the difference of the day Saturday. He was in good spirits, the matter of that Ben Pierson-Bob Lewis-Roz-and-Paul Warren kaleidoscopic foolishness wiped completely from his mind. He thought of Madge, perhaps a little too much of Madge, and after he had finished the beer he went inside and tidied up the breakfast things with a bachelor's habitual neatness, made his bed, shaved and attended to normal morning routine—doing all of this with a kind of stolid patience, and thoroughness, before he allowed himself to go into the studio and set the two pictures up side by side and study them, not with an artist's eye, but with a kind of male subjectivity that was pleasant, but also a trifle compelling.

And, after a time, he set both pictures against the wall, faces hidden, and then went outside. He had not had much exercise for a day or two—dealing with Ben Pierson could hardly be called exercise—and he thought that a small workout was in order. He took a machete and an axe and a pruning saw from his woodshed and went out into the wooded part of his property. For some time he had been meaning to clear out the undergrowth, even take out some of the saplings—cedar and hemlock, these particularly—that had no chance in the world of becoming anything but long skinny trunks with a little green bushiness on top.

And so he worked away the morning—the whistling axe, and the solid *thunk!* of its biting, the clean, sharp and fragrant chips that flew, the pleasant feel of sweat running down his chest and back, the physical delight, almost ebullience in the rhythm of muscles working smoothly almost as if they were bathed in oil. And, of course, the sense of accomplishment, the tidying up of his part of the forest, bringing light where no light had been able to penetrate, opportunity for growth where deformity had been inevitable.

But a man's mind was, in effect, like an electronic computer—nasty thought, needing the genius of an Artzybasheff drawing to make it palatable—that ran on some secret shielded power source of its own, and blinked its lights, and whirred softly to itself as it processed data in an inexorable kind of way, and came up with results that were real and true no matter how little you liked, or desired them.

And so, in the end, he made his decision, which, he admitted to himself, was part defiance, and part carnal urge, and part sheer puckishness of the sort commonly associated with George Hanks.

He put axe and machete and saw away. He went straight to the telephone. He called Gladys. She was pleasant to look at; he was reasonably sure she was available, and willing, probably eager; her prattle would be most amusing to turn loose on Mona Peters's party.

Gladys was at her apartment. Gladys was, quite obviously, flattered to hear from George Hanks in a non-professional way. George said, "Do you want to go to a party out here tonight, Toots?" Merely that.

Gladys did. She said so at length.

"You can sleep here," George said. There was no point in making the obvious statement that she would sleep in his bed and that he intended to be there too. Gladys understood.

"Well," Gladys said. She giggled. And then, "What shall I wear? For the party, I mean? A girl has to know, and I haven't met your friends—"

"We're not formal out here," George said. "A summer dress of some kind, the slinkier the better. I want to show you off." He was checking a timetable as he talked. "I'll pick you up across the bridge at—" He paused, running his finger down the columns. "There's a train out of Grand Central at 4:47. It gets in at 5:51. That's time enough. The party's at six-thirty. Tomorrow—well, we'll see about tomorrow. Bring a bathing suit. You can probably wear it this time."

He went in to shower, and amused himself by singing Gilbert and Sullivan—*The Gondoliers*—while he soaped and rinsed. The sense of physical well-being was strong after the exercise. He was glad he had thought of Gladys, which was a pun of sorts, but beneath George Hanks's contempt.

4
●●●●●●

WALLY PETERS had not spent the night on the sofa again. He felt that his point, whatever it was, had been amply proved. He and Mona had breakfast in the normal manner—Wally poured the fruit juice and made the coffee and got out the cold cereal and milk and carried it all into the living room where Mona waited with the napkins. Then Wally walked out to the end of the drive and picked up the paper.

It was a beautiful morning, bright, cloudless, warm. The river lay flat and shining, and even the bridge—subject of so much furor not really so long ago; object of hatred—had an ephemeral quality of loveliness, faintly haze-shrouded and seeming to float on the water as if sketched there by the hand of a Japanese artist. But Wally thought it prudent not to report this concept to Mona because Mona was not, and simply never would be, resigned to the fact of the bridge.

When breakfast was over, and the paper read, Wally carried the dishes into the kitchen, poured himself a fresh cup of coffee and started for the stairs. Mona said, "Oh, no." And then, "Honestly."

Wally came back into the living room to ask what that might mean.

"It's Saturday," Mona said.

"So?"

"Other men don't work on Saturday. They—help around the house."

"Oh."

"Honestly," Mona said. "We're entertaining tonight. Had you thought of that? And am I supposed to do simply everything, all by myself?"

"I thought everything was done. You had Madge and Mildred here helping all day yesterday."

"That's not true. Madge left early." And then Mona remembered that she still had not told him all, that the delicious bits of fact, probability, conjecture and sheer fancy had not yet been brought out, displayed, dissected, examined in thorough detail. There was so much, it was difficult to know where to begin. She took too long trying to find the starting place.

Wally said, "What isn't done? What do you want me to do?"

"Well." Mona made small fluttering gestures with both hands. "You know. There are always last minute things." And then, "But if you think you have to go to work, if you think that's more important—" She left the sentence unfinished, hanging.

The trouble was, always, that Mona's arguments and insinuations were unanswerable because you could never pin them down. It was like putting your thumb on a single shining drop of quicksilver; the moment you exerted the slightest pressure it broke apart into many small drops, each one perfect and whole; and these, in turn, if touched, turned into even smaller drops, also perfect, also whole, beautiful and shining, and skittering all over the table. A man could go mad chasing drops of quicksilver, or Mona's illogical logic. Wally said, "What kind of last minute things?"

"Well, you know, there are always errands."

Wally gave up. It was easier that way, and Wally was a peaceable man. And there were errands, a multitude of them; and, later, he could not for the life of him remember where all he had been that day because trips to the specialty grocery, and the supermarket, and the drug store, and the five-and-dime, and the ice plant and a few other places ran together in his mind and were impossible to sort out.

5

SATURDAY OR NOT, Louella returned to work during the morning. Sam was off somewhere, and did not come home for lunch. Louella read for an hour or two, and then went for a long walk. Several people saw, and recognized her striding along, head high, bosom thrust out. But it turned out that nobody seemed to be able to remember where, or when, or even which direction Louella was headed. As George Hanks had said, on Saturday there was no real reference of routine against which to remember things.

6

JOY'S PILLS had done the trick, stopped and then reduced the swelling of membranes before the terrifying stage of wheezing and incoherent vagueness had been reached. Allergic reactions were tricky things, of course, as the doctor who had prescribed the pills, and who gave her periodic shots, had explained.

He had used the analogy of a set of scales with a weight on one tray and small lead shot, one at a time, dropped slowly on the other. Eventually, he had said, a single shot tipped the scale, and then the reaction began. The single shot last night was the presence of the peonies, and it was more than a trifle frightening to think that she was apparently, despite the periodic shots, at all times that close to violent, and it was not beyond the bounds of possibility fatal, reaction. It was as if she were a bomb loaded, and set, and needing only the faintest touch of the detonator in order to explode.

But she would not for the world have told Bob of this sense of fright. Joy kept such feelings to herself, and if, sometimes, their pressure seemed almost too much to bear, that was the way things were and you had to put up with them. No one received, along with his certificate of birth, any guarantee that life was going to be easy.

And so, all during Saturday morning, Joy found herself moving a little slowly, a little carefully—which she told herself was silly—as if around the next corner might be waiting the single shot that would tip the scales again, detonate the bomb.

And Bob, only vaguely comprehending that she was troubled, and, of course, thinking that the trouble was himself, and Roz—that witch!—tried solicitude, offered help in all manner of household ways, and generally made a nuisance of himself just by being underfoot. And finally, in mid-afternoon, Joy suggested that he go off. "You could find a tennis game," she said. "Or play some golf. After all, you work all week in an office. You ought to be able to enjoy the outdoors on weekends. That's why we live in the country."

There was that, Bob admitted, and felt a vast relief that an excuse to get away from the house had been thus provided without his even suggesting it. He went off in his car, and it was not until some time later that Joy, going into the hall closet for something, and she could never afterwards remember what, found herself just standing there and staring because neither Bob's tennis racquet nor his golf clubs had gone off in the car with him, which was strange, within the framework of today's wary mood entirely too strange.

She did nothing in haste, commenced no action without thought. But the pressure of the fear she carried within herself on this day made thought, and delay, more difficult than usual.

After Thursday night's scene, Bob abject, pitiful in his shame, blurting out his confession and pleading wordlessly for absolution—after that, Joy would have sworn that the Roz Warren attraction was broken beyond all repair. But, was it? Had she been too hasty, too naïve in that belief?

She knew Bob's mercurial temperament, his pendulum swings from almost manic to depressive state, his little boy selfishness, his ego; beyond all, his ego. There was an elasticity to Bob which, in the advertising business, was one of his most valuable assets—the ability to bounce back from any failure or defeat no matter how devastating it might have seemed at the time, to emerge from the depths smiling again, and confident, eager to try once more. She found this quality admirable in many ways, sometimes even heroic; even though at other times, such as now, she saw it as mere emotional immaturity, irresponsible.

Perhaps on another day she would not have been so affected. But for Joy, as for others, this Saturday was a day apart. She went out to her own car, and, in her calm, expressionless way backed down onto the river road and drove off in the direction of the Warren's pleasant white house. She did not lie to herself by thinking it would do no harm to see if Bob, bouncing back from defeat, was preparing to attack again the citadel of Roz Warren, which was, really, no citadel at all in the sense of impregnability. Joy was aware that it might do a great deal of harm. But she had to know.

7

FOR MADGE, too, Saturday was like no day that had gone before. There was a kind of radiance in the air—silly concept, of course, but real nonetheless—a sense of anticipation warm as the feel of the sun itself. The broad river no longer seemed evil, and although she told herself that nothing, really, had changed, she knew deep within her that this was the falsity, and change itself the truth.

Such a ridiculous belief, that an unfinished picture of herself, however alluringly done, could alter even by a hairsbreadth the self-assessment she had carried in her mind all this time. And yet it had, and if last night's episode, all of it, seemed now completely unreal—herself, Madge Fuller, standing there on that dais, naked!—still what remained in her mind had the force of a dream, its details forgotten, but its emotion still strong.

She wished that now, in the light of day, she could see the picture again, find out if its effect remained. She had only to walk along the path, find George, ask his permission. He would understand. But she did not. Real, or imagined, what she had seen in the picture was too precious to risk. It was something to be cherished; mere illusion, perhaps, but illusion solid enough to build upon. "To think of myself as a big girl." She said it aloud, smiling.

Oh, she had seen something like this happen before. Not to herself, of course, but to Mildred Pierson. Mildred and Ben had no television set; intellectually, they scorned the medium, and saw no incongruity in the fact that they earned their living from it. But the attraction of self is inevitably too strong to be resisted, and so Ben and Mildred invited themselves here or there whenever a film was to be shown in which one of them had played a part.

And one night, in Martin and Madge's living room, Madge had sat and watched in Mildred's face the same process of transfiguration she had felt within her own being last night in George's studio. On the television screen Mildred had played the part of Maggie in Barrie's *What Every Woman Knows*. She had played it well, superlatively well. Jack Gould in the *Times* and John Crosby in the *Trib* had given rave reviews the following day. But that night, in front of the screen, Madge had watched the change in Mildred as she studied her own performance, lost herself in it. The lines of waspishness in Mildred's face miraculously smoothed themselves; the angry angularity of her cheeks softened; she became, before Madge's very eyes, gentle Mildred, compassionate Mildred, sweet, thoughtful, understanding Mildred. Unbelievable, and yet real. It had happened.

Still it was ridiculous. And yet laughter was easy on this Saturday morning, and a sense of gaiety could not be stifled. When young Johnny pranced home, filled with breakfast and the spirit of the night's adventure, bursting with it, wanting to recount every single enormous detail, even he seemed to be caught up in the new illusion. "Hey. What's with you, mom? You sort of— glow."

"Your father's coming home today. Maybe that's the reason." It wasn't. And yet, in a way, in a large way, it was, too. She wished that Martin's plane would hurry.

8

MILDRED PIERSON shopped that early Saturday afternoon. Normally she would have done her weekend shopping on Friday, but the necessity of helping Mona had upset that plan, and, what with one thing and another, compounded by the fact that she was rarely out of bed before eleven o'clock in the morning, it was two o'clock, or maybe three—she could not later pin the time down any closer than that—before she entered the supermarket, chose a cart, and began her gastronomic peregrinations up one aisle and down the next.

Mildred's tastes, and, out of necessity, Ben's, were exotic, and these days not limited by lack of money. It had not always been so, and sometimes it was hard to realize that the bad times were over—the times of waiting endlessly in a producer's office; of rushing from audition to audition; of taking tiny parts wherever and whenever they were offered or could be found and grabbed; the times of summer stock when the name actors and actresses, secure, enjoyed themselves in bucolic pleasures, while the others, the hopefuls, scratched and clawed and bit, in the nicest possible way, allowing no slight to go unavenged, no barest opportunity ungrasped; the Christmas times clerking at Macy's in order to put a few extra dollars in the bank. (Ben, one Christmas time, had brought that fine deep voice, along with much padding, to the role of jovial Santa Claus in Gimbel's toy department, an experience that had left him shaken for weeks.)

Out of those bad times, memories still vivid, came the knowledge that the world was, indeed, a jungle, that one fought, or one perished, that the teeth that showed in every smile could also bite, that pleasant words were mere masquerade. Preventive war—hit-and-run guerilla tactics, actually—was a fact of life. If one relaxed, one lost the touch.

Not for the world would Mildred have displayed actual temper in public. On the other hand, she was not an ingenue, and so her public image suffered nothing, in fact even gained a kind of homey quality, by the wearing of dungarees and sneakers and a short-sleeved plaid shirt, a kerchief on her head, and glasses perched partway down her nose as she prowled the shelves, compared frozen lobster bisque with vichyssoise, searched for and found the petit pois and the caffe nero, the imported bleu cheese almost hidden by that dreadful domestic stuff.

From time to time, as she was recognized, she smiled graciously, even exchanged village pleasantries, (It was warm today? It was, indeed, wasn't it?) or answered questions that demonstrated, in a satisfying manner, that finally, after all the striving and the clawing, she, Mildred Shaw Pierson, had become a *personality*. (Was she really going to Hollywood as it said in the local paper? She was considering the offer; she had not yet made up her mind.)

The store was crowded, all checking lanes filled. Mildred waited her turn in patience. Someone trundled a cart up behind her, and Mildred glanced, smiling. The smile froze, turned masklike.

Roz Warren said, "Hello, Mildred." With that slow, maddening smile. "You're looking well." Roz, in a crisp cotton dress, sandals on her bare feet, every hair in place, cool as one of those dreadful beer ads.

"Am I?" Mildred said. "Thank you, dear." And then, "It's so pleasant to relax in old clothes, don't you think?"

"At times." Smiling still, that incredible composure unshaken. Mildred said, "And how is the—baby?"

"She's fine. You must come see her."

Mildred's smile spread, showing a few more teeth. "Shall I bring Ben?"

"But, of course," Roz said. "Ben is always welcome. You know that."

And it was then that the man at the cash register said, with deference, "Miss Shaw. Your cart, please."

Mildred pushed the cart up to the counter. She began to unload it. Over her shoulder, she said, "So nice to have seen you, dear."

"Why," Roz said, "we'll meet again tonight, won't we? At the Peters'?"

"Possibly," Mildred said, and that was all.

9

MARTIN inched along in the traffic. In this one respect, if in no others, America, at least urban America, made no sense at all. Given a warm, sunny day, and a weekend, and the horror began. Every garage, public or private, promptly emptied; the urge to move, to go somewhere, was apparently inexorable, pure mass hysteria.

Someone, (was it Thurber?) had written once an imaginary dialogue between a man and a lemming, and the man's last question was why did the lemmings periodically start on a migration that ended inevitably in mass suicide? The lemming's answer was another question, covering the human race. "Why don't you?" the lemming asked.

At times like this Martin thought that the lemming had a real point.

Or maybe this was the migration that would end in mass suicide, and he was caught up in it. Maybe every single one of these cars jamming the road was headed for the Hudson River, the river itself and not a bridge; maybe each car, when it reached the river edge, would not even pause, but would plunge in, disappear, as if such behavior were the most natural thing in the world. If the Hudson River was not their goal, then where in hell were they all going, anyway? And why? And did they really think they would ever, ever get there? At this pace?

There was a gas station. Martin pulled into it abruptly. He left the car, went inside the office. No one was there; two men were busy outside at the pumps. No matter. Luckily, Martin had change. He telephoned the house, and Madge's voice, almost breathless, answered after four rings.

"Hi," Martin said. "I—"

"Marty." The gaiety in her voice was unmistakable, irrepressible. "I was in the shower! And what I grabbed turned out to be a hand towel!" And then, "Never mind. You're back. I'm—so glad, Marty."

"I didn't want you to worry," Martin said. "I'm caught in this damned traffic."

"Oh."

"No telling," Martin said, "when I'll get out there. I'll do the best I can."

And again, "Oh."

"You'd better go on to the Peters'," Martin said. "I'll come straight there. I'm sorry, but that's how it is."

There was a pause. Madge said finally, "All right, Marty. If that's what you think best."

Martin walked back out to the car. The highway was jammed, bumper to bumper, here and there off on the shoulder a stalled car, its hood up, overheated. But as soon as the car's engine cooled, off it would go again, joining the migration to nowhere. "Lemmings," Martin said. "Two-legged lemmings." He got into his own car.

10

BY SIX O'CLOCK Wally Peters was dressed—flannels, loafers, cotton jacket, plaid shirt with a button-down collar, black knit tie, almost standard county party attire. It was hot, but not too hot; he had debated the tie and jacket and decided that the weather did not justify leaving them off. Women, for some inexplicable reason, seemed to prefer their males done up in full uniform. As a matter of fact, the local women would probably have preferred the men in dinner jackets. There had been an attempt at that only last New Year's Eve, but George Hanks and Wally had said no, and Martin Fuller had gone along with them, and Bob Lewis; and so, in the end, only Ben Pierson and Sam Barnes and Paul Warren had turned up looking like Rotarians at a Waldorf dinner.

Wally checked the bar, found everything in order. He made himself a drink—which was a host's prerogative, wasn't it?—deciding first that he would be prudent to start on bourbon and stay with it rather than taking a chance on martinis. At Mona's parties you never knew when food would be served. Mona lit up inside like a Christmas tree at any party, particularly her own, and always enjoyed herself so much, not on liquor, merely on *joie de vivre*, that the idea of food slid out of her mind entirely. And so Wally thought he'd better stay with bourbon. What was that verse bit attributed to Dorothy Parker? "I cannot drink martinis/ Only one or two at the most./ After three I'm under the table/ After four I'm under my host." That summed up martinis pretty well. He wondered if Roz, by any chance, would drink martinis. Four of them, say. And he told himself that he was being childish again.

His drink tasted good. He carried it to the foot of the stairs. "Hey!"

"Oh, I'm coming," Mona said.

"You'd better not try to change your dress again. You've run clear out of time."

"I said I'm coming!"

Wally worked on his drink for a bit. He tried one of the cheese dips, found it palatable, tried the second, and then the third. And then his drink was empty and he went to replenish it.

"Wally!" Mona's voice indicated crisis.

Wally sighed. "I'll zip it up down here," he called. "And you'd better hurry. Someone's driving in."

"Oh!" It was a wail. Mona's heels tapped angrily on upstairs hall and stairs.

11

IT WAS six-thirty-five. In the railroad station yard George Hanks held the car door for Gladys. "I apologize, Toots. I'm usually punctual, and I dislike people who aren't. This time I slipped a cog." George rarely believed in explanations. To friends they were usually unnecessary; to others they were unimportant. As he got in beneath the wheel he said, "That's quite a dress. You do me proud."

Gladys giggled. "I really didn't mind waiting. I mean I knew something must have held you up. You're not the kind of man to ask a girl and then forget."

"No," George said, "that I don't do. I tie strings here and there to remind me."

Gladys said, "Tell me about tonight." And she giggled again. "The party, I mean. The people. Will there be other famous people there. You know, like you?"

"I'll fill you in as we go along. I'll make up a background if the character isn't interesting enough." He smiled. "I think you'll enjoy yourself, Toots. I intend to."

Saturday Night

1

ONCE, early in their acquaintance, George had described for Martin and Madge the local theory of parties. "Every night is Saturday night, and Saturday night is New Year's Eve. That tags it fairly well. Oh, there are some people who don't party much. But there's a hard core that does. It's a kind of incestuous coil, the same faces, the same cast, just different stage setting. Not every night, of course, but almost every weekend night, around and around. It's rather like taking in one another's washing."

And it was almost so. You knew whom you were going to see, and you could predict with fair accuracy how each was going to behave. It was a fair bet that Wally Peters and Bob Lewis would drink a little too much, sometimes more than a little; that Paul Warren would become more and more austere as the evening went on; that sooner or later Ben Pierson would sing at least one Spanish Loyalist song with great feeling and solemnity in that fine deep voice; that Louella would appear in one of her Bergdorf dresses, possibly brand new, certainly not seen more than once before, and the other women would look at Louella with envy—until Roz Warren appeared; that there would be no games of any sort, and record player music only infrequently; that there would be talk, talk, talk, rising in volume until whichever house the party happened to be held in echoed and reverberated, and the normal tone of voice became a shout.

There would be, almost certainly, some one episode that would stand out, mark the party as unique, to be remembered, as, say, the night Ben Pierson challenged Bob Lewis to a duel; or the night that it turned out that Joy Lewis—of all people!—could do the bumps and grinds as well as any burlesque queen (some of the men said better); or the night Mildred Pierson, in rare comic mood, did that devastating take-off on Tennessee Williams-type playwriting in a long, soul-searching and emotional monologue of complete nonsense.

Some parties would go on longer than others for no explicable reason. Except, of course, parties at Ben and Mildred's house, which always broke up early because Ben, as George Hanks put it to Martin and Madge, "has never allowed himself to comprehend that one bottle of gin, and a single pony of domestic brandy apiece will not keep a party of twelve going indefinitely. It isn't that he can't afford it. He can. And his miserliness drives Mildred wild. Still it continues, and I don't know why. God knows he drinks enough of anyone else's liquor. There are murky depths to our Ben."

Mona Peters would be everywhere, gay and carefree as a child, her voice the loudest, her laughter the readiest, her spirits a contagion. Roz Warren would smile her slow, maddening smile, and the men would flock to bring her fresh drinks, offer and light her cigarettes. Madge Fuller, for a reason she could never discover, would, sooner or later, be cornered by Ben Pierson, and, unwilling to give offense by rudeness, would have to listen to an interminable monologue on the proper way to mulch roses or force forsythia even as early as January. Sam Barnes would offer stock market advice to Wally Peters, who would listen carefully, storing up the information against the day when he might possibly have some money to invest.

This was the norm. Saturday's party began normally. It ended otherwise.

2

MILDRED AND BEN were the first to arrive, and Mona's zipper was still stuck. "The hell with it," Wally said, "I'll have to get a pair of pliers. After I let them in."

"Honestly," Mona said.

"You're decent," Wally said. "So a little more bare back shows than usual." He went to the door, greeted the Piersons and then went down to the basement for the pliers. When he came back, Ben was straining futilely at the zipper and Mona was giggling. The pliers did the trick. Wally hurried to the bar to get there before Ben did. Wally was aware of Ben's proclivities as well as the next man, and it was not that he begrudged Ben as much liquor as he wanted to drink, it was just that there was something irksome about the way Ben went about helping himself.

Mona said to Mildred, "Have you seen Madge? Since yesterday, I mean?" She giggled.

Mildred had completely forgotten her conjecture of pregnancy. She said that she had not seen Madge, but she had seen Roz Warren—and there was a small, uncomfortable silence.

Ben said, "What about Madge?"

And Mona giggled again. "Didn't you know? She's pregnant."

From the bar Wally said, "Oh, my God. How did that get started?"

"Well, she is," Mona said. And she looked at Mildred. "Isn't she?"

"For all I know," Mildred said.

Joy and Bob Lewis, and Sam and Louella drove in almost together. And then Madge arrived, alone, and explained that Martin was back from London, but having difficulty getting home from the airport. Sam Barnes said that was funny, because he had been in town that afternoon and the traffic hadn't been too bad coming out. "Of course," he added, "maybe it's different on the other side of the Triborough Bridge."

"Those island parkways," Bob Lewis said, "are pure murder." He headed straight for the bar. "Give me a drink, buddy-boy. I feel the need."

Mona said to Madge, "How are you, dear? Is everything all right?" And she added, truthfully, "You look simply lovely. You have a kind of—radiance." She made fluttering gestures with both hands.

Louella said quietly to Sam, "You were in town?"

"And I won't tell you why," Sam said, un-Sam-like. "You'll find out."

At the bar, Bob Lewis said, "Where's good old George Hanks, buddy-boy?" He had not seen George since that Thursday bit, and he had steeled himself to face him tonight and he wanted to get it over with.

Ben Pierson, still wearing the dark glasses, said to Madge, "I've been working in my roses."

And Madge, in her new ebullience, said, "Dear Ben. It's much too early to start telling me that."

And then Paul Warren arrived, alone, grave, austere as always.

At the bar, Bob Lewis whispered, "Where's the lovely Roz?" And he added to himself, "The witch."

Wally shook his head.

Louella said quietly to Sam, "Ask him, if you want. Or, I will."

Sam said merely, "Please."

Mona said clearly, "Where is Roz, Paul? Isn't she coming?" Her voice was almost a wail of disappointment.

Paul looked around the room in his austere way. He said politely, "Good evening, Louella. You're looking lovely, as always." And then, to the room in general, "I thought she'd be here. I was in town. I phoned her, and we agreed that she would come alone because I was afraid I'd be late."

Joy Lewis said in her calm way, "Madge came alone, for the same reason."

Sam Barnes said, "Did you hit traffic, Paul?"

"No more than usual," Paul said.

Gladys was an immediate hit in the slinky dress—strapless, white, clinging lovingly to every curve.

Still at the bar, Bob Lewis said, "Jesus! Good old George really finds them, doesn't he?"

Wally merely nodded. He wondered guiltily what it would be like to be a bachelor again. With George Hanks's money, that was, and prestige.

George said to Gladys, "And you've met Ben Pierson. Briefly, it's true, but perhaps you remember."

Gladys giggled.

Ben's face was stony. The dark glasses showed nothing.

George said, "I'm sure Ben remembers you, Toots." And then, "Evening, Ben." He held out his large hand. Ben took it gingerly.

George turned Gladys. "This is Paul Warren. Evening, Paul."

Paul nodded without expression.

"Paul," George said, "is a publisher. Louella Bloom, among others, is secure in his stable."

Nothing changed in Paul's face.

"You've heard of Louella Bloom, Toots?" George said.

Gladys giggled again. "I read all her books. Every one. I think she's wonderful."

Bob Lewis whispered, "Don't tell me she can read, too."

George said, "Well, here she is." He smiled at Louella, and drew an answering smile, one professional to another. "You'll forgive the build-up," George said. "Toots is interested in famous people."

Louella's smile broadened. "I'm sure your—lovely young lady has a name, George." She held out her hand to Gladys. "You flatter me, and I love it." She patted the sofa seat. "Sit here and tell me about yourself."

George wandered over to the bar. "Wally," he said. They shook hands. "Bob," George said. He held his hand out. "Long time."

"You know," Bob said slowly, and with intense relief, "you're a nice guy."

Mona said to Madge, "Don't you think you'd better sit down, dear?"

"What on earth for?"

Mona smiled in a secret sort of way.

Wally said, "What would your—uh—friend like to drink, George?"

George grinned, openly amused. "Why don't you go over and ask her? She looks even better up close."

Bob Lewis said, "Consider yourself told, buddy-boy." He felt better, much better, the hurdle of George Hanks behind him now. There was only Roz to come.

Roz did not come. It was Louella who remarked it aloud. She said to Paul, with no discernible expression, "Hadn't you better phone your house and see what's keeping Roz?"

"Well," Paul said. And then, "I'm sure she'll be along shortly."

Joy Lewis said, "Maybe she's had trouble getting a baby-sitter. I do sometimes."

"And I," Bob Lewis said to George, "sometimes have trouble driving them home. There's one old biddy who won't even ride with me. She walks."

"They're making roads narrower late at night these days," George said. "There is no doubt about it."

Martin arrived a little before seven-thirty. Madge flew to the door to meet him. Martin kissed her once, kissed her again. "I'm—sorry!" Madge said. Her voice was breathless. "I'm spilling my drink all over you!"

Martin smiled. His arm was still around her. "It's worth it." It was. He thought that Madge looked unusually happy tonight, prettier almost than he had ever seen her, which was maybe what came from not seeing her for a few days. He wanted to tell her how good she looked to him, but not here and now with all the people around.

George said aloud, "Offhand, I'd say the man needs a drink

after flying over all that salt water. Welcome back, friend Martin." He had watched Madge, without appearing to, ever since his arrival. He thought of the unfinished picture standing against the wall of his studio, and of the circumstances that had produced that picture. It was hard to get out of his mind Madge as she had been, posing, giggling. He said, "And while you're about it, Wally, maybe you'll build mine up a bit, too." And when it was done he walked over to talk to Gladys, concentrate on Gladys. He even tried to leer at Gladys.

Bob Lewis left the bar at last. He walked over to Ben. "I've been wondering," Bob said. "What's the dark cheaters bit? Are you doing a Method approach with an eye to playing Carmine de Sapio?"

It was eight o'clock when Louella said, "Really, Paul, I think you should phone." It was almost a command.

Mona said, "You know where the phone is. Unless—" and she giggled, "—you'd rather use the one in Wally's study."

"There's no need of that," Paul said in his austere way. He walked into the hall. He was gone quite a little time. He came back frowning. "Funny. There's no answer."

George, his eye on Madge again, saw, beyond her, Martin's mouth open and then close again, and he wondered what that might mean. He said, "Maybe the line's out of order."

"No," Paul said. "The operator says it's all right as far as she can tell."

George stood up. "Then we'd better find out."

Mildred Pierson said, "Aren't you being a trifle melodramatic, dear? After all, Paul is her husband." She paused, her timing carefully exact. "Although we know you are, of course, very fond of Roz."

There was silence in the room, not a sound, not a movement. George said, "Another time, Mildred. Hoard your malice until then."

Joy Lewis said, "There is the—baby. Someone should be there."

George walked into the hall. He was not gone long. Talk

stopped when he returned. He said, "I called the police. They're sending a prowl car over to see."

Mildred said, "Making a federal case of it, dear?"

Paul Warren said, "You are meddling just a bit, aren't you, George?"

"Perhaps."

"I'm not really sure I appreciate it."

"Suit yourself," George said. "It's your ulcer." He looked at Gladys. "Another drink, Toots? They're on the house."

Mona said, "Police? Honestly, George."

Ben Pierson took off the dark glasses, studied them solemnly, put them back on.

Martin hesitated. He had been standing with Madge ever since his arrival, and he did not want to leave her. On the other hand he did not understand George's attitude, which was direct, as always, and unconcerned about criticism, again as always, but with a difference in quality, a kind of un-George-Hanks-like gravity. Martin said quietly to Madge, "What's going on?"

"I don't know." And then, "Go find out, Marty." And she added, "Please." And this, too, was strange, coming from Madge.

The talk had begun again, a little louder than before. George was at the bar, and he saw Martin start across the room towards him, and he moved a little distance away from the bar, out of Wally's hearing. "How was the trip?" George said.

Martin nodded. "Satisfactory."

"I take it London's still there?"

"It was this afternoon." Martin was puzzled. There was nothing in George's face, or in his voice, and yet the impression George gave was almost resentful, almost unfriendly. "What's up?" Martin said.

"Up?" George said. "The opposite of down?"

"Come off it, George." And then, with some surprise, "You're pulled up as tight as a fiddle string. What goes on?"

"You can't guess?" George said.

"No."

"I wonder." Slowly, visibly, the big man relaxed. And then,

"Call it a hunch, friend Martin, George Hanks and his crystal ball—"

And from across the room Mona's voice rose in its delighted way, "But you simply can't keep it a secret indefinitely!" And she giggled. "I mean, when a girl's pregnant it does begin to show!" There was silence in the room.

Madge said slowly, distinctly, spacing the words, "What did you say?"

George said to Martin, "Your cue, boy. It looks like one of those evenings."

Martin recrossed the room. He said, calmly enough, "Something I ought to know?"

Madge said, "I haven't the faintest idea."

Mona giggled again. "Yesterday, when you left here so mysteriously and went to the doctor—"

"But I didn't go to the doctor," Madge said. She began to smile. You couldn't take offense at Mona, because no offense was intended. Mona frequently got things twisted. "You—"

Mona said, "You said you had an appointment."

"I did," Madge said, and the smile was suddenly gone. "But it wasn't with a doctor."

"But you were so mysterious, dear."

Across the room George Hanks said, "Jesus Christ."

Madge said, "I am not pregnant, period. Does that settle it?"

"Oh, dear," Mona said. "And I was so sure. You look so— radiant, everybody's noticed it, and I was sure—"

George Hanks said, "Apparently, for once, you were wrong, pet, thereby sullying an otherwise unblemished record."

Bob Lewis said, "Beautiful, George, beautiful. The exact—" He stopped, crouched a little to look out beneath the window shade. "Somebody's coming. The fair Roz, at last?"

Mona flew to the door. She opened it. She seemed to shrink, childlike. She stepped back. A uniformed policeman followed her into the hall, into the living room. "Mr. Paul Warren?"

"Here," Paul said. He was frowning. "What is it, officer?"

"I'd like to talk with you, please. Outside."

And when they were gone out onto the porch, Mildred said, "You seem to have stirred something up, George dear. One of your better efforts."

George set his glass on the bar. His taste for whiskey was gone. He said slowly, "You are a bitch, aren't you, Mildred? I think your blood is pure vitriol." He started for the door. The policeman met him in the hall.

"Mr. George Hanks?"

"That's right," George said. "I called you."

The policeman nodded. "Then you won't mind coming along with us?"

"No," George said. "I won't mind." He turned back into the room. He caught Martin's eye. "Look after Toots for me, will you?"

Martin said, "Of course."

George almost filled the doorway as he walked out into the darkness.

3

IN THE SILENCE Mona said, "What on earth do you suppose—?"

Wally said, "Why don't you shut up? For once?"

Mona said, "Honestly."

Mildred said, "Take me home, Ben. I won't stay here to be insulted."

Bob Lewis said, "The insultor was George Hanks, Mildred dear. And he gone."

Mildred said, "Come, Ben." And then, in sudden impatience, "And take off those silly dark glasses."

"Curtain line," Bob Lewis said. He walked not quite steadily back to the bar. "Another small potion, buddy-boy?"

Louella said, "I think we'd better go, too, Sam."

Sam nodded.

Mona said, "But all that food! You can't! You simply can't!" She looked around desperately. "Madge! Martin! Joy!"

Madge's hand was in his. Martin gave it a small squeeze. He looked down at her. Madge said, "I think we should stay, Marty. At least until George comes back."

Martin nodded. He glanced across the room at Gladys.

Gladys merely looked bewildered.

And a little later Mona's voice rose again in a wail, "Can't anybody think of anything at all to say?"

Wally came back out of his drink. "Only you," he said.

4

THE PLEASANT white house was ablaze with lights. There was an ambulance in the drive, and a second prowl car. George rode in the back seat with Paul Warren, the two policemen in front. No one had spoken. Paul's lips were a thin straight line, and his face held no expression whatsoever.

They got out of the car and climbed the porch steps, walked inside. There in the front hall Paul Warren stopped. He shook his head. His lips worked, but no sound came out. One of the policemen said, "You can wait down here if you'd rather, Mr. Warren." And Paul walked into the living room and sat down heavily.

The policeman said to George, "You know Mrs. Warren, don't you?"

"Yes," George said. And he added, "I did." He followed the policeman up the stairs, down the hall towards the master bedroom.

The policeman said, "My name's Parker, Fred Parker, I'm a lieutenant." And, incongruously, "I used to watch you play ball. At the Polo Grounds and then at the Stadium." There was a sound behind them, a baby's cry. "We brought a nurse over from the hospital. The kid was crying her lungs out." At the bedroom doorway he stopped. He looked at George. "Not very pretty," he said. "It never is. We want your identification. Just for the record."

George nodded. He walked in.

Roz was there, on the floor, the lovely long clean legs sprawled in disgraceful awkwardness that Roz would never, never have permitted. George had a desire to straighten the legs, by this much at least diminishing the indignity of death. Roz's body wore mules, and panties and a bra. On the right side of her naked back, low down in the kidney area, there was a small dark blemish; the wound had bled little.

There was a hospital intern, white suit and all, and he said, "The damndest thing. The bullet went clear through her, and came partway out, only partway. It's caught in the net of her brassiere. It looks like she has two nipples on that left breast." And then, "Jesus, what a body. She must—"

George looked at the intern, and the intern was silent.

Lieutenant Parker was watching George. George said, "Yes. Rosamund McCartney Warren. Is that all?"

"For the identification, yes," the lieutenant said. "But there are a few questions—"

"Yes," George said. "I thought there would be."

They sat in the living room. Paul, on the sofa, was a man stunned. He watched, and did not seem to see; listened, and did not hear. And after a few moments George got up from his chair and went out to the pantry and mixed a stiff drink of scotch, brought it back and put it in Paul's hand. "Drink it," he said. And then he sat down again.

Lieutenant Parker said, "You must have had some idea, Mr. Hanks."

"You might as well make it George. It's easier. Because I called you, you mean?" He nodded. "Let's say I had a hunch that something might have happened. If she, Roz, was still here, she would answer the phone. She did not. If she was gone, then someone would be here to look after the baby, and the baby sitter would have answered." He spread his large hands. "Nobody answered, so something was wrong." He looked at Paul. Paul held the drink in both hands. He stared into it.

Lieutenant Parker said, "But why was it you who called us? Mr. Warren might have been worried, and called, but you—"

"Let's say I'm a meddler," George said.

"This isn't a joke, you know."

"I wasn't joking. I'll let you know when I am."

The lieutenant was silent for a few moments. Then, "Did you expect something like this to happen? Is that it?"

"I don't know," George said. He doubled both hands into large fists, studied them. Then he opened the hands and rested them on his thighs. "There was the—possibility. The depths were seething, although maybe you won't understand that."

"Try giving me a few hints."

George shook his head. "It wants thinking about, sorting out."

The lieutenant said, "You aren't going to do anything silly, are you, Mr. Hanks? George?"

"I frequently do. That's not a joke, either."

"Did you have anything to do with it?" the lieutenant said then.

"Would I tell you, if I had?"

"You might. They do sometimes. It depends on how tough they are inside, where it counts."

"For the record," George said, "I didn't have anything to do with it. I haven't seen her, Roz, since Thursday night." He nodded at Paul, who still stared, unseeing, into his glass. "He was here. We had a drink."

The lieutenant said, "You knew Mrs. Warren well, didn't you?"

"I did."

"I mean, very well. You know how villages are."

"I know," George said.

"And," said the lieutenant, "weren't there others who knew Mrs. Warren very well?" And he added, "I'm not just trying to make gossip."

"I know that, too," George said. "The garbage can is kicked over now, and the pigs can start rooting. Pity."

"Is it?" the lieutenant said. He stood up then in sudden decision. "I'll send you back to the—party, if that's where you want to go. I'll want to talk to you later again, of course. You'll be around."

"I'll be around."

"One thing," the lieutenant said. "If you get any ideas, we're the people to bring them to." And he added, "I'm not joking, either."

"I didn't think you were," George said.

5

DOWNSTAIRS the house was dark, the party already passed into county history. Wally, in pajamas, sat on the edge of the bed with a cigarette and a nightcap. Mona was in the bathroom, and what she could be doing all that time was more, far more than Wally could understand. Wally thought that he had better take a sleeping pill, if he could ever get into the bathroom to get them, because otherwise it was a leadpipe cinch he'd just lie awake in the darkness and think about the whole bloody mess no matter how hard he tried to shut off his mind.

Roz dead—it was unbelievable. These things happened, of course, otherwise he, Wally, would have to find another way of earning a living because people simply would not believe books about mayhem and violence and murder. But—truism, of course —when it happened to someone you knew yourself, not just a name in the newspaper or a character in a book, the feeling of disbelief just would not be denied. And when it happened to somebody like Roz, who was the epitome of *aliveness,* then the entire operation moved into the realm of fantasy.

Wally was not unintelligent. He was not naïve. And his imagination was vivid enough, in this instance too vivid. He knew what to expect—the local gossip, the newspaper stories, the peeking and probing and prying by the police; God knew he'd worked this all out on paper often enough in as much shocking detail as he could manage—and the knowledge frightened him, brought a kind of hollow feeling into his stomach that was qualitatively no different from the feeling of physical fear. Because he was going to be right in the middle of the mess, and he had no way of knowing where it would all end, or, more important, how he, Wally, would stand up—as a person, as a man, as an allegedly superior creature of civilization. And it was this sense of the unknown, the unknowable, that was worst of all.

He was still sitting there on the edge of the bed when Mona, at last, came out of the bathroom. She wore a silk dressing gown Wally had given her, extravagance arising out of some larger-than-expected royalty check now long since spent. Mona's face was bright, not at all a mirror of Wally's mood. She said, "Honestly. Have you ever seen so much confusion?"

Wally admitted that he had not. He thought of that sleeping pill, and decided it could wait until he finished his drink.

"She's dead," Mona said. "Shot. Murdered! And lying there in panties and a bra! And mules!" George had been strangely, even unnecessarily, clinical in his report. Mona did not understand it, but she would not for the world have altered it. It had not taken much prying at all to get the whole story, chapter and verse; it was almost as if George had been determined to tell whether he was urged or not. "Wally."

"Mmm?"

"Look at me."

Wally raised his head.

Mona said, "Don't you find it—exciting?"

"Frightening."

"Honestly," Mona said. "Sometimes you deliberately misunderstand what I say."

Wally's face was blank, bewildered. "Come again?"

"Exciting, silly." Mona moved closer. "Don't you know what the word means?" She was smiling.

"Well," Wally said, and was silent. He made no move.

Mona undid the belt of the silk dressing gown. It fell open.

Mona was naked. She let the gown drop to the floor. "Exciting is the only word. Don't you see?" She moved even closer, smiling still, confident. She bent over him and her shoulders began to move with slow deliberation, brushing her breasts lightly against his face. "Don't you see?" It was a whisper this time.

Wally reached for her in a kind of blindness, drew her down to him. This was what Mona gave him, this was the dowry she had brought to their marriage. Other people might see no more of Mona than silly tongue and childishness, fluttery gossipy helpless foolishness; the knowledge of what lay beneath was Wally's alone, his secret and his treasure, more precious for being hidden from the world. Here, now, with Mona, the real, secret Mona, he was complete.

And, later, just before sleep came, Wally said suddenly, "Necrophilia."

And Mona said, "What on earth is that?"

"Never mind. Go to sleep. It's just a word."

6
• • • • • •

IN THE STUDIO George said, "Do you want a drink, Toots?"

"I don't think so, thank you." And she added, "You go ahead."

"No," George said. "Liquor isn't quicker this time. It isn't anywhere near quick enough." And then, "That was a rough time tonight. For you, I mean. I apologize."

"It—doesn't matter. It wasn't your fault."

"Maybe it was," George said. "I don't know. I haven't got it straight yet." And then, inactivity impossible, he walked the length of the studio in that light and yet ponderous way, turned at the far wall and came back to the girl. "You're no part of this," he said. "And you're better out of it. I'll drive you into town."

"You don't have to do that."

"I don't have to do anything." He paused. "Check that. I'm

just kidding myself. I'm not really any freer than anybody else."

"I don't understand what you mean."

He smiled then, gently, without mockery. "I'm pitching curves at you, Toots. Forgive me. I'll stop. Do you want to go back to town?"

"Do you want me to?"

His smile spread, turned inwards now, upon himself, his thoughts. "Strangely enough," he said, "but not in the way you may think, I don't want you to go. Is that another curve? If it is—"

"No," Gladys said. "I understand that. You don't want to be alone." And she added, "Some things I can understand. And I'd like to stay."

"Thanks," George said. The smile was gentle again. "Go to bed."

"All right." She glanced at him. "Are you coming?"

"I don't know." He spread his large hands. "I just don't know."

She walked to the bedroom door. There she stopped, turned. Her face for that brief moment was quite close to the idealized face George had drawn in the picture—the vacuousness gone, replaced by understanding. "It doesn't matter, you know," she said.

She lay awake for some time in the large bed. And then, at last, she slept. When she awakened she was still alone, and the studio lights burned on. She got out of bed, put on her robe. Her bare feet made little sound as she walked out, and George did not even look around.

He was at his easel. His cotton jacket and tie were tossed on a chair, and his shirt was open at the throat, the sleeves rolled up on the blacksmith's arms. He was scowling in concentration and he did not seem to notice when the girl came around behind him to stand, to look past his shoulder at the picture on the easel.

It was the picture of Madge, finally finished now, every flesh tone, every shadow, every curve complete. Out of Madge's giggles George had drawn soft laughter, anciently secret, lifting Madge's lips, lighting her eyes, bringing a glow to her entire being.

"She's—lovely," Gladys said.

George said, without even glancing at her, "Did you ever hear of a man named Goya, Toots?"

"No."

"He was a painter. He did a nude of a duchess, the Duchess of Alba." He smiled. "As a matter of fact he did two pictures of her, one of them nude and the other clothed. There's no point to the story. I'm no Goya."

Gladys still studied the picture. She said, "Was he in love with her? The duchess?"

George turned slowly. He looked at the girl for a long time. Then, "So they say." The smile was gone. He put down his palette, stuck the brushes in an open jar. He undid the easel clamps and took the picture down, carried it over to the wall, set it with its back to the room.

"It's late," Gladys said. "Come to bed." She walked away, silent on her bare feet.

In the darkness George got into bed beside her. "Toots—" And then, "No. You've graduated from the Toots stage."

Her voice was gentle and without reproach. "Go to sleep. You're tired, and upset. Goodnight."

He felt soothed, eased. Strange. "Goodnight, honey," George said. And then, almost humbly, "Thanks." Miraculously, sleep came.

7

MILDRED PIERSON lay on her back staring up into the darkness. In the other bed Ben was awake too, and Mildred knew it, although there had been no word, or even movement for some little time. Mildred said, "What are you thinking?"

There was no answer.

"Ben." And then, "Do you know what the police wanted with Paul, with George?"

"I know." In the fine deep actor's voice.

Mildred waited, but he said no more. "Tell me," Mildred said. There was a silence this time. Then, at last, "Roz is dead."

Mildred closed her eyes, squeezed them tight until strange lights and patterns flashed on her retina. She opened her eyes again. "Why do you think that? Why, Ben?"

"I *know,*" Ben said. And then, with finality, "Goodnight."

8

SAM BARNES said, "Are you going to read tonight?"

"No," Louella said.

"It was quite a—mess, wasn't it?"

"Understatement, Sam."

"People can be so—bitchy."

"I didn't think," Louella said, "that I'd ever hear you use a word like that."

"They are."

"Of course they are. There's that quality in all of us if you scratch deep enough."

"In you?" And then, "Yes."

"You've seen it, Sam."

"Why is it there? In everybody, I mean. You understand these things better than I do."

Louella said, "When most people ask a question, they don't really want an answer. You do, don't you, Sam?" She was silent for a few moments. "Everybody," she said then, "carries his own private picture of himself in his mind. It may be close to reality, as George's is, or it may be as far-fetched as Ben Pierson's. But it's a—sacred thing, that personal picture. When it is violated in any way, then the bitchiness comes out, pure revenge. I think that is the basic reason, Sam."

Sam said, "Do you have a private picture of yourself?"

"I said everybody."
"Even me?"
"You have your picture, Sam."
There was silence. Sam said at last, "It's late. Go to bed, Louella. I'll close the door so I won't disturb you. I have some —work to do."
Louella said, "I don't think you have any work, Sam." She paused. "You're troubled. Do you want to tell me?"
"Goodnight," Sam said. He closed the door gently.

9

MADGE SAID, "I—planned a different welcome for you, Marty. But I—couldn't go through with it now. Not after hearing about Roz." She was silent for a few moments. "The way George talked about it. It was almost ghoulish. And George isn't like that."
"No," Martin said, "he isn't."
"Why did he do it?"
"I don't know."
"You've been wondering, too? It was as if he was trying to shock us. That was the feeling I had. I still have it. Why would he do that?"
"I don't know."
"Was he trying to—frighten somebody?"
Martin looked at her.
"Was he, Marty? Trying to frighten somebody into—saying something, doing something?"
Martin said, "Why would he try to do that?"
There was brief silence. Then, "Marty," Madge said, "was it only traffic that kept you so late?" She watched him frown, and then smile.
"Did he frighten you?" Martin said. The smile spread. "It was only traffic, two-legged lemmings in compulsive migration."

"Marty," Madge said, "I think you're lying to me. Please don't lie. Not ever again."

Martin said, "Hey." And again, "Hey."

"Goodnight, Marty."

10

BOB LEWIS said, "Did I win first prize: For boy having best time at party?"

"I think you did," Joy said.

"Does that make me the local champ?"

"I rather think it does."

"Shoes come off easy. It's the socks that are the troublemakers. Somebody ought to design a new sock, maybe with a zipper."

"Let me help."

"You're a good girl. Do you have a preference, left foot over right, for example?"

"I'm ambidextrous."

"That has other meanings. But you wouldn't know about that. You're pure. Funny word, isn't it? But you are."

"Stand up, and I'll help—"

"Pants are easy. Just unbuckle, unhook, unzip—and there they go. Sailors wear bell-bottomed pants so the feet come out easier. Sound idea. The world is full of sound ideas. You wouldn't think it, but it is. Like—like—" He was silent.

Joy said, "Like killing Roz Warren?" She watched his eyes come into sharp focus, the drunkenness for the moment recede. She pushed the question again. "Is that what you meant?"

The moment was gone. "Pajamas ought to be re-designed, too," Bob said. "Hard to get into and they twist every time you turn over." And then, "Good old honey-bee Roz."

Joy said, "I'm glad she's dead." Joy did not know then, or ever, if the words got through to him.

This was Saturday night.

Sunday

1

SUNDAY MORNING in the county was usually quiet, in this respect as different from Saturday as Saturday was from the balance of the week. There were, not infrequently, hangovers of varying degrees, and these did not tempt a display of furious activity. There were, too, the Sunday papers—*Times* or *Trib;* or, for Sam and Louella, both—with the multitude of special sections to be read slowly, savored. And then there were usually things to be done, small Sunday-type things concerned with house or garden—not major projects such as painting or papering a room or spading an entire flower bed, but the lesser items of gluing together that broken ashtray, or fixing that shutter that banged in the night, or tying up the one branch of the rambler rose that had grown beyond the limits of its own strength. Few of the people in George's fourth group went to church or even thought about it.

"Karl Marx," George Hanks said once, "wrote that religion is the opium of the people, and, like a lot of the things he wrote, the statement has a tiny germ of truth wrapped up in overwhelming nonsense. Religion can be a drug, of course. So can liquor to an alcoholic. But not very many people drown themselves in either one."

And Martin said, "Disraeli touched on the subject in one of his novels—*Endymion*, I think. One of his characters said that sensible men were all of the same religion, and when he was asked what the religion was, he said that sensible men never told."

"I can see," George said, "that I should have chosen an English professor for a father."

They never discussed the subject further, and yet their views were quite similar. George's code of behavior, his sense of professionalism, was founded upon the rock of self-reliance. This is not to say that George considered himself omnipotent; he did not; a large share of George's strength lay in a realization of his weaknesses. Professionalism, rather, meant that there were no excuses, that what a man did, or did not do, was his and his alone; his fault if he failed, his satisfaction if he succeeded. A man could, and did, ask advice on occasion, but the responsibility for decision and result rested solely within himself. A man was what he was, which by no means implied that he was powerless to change, and, within the limitations of his own entity, he strove, struggled, conquered, failed entirely on his own. George respected faith in others, if that was what they chose, but found no particle of faith in himself—a lack that had never bothered him. Like Disraeli's sensible man, George never told of his own concepts; to tell, and by telling to run the risk of proselytism, would have been unwarranted intrusion on another's basic responsibility, and, hence, negation of the code.

Martin had reached almost the same conclusion by a different, typically intellectual process. Once, long ago, he had read or heard the thesis that everyone did always what he wanted to do, and he had examined that thesis over a period of years and found it to his own satisfaction true.

That man did always what he most wanted to do, meant, really, that he chose the course that solved best for him the complicated equation of life itself, that resolved the almost infinite number of forces acting upon him, forces from without and from within.

There was no simple way to evaluate these forces, or even to break them down into categories. They existed, they exerted their pressures, they could not be ignored. But neither could they be tabulated. What a man did in the end was what felt most nearly comfortable to him, or least uncomfortable, whether it was robbing a bank or digging a ditch or painting a picture or getting drunk.

The man who dug the ditch complained, perhaps, that he would rather be doing something else, but the plain truth was that when the forces were as closely balanced as they could be—economic forces, physical, mental, emotional; hereditary and environmental —the man, even though unhappy digging the ditch, yet did it because he did not want enough to do anything else, to face the alternatives that would arise from not digging the ditch.

To Martin there was a sense of inevitability to this and to everything else, each thing that happened stemming naturally from all else that was happening and that had happened, *ad infinitum;* and this sense of inevitability was as close as he could come to a religious concept. And yet, like George, he believed that each man, any man, could within limits control his own destiny by his actions, thereby affecting the relationship of cause-and-effect, and by this infinitesimal amount altering the entire course of human events. The capacity, and the responsibility, lay within each man. It was a question of choice.

2

ON THIS Sunday morning, Ben Pierson went to church for the first time—except an occasional Christmas Eve—for almost as long as he could remember; it was certainly the first time during his adult life.

He wore the dark glasses, along with a blue suit and a white shirt and a subdued necktie. He was not furtive, but neither was he overbold; he nodded with a kind of funereal gravity to the two men standing at the door, ignorant of both their names and their functions, and then took a place in one of the rear pews.

He rather enjoyed the service, although the crew-cut young minister was, in Ben's professional opinion, something of a ham, and an amateur at that; and his references to Camus, Pasternak, Brahms and Handel all in one completely unintelligible sermon did seem stretching matters a bit. The minister was obviously conscious of the alleged intellectual level of his audience, some of whom Ben knew by sight and reputation, and trying hard.

The mixed choir was not bad. The choir director, who was also the organist, did distract a trifle by her bobbing and bouncing and almost frenetic head-waving, but this Ben could forgive in view of the impossible set designing; the organist should, of course, have faced the choir instead of having her back to them.

Ben could not remember the words of the hymns, but a hymn book was right there in the rack in front of him. And his ear was impeccable, and the tunes came back without effort. He allowed that fine voice to roll out through the small church, thereby bringing a gleam to the eye of the organist who spotted him, and marked him down for later approach and possible capture.

When the collection plate was passed, Ben dropped into it a ten dollar bill, folded small that its denomination might not show.

He left as soon as the service was over, slipping out even before the crew-cut young minister could reach the door and take up his stand. Ben drove straight home, neither fast nor slow. He felt no better, no nearer to a sense of peace.

3

WHEN GEORGE HANKS awakened, Gladys was already up, and showered, and dressed, if that was the term, in one of her swim suits. "It's a lovely day," Gladys said. "I'd like just to lie in the sun, if that's all right. I mean, in town, there isn't really any place where a girl can sun herself without people, men, peeking or just plain staring, and there's one man who actually uses field glasses—"

"Anything you like," George said, and he almost, but not quite, added, "Toots."

George put on the denim shorts and sandals and pulled a tee shirt over his enormous shoulders. He found Gladys bewildered in the kitchen. "I guess," Gladys said, "that you do things different than I do. The way you cook, I mean. All these pots and pans hanging and these little jars and things, and I couldn't even find a can of coffee—"

"Honey," George said, "you just go out and lie in the sun. I'll shout when breakfast's ready."

"I just have fruit juice and coffee. I mean—"

"Not this morning," George said. He patted her haunch. "Scoot."

Gladys was momentarily perceptive. "You feel better this morning. I'm glad." She walked out into the sun.

It was true, of course. He did feel better, much better, a sense of physical well-being too strong to be ignored. The coffee smelled good, rich, fragrant, tempting; and the local sausage broiling slowly. And there was a kind of sensual pleasure in mixing the thin lumpy batter, ladling a spoonful into the pan, flowing it around with gentle motions of his thick wrist until it was evenly spread, watching the small bubbles form and break, the edges begin to curl ever so slightly; flipping each pancake—*crêpe*, really; not pancake at all in the usual sense—with a single motion of the spatula, flipping it again out onto the warmed plates.

Basically man was an animal, of course, although most people tended to forget this, or denied it; and man's physical reactions continued in the face of almost any provocation or threat. The condemned man ate a hearty meal—George had an idea that this was more often the case than not.

He set two places at the round hutch table in the sunny corner of the kitchen. Then he summoned Gladys, and held a chair for her, and smiled when she said that she couldn't, she couldn't possibly eat that much breakfast, because she wasn't used to it, and, anyway, a girl had to watch her figure—

"Suit yourself," George said. His voice was gentle, unbarbed, the memory of the girl's understanding and companionship warm in his mind. "But you can't insult the chef by refusing even a taste." He watched her nibble a bit of the thin French pancake with just a little melted butter and a touch of maple syrup; she tried the sausage. She looked at George.

"Well," she said. And then, "It's so good."

George said, "Don't be embarrassed, honey. We're all animals."

Gladys giggled. "That's a dreadful thing to say."

George sent her out into the sun again while he tidied up. Then he made the bed, and shaved. He carried a can of beer outside, and sat down on the low rock wall. Gladys watched him. She said, "You seem to be—waiting."

"I am."

"For what?"

He shook his head, smiling. "Don't let it worry you." And when he heard the footsteps coming up the path he said merely, "There's more lawn on the other side of the house, honey. Go lie there."

It was Martin. George said, "I expected you. Get yourself a beer, and then we'll talk about it." And when Martin had returned from the kitchen, beer in hand, "How's Madge?" George said.

Martin sat down on the rock wall. He said, "She called Paul Warren. I don't know if she got him out of bed or not. She wanted to know if there was anything she could do—for him, or for the baby." And then, almost sharply, "I suppose you expected that, too?"

"Being Madge," George said, "yes."

"Maybe you know her better than I do."

"Relax," George said. He grinned. "Or don't relax." He sucked on his beer.

"She said something last night," Martin said. "She said that it seemed to her that you were trying to frighten us all when you came back to the Peter's house."

"And what did you think?"

Martin said, "And she also said that she thought I was lying to her when I told her it was only traffic that held me up."

"Was it only traffic?" George said.

"God damn it—"

"You'd better make up your mind," George said. "If you've thought about it, you'll see that. Shall I draw the picture?"

Martin studied him for a long time. Then, "I guess you'd better."

George said, "The time your flight got in can be checked."

"Obviously."

"And they keep a pretty close watch on traffic conditions—radio cars, helicopters. They can make a good accurate guess on how long it ought to have taken you from Idlewild out here."

Martin said slowly, "You mean the police, of course."

"I mean the police. Don't underrate them. That lieutenant has ideas. That's what I meant when I said you'd better make up your mind."

"Look," Martin said, "I phoned Madge from a gas station on the other side of the Triborough Bridge. I told her—"

"Can you prove that?"

"That's silly. I talked to her—"

"Can you prove where you phoned from?"

Martin was silent. Then, "No." And he made himself smile. "A tempest in a teapot."

"You're wrong," George said. And it was then that he talked at some length of the waiting period that began Thursday morning, used the analogy of the strange dogs and cats penned up together with a thunderstorm brewing, mentioned the Ben Pierson episode at the New Jersey bar. And he added, "You were back yesterday in plenty of time. You could have killed her just as easily as any of the rest of us. We're all in it together."

"I wasn't back in plenty of time. I—"

"Stop trying to kid yourself, and me. I think you wanted to see Roz before the party. I think—"

"I didn't see her."

George was silent for a few moments. He looked down at the folded beer can at his feet, kicked it idly. Then he looked up again. "Maybe you didn't. I don't know. I wouldn't expect you to tell me if you had." He paused. He smiled faintly. "But don't lie to me about the time. I know how long it takes to drive in from Idlewild even with traffic." The smile spread a little. "I don't object to lying on moral grounds. I do object to it when it insults my intelligence." He paused. The smile was gone. "The police won't see it that way. They'll just see it as a lie."

Martin was silent for a long time. Then, "You're right, of course." He said it slowly, heavily, "I did want to see her. Roz. I drove to the house. The lights were on. I sat in the car for some time, because I thought that Paul was probably there too." He paused. "Funny, I hadn't even considered Paul. I had thought only about Roz, what I'd say to her."

"Nobody ever really thought about Paul," George said. And then, "Go on."

"I decided finally," Martin said, "that it had to be done, Paul or no Paul. So I went up and rang the bell. There was no answer. I assumed they had gone to the party, so I went on too. I didn't think about the baby, that there ought to have been a baby-sitter at least."

George stood up. He picked up the empty beer can, worked it in his big hands. "When the police come around, you'd better tell them."

Martin nodded. "And Madge—"

"What you do about Madge," George said, "is your own business." And then, "Dammit, I'm not God. I'm not even Dear Abby." He walked off, around the house, to the lawn terrace where Gladys was.

Martin, frowning, watched the broad back until it disappeared.

4

LIEUTENANT PARKER was polite, sitting there in the sunny, pleasant, and obviously expensive room with Louella and Sam. He had used no shock tactics; with people like these they rarely produced results. And yet it seemed that he had shocked them, the man at least; the woman had the kind of poise that did not come apart easily. A damn good looking woman, too, although with overmuch assurance for the lieutenant's taste.

Sam said, "I had—no idea, lieutenant. That she, Roz, was dead, I mean."

The lieutenant said, "Why did you and Mrs.—Barnes leave the party?" He had almost said Mrs. Bloom, which would not have helped matters at all.

"Why do you ask that?" Sam said.

Louella said, "The party had already begun to come apart at the seams, lieutenant. Claws were showing. Tempers were beginning to rise. It was not pleasant, and so I suggested that we leave. Another couple did the same."

"That would be the Piersons," the lieutenant said. And then, "It was only that? The—claws and tempers?"

Louella said, "I'm not sure you understand, lieutenant."

"I doubt if I do, Mrs. Barnes. You people who move out from the city are a little—out of my line. I'm just a village boy."

Louella smiled. "Self-deprecation, lieutenant? Is that the way you want us to think of you, as a naïve bucolic." She nodded. "Very well. There was no screaming, lieutenant. There was no physical trouble of any kind. Certain people—sniped at one another in the nicest possible way without even raising their voices, but it became uncomfortable, and so, when the interruption came, your arrival, your departure with Paul Warren and George, we took the opportunity of leaving ourselves."

"Thank you, Mrs. Barnes."

"Not at all."

Sam said, "When was she killed? I mean, do you know that?"

"Not really," the lieutenant said. "Within a matter of a few hours, we know, but no closer than that."

And Louella said, "So, obviously, you would like to know, wouldn't you, lieutenant, what each of us was doing during the late afternoon?"

"It would be a help."

"I went for a walk," Louella said. "I do frequently when I'm working. I had no destination. I merely walked."

"On Sunset Road, Mrs. Barnes?"

"Is that the name of it?" Louella said. "I didn't know. I walked past the Warren house, yes. That was what you meant, wasn't it?"

The lieutenant said, "Do you happen to know the time, Mrs. Barnes? It would be a help if you did."

"I have no idea," Louella said. "I was thinking of other things." She paused. "I didn't kill the woman, lieutenant. If I had, it would not have been with a gun, I promise you."

Sam said, "Louella." There was silence.

The lieutenant said, "Would you mind telling me where you were, Mr. Barnes?"

"I was in town. The city. I—" Sam stopped there. He shook his head in helplessness. "No. I wasn't in town, although that's what I told my wife. I'm sorry, Louella. I was here in the county. I had an—appointment."

The lieutenant said, "Yes, Mr. Barnes?"

"With a doctor," Sam said. "Dr. Rogers, William Rogers. He's—"

"I know Doc Rogers," the lieutenant said. "He's been out here a long time."

Sam said, "Oh. I—" He stopped again. He spread his hands. "I didn't see the doctor. I had the appointment, but I—didn't keep it." He was silent.

The lieutenant said, "Why was that, Mr. Barnes?"

Sam shook his head. "That is my business, lieutenant. It's enough that you know that I had the appointment, that I didn't keep it, that I was here in the county all afternoon, just driving around, thinking. I have no—alibi, if that's the word."

Louella said, "Is that all, lieutenant?" Dismissal, plain and clear.

The lieutenant nodded, smiling faintly. "I think so, for now." And he added, "Thank you."

And when he was gone, and they sat again alone in the sunny pleasant room, Louella said, "I think you'd better tell me, Sam."

"Tell you what?" But he got no answer, and had expected none. He said then, "All right. I was going to see the doctor to find out about myself." He hesitated, embarrassed.

And Louella said slowly, "I think I understand. To find out if Roz's child could be yours, Sam? Is that it? To find out if you are actually capable of fathering a child?"

The embarrassment was gone. He faced her steadily. "Precisely."

Louella said gently, "Why didn't you keep the appointment?"

There was a little silence. "You're not usually obtuse, Louella," Sam said then. "I think you know the answer. I think you just want to make me say it."

"Sam—"

"I didn't keep the appointment," Sam said, "because I was afraid to find out whether I'm a man or a—eunuch. Satisfied now, Louella?"

5

JOY WAS on the telephone when Bob Lewis came down stairs. It was already mid-morning. Joy said into the phone, "Of course. We'll be here." She hung up.

Bob said, "Who in God's name was that? And call them back and tell them we won't be here, at least I won't. Tell them that I just cut my throat with a dull and rusty knife."

"That isn't very funny," Joy said. "Not this morning." And then, "I'll get you some coffee. I kept it hot."

Bob followed her into the kitchen. He said, "Look. I was a bad boy last night. I got potted. I'm sorry. Trouble was I'd had a few during the afternoon, and—"

"Is that where you went?" Joy said. "To a bar somewhere?" Her voice was calm, too calm.

"I had a few at the Tavern," Bob said. "Only a couple, really. But apparently they sneaked up on—"

Joy said, the calm still holding precariously, "Were you there all afternoon? From the time you left here?"

Bob said, "Why is it that women can't talk and act at the same time. The coffee, woman, the coffee." He took the cup from her hand, swallowed eagerly. "Jesus, it's hot. But good."

"Bob."

"No," Bob said, "I didn't spend the afternoon there. I figured I'd better not have too many. So I left and went for a drive—"

"Where?"

"Around. 'Where did you go? Out. What did you do? Noth—' "

Joy said, "The phone call—"

"Oh, Jesus, yes. Call them back. Tell them I've—"

"I can't."

"Will you tell me why the hell not? It's perfectly simple. All you do is dial a number, and then you say—"

"It was the police." And the calmness was entirely gone now; what remained was only tight control teetering on the brink of hysteria. "They—he, a lieutenant, wants to talk to both of us. Just a few questions, he said. It would be—helpful if we could tell him what we did, and where we went yesterday afternoon. Can you tell him?"

He tried to set the coffee cup down on the stove top, but his fingers fumbled the simple movement and the cup overturned, and he merely stood there watching while the coffee spread, ran over the stove's edge, hissed angrily on the still-hot burner. He turned around then. He said, "I can try." God knew if there was one thing he could do it was talk off the cuff. "You were here, weren't you?" And then, "Weren't—?"

They both heard it, the sound of tires in the gravel of the drive.

Joy said, in a voice he had never heard before, almost a monotone, completely expressionless, unreal, "Do you know, Bob, I'm going to scream." Joy did.

6

IT WAS some little time after breakfast that Mona had her idea. She put down the *Trib,* through which she had searched assiduously and found nothing about Roz Warren. It was simply maddening to be left in the dark this way. It was not fair. She jumped up from the sofa and flew upstairs, pounded on the door of Wally's tiny study. "Wally. Open the door. Locking it. Honestly."

Wally let her in. He felt good this morning, larger than life, confident. Last night's fears had washed away in Mona's arms. And the story was going well.

Mona said, "Yesterday, when you were doing all those errands—" She paused. "Did you see Roz?"

"No." And he saw the disappointment in Mona's face. "I was busy."

"But you went so many places."

"I didn't see her. At least, I don't think I did."

"It isn't like New York," Mona said. "I mean, there you simply never see anybody you know. I've never understood how that can be because you see so many people and they can't all be strangers. I don't think there are that many strangers." To Mona it sometimes seemed that what existed outside of her ken was entirely unreal, mere stage setting, not really to be taken seriously. "But here it's different. I mean you simply can't walk along Main Street without bumping into simply everybody you know."

Wally thought that the implied comparison between Main Street and Trafalgar Square or the clock in Grand Central was a trifle far-fetched, but he let it go. "As far as I know, I didn't see Roz," he said.

"But you aren't sure."

"If I saw her, I didn't notice her."

Mona's dejection was plain. She said, "What in the world were you doing all that time?"

Wally smiled. "Look. I have to get to work."

"Honestly."

"If it will make you feel any better," Wally said, "I was past the Warren house three or four times, but—"

"Oh!" Mona said. "You were?" She jumped up from the chair, flew out of the study, down the hall, down the stairs.

Wally said, "Hey!" although he knew that it was futile. And then he closed the door and turned back to the typewriter.

Mona was back in a few minutes. "Open the door. Wally!" And when she was inside again, "The nicest man." She giggled happily. "I mean it makes you feel better, much better, when you know you have such nice people working for you."

Wally shook his head. "I'm clear out in left field. Who?"

"Why, the police, silly. I told the man that my husband was at the Warren's house yesterday afternoon. I mean, I knew they'd want to know, and they did, the man was so nice. He asked me all about it, and I told him that he'd better talk to you, and he said *he* wouldn't, but that another policeman named—it doesn't matter what his name is, I forget it, but he's a lieutenant, and he's coming to see you." The words stopped at last. There was a pause. Mona said, "Why, what's wrong? Don't you want to *know* what's happening? And how else could we find out?"

Wally closed his eyes. "Oh, my God!" he said.

7
•••••

THE BODY lay on a white table in the county morgue. The light was glaring, pitiless. The man with the tripod camera had taken four pictures—front view and back view; in the bra and panties, and nude. He said, "She must have been quite a dish."

And the morgue attendant said, "She's just meat now. You all through?"

"Routine is satisfied," the photographer said. "At least that's how they'd say it in *Dragnet*. Between you and me, I don't know what the hell good pictures do except to give the jury a thrill. If there ever is a jury." And then, idly, he picked up the net brassiere. "Funny," he said. "Why would she have a safety pin here in the strap? The strap isn't busted or anything."

The morgue attendant said, "Look. Don't waste your time trying to make sense out of anything any woman ever does. Especially this one. She got herself dead, didn't she?"

"My, my," the photographer said, "aren't we sour on life today?"

8

LIEUTENANT FRED PARKER was not a brilliant man, and well aware of the fact. He had not lied when he told Sam and Louella that he was a village boy; he had been born and had lived all of his life, except for four years in the army, within the corporate limits of the village. In the army he had risen to the rank of sergeant, buck sergeant, and from time to time, when he thought about it, he supposed that it would have been about the same as in the army if he had ever succumbed to temptation and taken examinations for the city police force. Sure, the city force paid better, but it cost more to live in the city, too. And here in the village he had a nice little house, and people knew him, and he was a lieutenant, which maybe wasn't much, but he liked it. Sometimes when he phoned the city police to ask for their cooperation on something or other he thought he detected a smile behind the voice of the city cop when the cop used the title *lieutenant,* but Fred Parker didn't mind as long as he got his cooperation.

He had gone through grade and high school right in the village—junior high had not existed then. Like most kids he had fooled around with football and baseball and things like that, and in high school he had been a pretty fair halfback, maybe even better than pretty fair, but he had never had any illusions that college scouts would come around looking for him, and they had not.

These days he did a little bowling, and a little hunting in season, and that was about it, except for maybe once a year a day trip with four or five other fellows out to Long Island or down to one of the Jersey ports where the charter fishing boats operated. Two or three times a season he went in to the Stadium to watch the Yankees play, now that the Giants had moved out to Frisco; and he usually managed to attend one or two of the football Giants' pro games, although sitting home in front of the television set was a lot more comfortable. That Stadium could get awful cold at times.

He enjoyed television—Ed Sullivan, the westerns, *Dragnet*, that kind of thing. And sometimes he watched *Playhouse 90* or one of the others, and so Mildred and Ben Pierson were not unknown to him, at least by sight. In real life they were a couple of screwballs, that was for sure, but, then, Fred supposed that most actors were.

As far as that went, most of these people who moved out from the city were screwballs. Not the ones in the developments; they were Fred's kind of people and he understood them all right. But this other bunch, the ones who seemed to revolve in orbit around the dead woman, they were real characters, every one of them. Like that Lewis woman who screamed and just went on screaming and then all at once settled down and was normal-seeming as could be. And her husband with the hangover so thick you could cut it with a knife—Vice President of an advertising agency, for God's sake! No wonder those quiz shows were rigged—who had to try three times before he could get flame and cigarette together. And that good looking woman writer, Louella Bloom Barnes, who had as much as said that she would have killed Mrs. Warren with pleasure, only she would have done it differently so death would not have come with ease. And now that other writer, Peters, with the bubbly wife. Peters had been scared, good and scared, and what could a man make out of that?

Fred had purposely saved George Hanks, set him well down on the list. George Hanks was an artist—a real good one, Fred thought, on the basis of his things in the *Saturday Evening Post* and *Playboy* and *Esquire*—and artists were notoriously wacky, of course. On the other hand, a man who had played the kind of middle linebacker George Hanks had played, pro lineman of the year and that kind of thing, had to be basically real, hence understandable to a man like Fred. George Hanks just couldn't be wholly like the rest of the crew, at least Fred hoped he couldn't because, God knew, Fred needed to encounter a little normalcy before he, too, went nuts. What in the world made those other people tick, anyway? And how could they all manage to make the kind of living they did? It hardly seemed fair.

Fred drove up through the trees to the parking circle in front of the studio. He could remember when this had been the stables of the Vanden estate, somewhat run-down as the Vandens themselves had run down in the way quite a few of these old Hudson River Valley families seemed to do. And he had to admit that what had been done to the stables had turned them into something most attractive—that big north window where the hay loft doors had been, and the new stone work, and the chimney added, made out of used brick that looked fine, but was, Fred knew, the very devil to work with because the edges were all uneven. He had heard that George Hanks had spent close to thirty thousand fixing the place up, and he had thought the figure exaggerated, but maybe it wasn't, all that work with prices the way they were these days. It would be nice to have thirty thousand dollars to put into a house, or just to have thirty thousand dollars, period. Fred sighed, and told himself that he'd better get down to work.

There was no answer to his knocking, so he walked around the studio, admiring the low rock wall and the lawn and the flower beds. He found George out behind, sitting there in the sun with a can of beer in his hand, and for a moment Fred didn't know whether to duck back out of sight or not because, Jesus, that girl lying in one of those folding chairs had on only a little G-string sort of thing below, and up top hardly enough to cover a couple of lemons let alone breasts her size. But he had a job to do and so he stood his ground and coughed discreetly.

George said, "Hi, lieutenant." And he got up from the low wall, not at all embarrassed. "I imagine the lieutenant wants to talk to me, honey." And that was all. He led the way back around the studio. To Fred he said, "Pull up a piece of wall. I'll get you a beer."

Fred felt better. At least this one you could talk to, not that that meant he, George, was beyond suspicion of course, because he wasn't. The way Fred had heard it George might have had as much reason to kill Mrs. Warren as anybody else, sex being the explosive force it was. But at least George was somebody you could talk to.

George came back with the fresh beer. He handed it to Fred and sat down. "Shoot." No questions, no wind-up; Fred liked that, too.

Fred said, "I'm not a tricky cop, Mr. Hanks—George. I'm just asking a few questions, trying to get a picture of where people were and what they were doing yesterday afternoon."

"Any particular time?"

"Let's say late afternoon, the last two, three hours before the party."

"I was here," George said. "I was working. There was a picture I wanted to finish, and I got interested in it and didn't pay much attention to the time. As a matter of fact I left the—young lady out back standing in the station across the river for over a half hour because I hadn't noticed what time it was." He paused. "I was all alone. I had no phone calls. I can't prove I was here, lieutenant."

"Most people call me Fred." And then, "Did you finish the picture?"

"No," George said. "I didn't finish it until last night, late, after

I came home from the party." He saw the question in Fred's face. "Gladys came home with me," George said. "She went to bed. I stayed up and worked." And he grinned suddenly. "And if you find that hard to believe, why, so do I, but it's how it happened."

"A man gets upset," Fred said, "he does funny things. My wife had an operation a year ago. It wasn't serious, but it could have been. The lump could have been cancer. While the operation was going on, I went home. I defrosted the refrigerator. It was all I could think of to do."

George studied the man with new interest. He said slowly, "You're asking why I was that upset?" He was silent for a few moments. Then, "It's a little complicated. She, Roz—" He stopped there. He raised the beer can, drained it. He closed his hand and the beer can collapsed. "That was one hell of a woman." And he looked at Fred. "Do I shock you? Talking like that about another man's wife?"

"I can stand it."

"Waste," George said. "Can you understand that? In physics they teach you about the conservation of energy, or at least they used to. You don't destroy something, you convert it into something else. You burn wood, you turn it into heat, the energy isn't wasted. But you kill Roz Warren and there's nothing left except the body, and no matter what you may have heard, the body was only a part of her. All the rest, and there was a lot, is gone, destroyed, wasted. That's what I meant." He held the flattened beer can in both hands now and folded it double without apparent effort, without even seeming to realize what his hands were doing. He dropped it on the lawn.

Fred was silent for a moment. His eyes were on the beer can.

George looked down. He said, "Oh, sure, I'm a big strong fellow. So?"

Fred said, "Do you own a gun?"

"No gun," George said. "I don't like to kill anything."

Fred smiled. "Woodchucks? What they do to a man's garden."

"I like them," George said. "They look like little men in baggy tweed suits. I like to see them sitting along the parkway watching the cars go by. I think they're probably wondering where everybody's going in such a hurry, and why. No gun, lieutenant—Fred."

Fred was silent for quite a time, thoughtful. Then, "You watch a man play football, especially when the going gets rough the way it does in the pros sometimes—" He paused. "You think you get to know something about the man." He paused again. "I watched you, quite a few times. Maybe I'm wrong, but I don't think so. I can see you losing your temper and taking somebody apart with your bare hands. But I can't see you shooting someone, a woman, when her back was turned." He seemed faintly embarrassed. "As I said, maybe I'm wrong."

George stood up. "I'll get another beer. I have a thirst today." And when he was back again, and seated on the low wall, "You have something on your mind. You're not just making conversation."

"No," Fred said, "I'm not." He sighed. He looked at George. "I'm over my depth. I don't begin to understand these people. Maybe you do. The way they behave, the ones I've talked to and I've talked to most of them who knew Mrs. Warren well—the way they behave I'd be tempted to think that every one of them killed her. If they were the kind of people I understand, that is. But they aren't. Mr. and Mrs. Pierson sat there and looked at me and then went into a performance you'd pay scalper's prices to see on Broadway, a real tear-jerker, Eliza crossing the ice, bloodhounds and all—you think that's funny?"

"Don't you?"

"Well, yes," Fred said, "I suppose so." And then, "It may sound corny, but I'm trying to do a job. I didn't know Mrs. Warren. I heard a lot of things about her and maybe they were true and maybe they weren't. It doesn't make any difference. You say it's a waste, and I'll take your word for it, but that doesn't make any difference, either. Somebody killed her. That somebody has to pay for it. That's what the law says. I represent the law. So it isn't really very funny to me. Maybe I'm funny, sitting here drinking beer with you. That's all right. I don't mind. But the job isn't funny."

It was strange where they turned up, the pros, the ones who had grown out of the habit of thinking and behaving like amateurs. George said, "You're asking me to help?"

"I am. I said it before, maybe I'm wrong about you. But a man has to start somewhere." He shook his head. "I'm probably ruining what's left of your weekend. I'm sorry about that. But—"

"Gladys will keep," George said. He was grinning again. And then the grin disappeared. "Tell me what you've found. Maybe I can help you sort it out."

9

MADGE CAME into the living room dressed in a dark summer print dress, white gloves, bag and all. Martin said, "What in the world—?"

Madge said, "I asked Paul Warren if there was anything I could do—"

"George," Martin said, "told me that being you, it figured."

"Did he?" Madge's smile was gentle. "Dear George." She missed Martin's faint frown. She said, "Paul is completely broken up. I can't blame him. He's—lost. There's a woman taking care of the baby, I don't know where she came from, but she's there, and that's what counts. And she can cook for Paul too. So that's taken care of. But when I asked Paul about funeral arrangements he hadn't even thought about them, and I told him that if he wanted me to I'd—take over."

"You're a stranger," Martin said suddenly. "A very lovely, wholly competent stranger." He was smiling, and yet his voice held the ring of truth. "I'm baffled."

"Are you, Marty? I'm—glad."

"You're taking over," Martin said. "Just like that. You're going into the ghoulish detail of—arrangements. You're going to make the decisions, take the responsibility—"

"Someone has to, Marty."

"Yes. Someone has to. Roz can't do it, and so you're going to. Why? You didn't care much for her. You didn't know her well."

"Maybe I knew her better than you think, Marty."

Martin studied her. He said, "More surprises? What does that mean?"

"It doesn't matter." She tugged at the cuff of one glove. "Mona called. Listen to me, Marty. A police lieutenant went to their house, talked to Wally, asked him where he was yesterday afternoon."

"Knowing Wally," Martin said, "I can imagine his reaction."

"Marty. Please. He, the lieutenant, is talking to everybody who —knew Roz at all well."

"George said as much. He said we're all in the club, which was no better than routine George Hanksism."

Madge said, "What are you going to tell the police, Marty?"

"The truth. What else?"

She was silent, watching him, studying him. And, again, the feeling was strong in his mind that she was a stranger, as he had said a lovely, wholly competent stranger. It was an eerie feeling, unnerving. Martin said, "You still don't believe me, do you?" And then, "You're right, of course. I stopped on the way in from the airport. I stopped at the Warren's house. I wanted to see Roz. Shall I tell you why?"

"Not unless you want to, Marty."

"The omniscient George Hanks," Martin said, "made me see the light. He convinced me that it was silly to lie to the police."

Madge let her breath out slowly. "Bless George," she said. And then, "I'll go along now." And she found a smile and put it on. "I'll go off to try to be that—wholly competent stranger."

"I put another adjective in, too. It was *lovely*."

Madge walked quickly to the door, and out, down to her car. She wanted to laugh, and she wanted to cry, both, which was a silly state of affairs, wasn't it? "Too, too silly." She said it aloud. For a big girl, that was. Bless George Hanks.

10

THE DAY was bright, and hot, and so the dark glasses did not seem at all out of the ordinary. Ben had changed from the blue suit to flannel trousers and a cotton plaid shirt, long-sleeved to cover the length and thinness of his arms. He could have taken the car, but he preferred to walk. Mildred, studying him, had said, "Are you all right, Ben?"

"I'm fine."

"You're quiet."

To this Ben had no comment.

"Why did you go to church, Ben? You've never done that before in all the time I've known you."

"Maybe I should have."

"Ben." And then, "Where are you going?"

"I'm going to see Paul. I'm going to offer my condolences."

"Really, Ben."

It was pleasant walking along the narrow winding road. There was no wind; the trees and even the wild grass in the fields were somnolent, at peace. Years ago and hundreds of miles away it had been like this, quiet, calm, a Sunday hush on the land, and if, despite a president's pious statements, there had not been two chickens in every pot and sometimes not even one, there had been other things; and now, viewed from this distance in time and place, Ben could see how important those other things actually were. In those days life had been simple, if irksome. Right and Wrong had existed, written in words of fire, and everyone knew the difference, or, if he pretended that he did not, he was swiftly shown the light.

In those days he, Ben, had not even been aware that this vast country contained a multitude of people to whom the Rules were not that simple; people who could, with their clever tongues and their hair-splitting minds alter, twist, distort, or at least seem to, what was *unalterable*; people who smiled, or openly scoffed at *truth;* people to whom solemnity and belief were a mockery; people whose lives were devoted to the pursuit of the witty, the bright, the amusing, the gay. George Hanks-type people; Roz Warren-type people. He, Ben, had lived amongst them too long. He saw that now.

There were half a dozen cars parked along the road by the entrance of the drive that led to the pleasant white house, and Ben, seeing these, and understanding their significance, was tempted to stop, to go away, to return at another, less conspicuous time. But he gathered himself and marched up the drive anyway.

Men to match the cars were clustered around the front door, arguing with a village policeman who looked as if he had taken about all the abuse he was going to put up with. One of the men said to the policeman, "Sooner or later we're going to talk to him, buster. He's a big shot publisher and he can't hide forever. He has a wife with the looks she had, and she gets herself killed, people want to know about it."

And another of the men looked at Ben and said, "Who are you?" And then, "Hey. Wait a minute. I've seen you on TV. You're—"

Ben said to the policeman in that fine deep voice, "I'm a friend of Mr. Warren's, officer. I came to offer my condolences." And he looked with scorn at the other men. "I'm not one of the —jackals."

Somebody said, "Dig him. Which one of the Apostles does he think he is?"

The policeman said, "Sure, Mr. Pierson." He stood aside. "You can go in." And then, in a different tone, "Maybe in the city you newspaper guys are real important. I wouldn't know."

"Oh, for God's sake," one of the men said. "You think you're going to lock somebody up?"

"No," the policeman said. "I'm going to clobber somebody,

and I don't much care who I start with." It was the last Ben heard as he closed the door.

It was cool in the big house, and quiet, and, after the bright sunshine, dim. From the living room Paul said, "Hello, Ben. Come in."

He was on the sofa. Ben was shocked at the sight. Paul's gray hair was rumpled. He had not shaved, and the stubble entirely black, gave his face an unwashed appearance. He wore still the tie he had worn last night, the knot pulled down, his collar unbuttoned. There was a half empty glass on the coffee table in front of him. "Sit down, Ben. I'm not drunk, if that's what you're thinking. I've been spacing the drinks. You can keep going indefinitely that way." He paused. "My manners. Will you have a drink, Ben?"

Ben shook his head. He sat down. "I came to offer sympathy."

"Very decent of you."

"I went to church this morning."

One of Paul's eyebrows rose a trifle. "Did you pray, Ben?"

"I did."

"For whom?" There was a pause. "And to whom?"

"You're laughing at me, Paul. Why?"

Paul said, "Funny. I said the same thing to George Hanks, accused him of laughing at me. It was right here, in this room. Did you know that, Ben?"

"I didn't know."

Paul said, "Why do people laugh at each other? Do you know the answer? To build themselves up? Maybe that's it. It doesn't matter. For whom did you pray, Ben? I withdraw the second question."

"For Roz."

"Good of you." Paul was silent for a moment. Then, "She laughed a lot. No, strike that. She didn't laugh. She smiled. Do you remember her smile, Ben?"

"I do."

"La Gioconda. I've never understood what was mysterious about that smile. It's perfectly simple, understandable. Mona

Lisa was a woman. She was smiling because men amused her, all men, probably even da Vinci himself."

Ben said, "Don't scoff, Paul."

"It offends you? I didn't intend that. I'm not scoffing at you, Ben, only at myself. And that's funny, too, because Roz said that George Hanks was laughing at himself, not at me, only I didn't believe it. Roz—" Paul stopped there.

The succubus was exorcized, Roz's martyrdom now achieved; Ben could afford to be forgiving. "Roz was a lovely woman."

"She was that," Paul said. And then, "I miss her. God, how I miss her." He picked up the drink, studied it for a long time, sipped it at last and then set it down. "Thank you for coming, Ben. And thank you for your solemnity. I don't think I could have stood any more—amusement."

When Ben walked outside the newspapermen had retreated as far as the end of the drive. They clustered around him. Like vultures, he thought. He walked through them on his long legs as if they did not exist. And one of them, watching, said, "You know, a cross on his shoulder and a crown of thorns wouldn't be out of place at that. On him they'd look good."

Ben had found his peace at last.

11

FRED PARKER SAID, "So there it is. Nobody seems to know where they were yesterday afternoon, or at least they can't prove it. I haven't talked to Mr. and Mrs. Fuller yet, but I suppose it'll be the same with them. Or with her, anyway. He flew in from London, I understand, and went straight to the party." He looked at George.

"You'd better ask Martin," George said. He smiled faintly. "You won't find him throwing a tizzy at you the way the rest of them have."

"That," Fred said, "will be a relief." He was silent for a few moments. Then, "To be plain about it, every one of the men had, at one time or another, been in Mrs. Warren's bed, is that right?"

"The answer is yes," George said. "You wouldn't believe me if I said anything else."

"And," Fred said, "all the women knew it?"

"I don't think there's much doubt about that."

"Maybe you wonder," Fred said, "why I haven't even given a thought to anybody outside that group, a tramp, say, or a burglar. I'll tell you why. It's simple enough. There are a lot of nice things in that house. And maybe you didn't notice, but Mrs. Warren's jewelry was right there on her dressing table—earrings, a bracelet, a necklace. And her evening bag was there, too, one of those little things women carry, and it was already packed, if that's the word. It had close to two hundred dollars in it, God only knows why. I can't see somebody breaking in, going upstairs, maybe surprising her and shooting her, and then running off without taking something. Can you?"

"No," George said.

Fred said, "The gun that shot her was a thirty-eight, Police Positive. That doesn't help at all. The gun could be anywhere—" He gestured. "That's a big river out there. And anybody could have shot it, a man, or a woman. You take a service automatic, or even one of those nasty little .380's, and most women can't even pull the slide back to jack a shell into the chamber. But anybody can cock a Police Positive and then pull the trigger." He smiled faintly. "And nobody, of course, admits to having a gun. There isn't a pistol license in the whole crowd. But somebody had one."

"I can't help you," George said.

"Maybe you can in another direction. You knew Mrs. Warren. Which would she be likely to let into the house when she was dressed that way, or undressed, just bra and panties—a man she knew well, or another woman?"

George thought about it. "Neither," he said.

"That doesn't make sense, because she let somebody in."

"You have to know the woman," George said. "She was fastidious, impeccable, always. She—" He spread his large hands. "She would have put on a robe for anybody, man or woman."

"She didn't always keep her robe on with men. I'm not trying to be funny."

"No," George said, "she didn't. But when she took the robe off, there was only her under it." It was not easy, explaining, remembering. He said, "Look. There was no pretense in her. Not in that way. There was no coyness. She was not a tease, that was the last thing she was. Bra and panties don't fit. They would have—cheapened her, and she was not cheap."

There was a little silence. "Okay," Fred said then. "That leaves her husband—"

"No."

"Dammit," Fred said, "every woman lets down in front of her husband."

"Wrong," George said. "Roz and Paul had separate dressing rooms, separate baths. Paul is a vain man, and is there anything sillier-looking than a man walking around in a shirt and shoes and socks and garters? Roz respected his privacy. He respected hers."

Fred stood up. He sighed. "Okay," he said. "Thanks. The only thing is, the way you see it nobody could have gotten to her. But somebody did."

George nodded. He said slowly, "I've called it as I see it."

"A man," Fred said, "can't do better than that. Go back to your young lady. Better tell her not to get too much sun. City people do sometimes."

George walked around to the back terrace. Gladys was still in the lounge chair. He smiled down at her. "I've given you a fine time in the country, haven't I? I'm sorry."

"You're a nice sweet guy," Gladys said. "I thought you were a character at first. But you aren't, really." She came up out of the lounge chair in one long smooth movement. She adjusted the tiny halter of the swim suit. "What time are the trains?" And she smiled without giggling. "I'm not mad. Don't think that. It's just that with so much on your mind you don't even see me. I understand, and I don't mind."

"Honey—" George began.

This time it was a giggle. "Of course," Gladys said, "if you want to ask me out again when you don't have quite so much on your mind—"

"A promise," George said.

12

FRED PARKER DROVE only as far as the next driveway, turned in to the Fuller place. He sat in the car for a little time, just turning over in his mind what George had told him, trying to fit together the bits and pieces of fact and character and pure conjecture; under no illusion that an answer would appear, merely, in a sense, staking out the foundations, setting them, in order that, sooner or later, a structure could be built that would stand.

And then, on the car radio, he called the village station, told them where he was, asked if there was anything new. There were a few items, nothing really startling, but then Fred had not expected anything startling. The sifting and the sorting was going on and would continue to go on in a multitude of ways and directions, turning up this and that and the other thing, most of it not important and probably not even necessary to find out, but how was a man to know how deep to probe at this stage of the game?

The sergeant said, "Mrs. Lewis was seen in her car yesterday about four-thirty over at the Warren house. She may have gone in, or she may not. Shall I send somebody over to ask her?"

Fred thought about it. "No," he said then. "She screams. And if that sounds funny, maybe it is. Leave her alone for now." George had given him a thumbnail sketch of Joy Lewis, describing her as a woman unnaturally placid on the surface which made you wonder how much turmoil was bottled up underneath.

To a woman like that, who had flipped once, silence and apparent disinterest from the police might, just might provide the most insidious kind of pressure. If she was involved, that was good. And if she was not involved, why, that was too bad, and Fred did indeed feel a kind of pity thinking about the possibility, but that was how things were when something like murder was done. Check that. There was no such thing as something like murder. Murder was in a class by itself.

The sergeant said, "Mr. Warren said he spent the afternoon at his office in town. Apparently he did. They keep one elevator man on Saturday, and he signs people in and out. He took Warren up in the elevator at one-thirty, brought him back down at six."

"Anything else?"

"Not yesterday," the sergeant said, "but Friday afternoon Mrs. Fuller went to see the Warren woman, stayed a half hour or so. Tim Potter drives that RFD route, and he saw the Fuller station wagon and recognized it as he went by one way and came back the other. Everybody's getting in the act."

Fred said, "Of course they are. When did we last have a killing in the village?"

And the sergeant said, "Yeah. Big deal." And then, "Lou, at the Tavern, says Mr. Lewis was in yesterday, like he said, and had a couple, maybe three, and then left. So that checks. Nobody has turned up who saw Mr. Barnes driving around. The doc says Barnes did have an appointment, but he didn't keep it, and Doc doesn't know what it was for, and Doc says to tell you that even if he did know he wouldn't say."

Fred smiled faintly, thinking of the doctor in whose mind and memory were locked all manner of things that could make life uncomfortable, even downright unbearable probably, for a fair segment of the village population. The knowledge of these small personal secrets was safe in Doc's care; it would go to the grave with him one day.

"And," the sergeant said, "Pierson, he's the actor, was just out to see Warren, to offer his sympathy, Sammy Parks says. He didn't stay long. And did you know that he, Pierson, went to church this morning? Nobody's ever seen him there before."

"So?" Fred said. "I didn't know that." He was silent, thoughtful.

"That's all I have," the sergeant said.

Fred got out of the car and walked up to the porch of the house. Martin was standing there waiting for him, which could mean something, but probably meant nothing, Fred thought, because almost anybody, seeing a police car parked in his drive, would come to the door to see what was up. Still— "I'd like a little information, if you'll give it to me," Fred said.

And Martin nodded. "I will. But I'm not going to enjoy it." They were inside now. Fred sat on the sofa, Martin in a leather chair. "You want to know," Martin said, "whether I went straight to the party from the airport. I didn't. When I called my wife and told her the traffic was holding me up, I was being quite honest. But once I got past the Triborough Bridge it was clear sailing, and so . . ." He told it as he had told it to George, without much inflection, with little emphasis—how he had sat in the car in front of the Warren house trying to make up his mind; how, finally he had rung the bell and had no answer and gone on to the party. He said, "That's it." And then, "Will you tell me one thing, lieutenant?"

Fred watched him, and waited.

"She," Martin said, "Roz, was there, in the house. That's the way it has to be. But was she already—dead? Or could I have done something for her if I'd used my head, if I'd seen that something was badly wrong because the baby wouldn't have been left there alone?"

It was strange, Fred thought, how each of them reacted in his own way. And this one was thinking not so much of himself as of the dead woman and whether he could have helped her, and Fred found himself liking that. "She was dead before she hit the floor, Mr. Fuller. You couldn't have done anything for her. Neither could anybody else."

Martin said, "Thanks." And that was all.

"You knew her well, didn't you, Mr. Fuller?"

"You know I did. Intimately. That's the usual word."

Fred said, "I don't peek through keyholes because I enjoy it. I outgrew that a long time ago." And he saw Martin's face soften a trifle, some of the resentment fade. "Will you tell me about her?"

"Tell you what?"

Fred said slowly, "I guess you'd say she was a remarkable woman, having as much effect as she did on so many people—"

"She was a remarkable woman. And it was not just her face and her body, lieutenant."

George Hanks had said the same. And George had also said that this one, Fuller, wouldn't throw a tizzy the way some of the others had, and Fred thought this was true. He said, "You know what she was wearing when we found her, Mr. Fuller?"

Martin said, "George Hanks described it, in detail, last night when he came back to what was left of the party."

"So?" Fred said. "I didn't know that." No matter, for now. "Knowing her, Mr. Fuller, would you say she'd have been more likely to be dressed that way in the presence of a man she knew well, or another woman?"

Martin shook his head. "Neither one. Somebody surprised her. That's the only way it could have been." And he paused, searching for words to make clear what he knew to be true. "Look, lieutenant, this is going to sound strange. She was a modest woman. I know that's hard to believe, but it's true. She was modest in the same way Eve was modest before she ate the apple, if it was an apple, and found out what shame was. Roz was modest dressed; she didn't need to be otherwise to attract. And she was modest naked, which may sound like a contradiction in terms, but it isn't. She wouldn't have—stooped to underwear in a man's presence. I think it would have been, to her, the same as being seen with her hair done up in curlers. And she was never that close to any woman, close enough to be just girls together. The other women didn't like her much."

Fred said, "Did your wife like her, Mr. Fuller?"

"I don't think so." And then, thinking of Madge, feeling again that sense of strangeness and of change in her, "I don't know, lieutenant."

Fred said, "Would you know why your wife went to see Mrs. Warren Friday afternoon?"

"Madge—?" Martin stopped there. He was silent. He said then, "I wouldn't know, lieutenant. I was in England. My wife is off now making the funeral arrangements. When she comes back, you can ask her."

And it was then that the phone rang, and Martin went to answer it. He turned, held it out. "The desk sergeant. For you."

The sergeant's voice, to Fred's ear, held a blend of triumph and incredulity. "Pierson," the sergeant said, "the actor fellow, lieutenant, who went to church this morning, remember?, and then went out to see Mr. Warren, offer sympathy—"

Fred said, "What about him?"

"Why," the sergeant said, "he just walked in. He's cold sober, at least I think he is even if he does look a little wacky. He says he wants to confess. He says he killed her. He says he wants to be punished."

13

IT WAS mid-afternoon when Madge returned home. Martin was not in the living room, nor was he upstairs. Madge located him finally down in the basement room he had rigged up as a workshop. He had the electric clock from the kitchen spread in pieces on the bench and he was working carefully, deftly with a tiny oil dropper. Madge said, "Am I—interrupting, Marty?"

"Of course not. I'm just taking some of the noise out of this thing. The bearings were all dry."

"It has been noisy," Madge said, and she thought how ridiculously banal the conversation was, how pointless; two people, herself and her husband, taking refuge in almost meaningless words. Because they were—civilized people? Was this then the end-product of civilization, this surface calm, this concentration on unimportant detail? And if it was, what happened to the elemental feelings? Were they irrevocably submerged? She said, "The sweater is lovely, Marty. You were sweet to get it for me. And the scarf."

He looked up from the bench then, smiled faintly, nodded. Madge had changed from the print dress to the new sweater and a flannel skirt. Martin said, "It is the right size, isn't it? I was worried."

"It's perfect."

"A little hot for summer."

"But the nights will be getting cool."

"Yes." He was busy with the clock motor again.

Madge said, "Marty. Ben has—confessed."

"I know."

"I saw him."

Martin turned slowly. "Where? And why? Particularly why?"

"I went to the police station. I had to see the lieutenant—"

"For God's sake, why?"

"You can't have a funeral without a—body."

"Oh."

"And the police had to give their permission."

"I see." He did not turn back to the bench. He stood there, the clock motor in one hand, in the other the oil dropper held as if it were a hypodermic syringe. Even his attitude was strangely clinical. "Did they give their permission?"

"Yes."

"And Ben was there? That was how you saw him?"

"I asked to see him. I wanted to know if there was—anything I could do."

Martin said slowly, wonderingly, "Little mother of all living." And then, "Why, Madge?"

"I hoped you would understand."

There was a long silence. "I don't," Martin said. "If Ben killed her—"

"That's just it, Marty." She paused. "No one person killed her. We all did." She turned away then. Over her shoulder as she started up the stairs she said, "The funeral is tomorrow at eleven o'clock. It—seemed best to have it as soon as possible. I have to notify people." She was gone up the stairs.

Martin turned back to the bench. His hands, of their own volition, moved together, juxtaposing motor and oil dropper, working on, lubricating each small bearing; hands were like small independent animals with knowledge of their own. He had never thought of it that way before. Upstairs, faintly, he could hear Madge's voice on the telephone, the wholly competent stranger taking charge.

14

THE NEWSPAPERMEN had deserted the Warren house for the police station, and so there were no cars when Louella drove in. She was outwardly calm, composed. A strange woman answered the door and looked at Louella and was visibly impressed, but hesitant. "I don't know if Mr. Warren wants to see anybody—"

Paul's voice, from the living room, said, "Who is it?" And when Louella answered, the voice altered abruptly. "Come in, please. Do."

He was standing to greet her when Louella walked into the room. She studied him with cool impersonality. "You ought to be ashamed of yourself, Paul. The least you can do is behave like a man."

He was silent for a few moments. He seemed to collect himself. One hand touched the loosened tie. "You're right. As usual, Louella."

"Go shower," Louella said, "and shave. Make yourself presentable." She sat down. "I'll wait."

In her consciousness there was that dichotomy again, infuriating and impossible to avoid; one part of her mind watched, recorded every word, every gesture, every feeling. It was as if that part of her mind were saying silently, "There I am. That is the way I behave, react, given the facts, the circumstances. And there is the man, and this is what he does under the stimulus applied." No sense of triumph in domination, no emotion at all, merely a watching, recording, missing nothing, storing up the knowledge gained against future story need. Impersonal. Horrible. But she could not make it stop.

When Paul came downstairs again, showered, shaved, more or less his usual impeccable self, Louella was still sitting, waiting, showing nothing.

"I apologize, Louella," Paul said. "I've been—wallowing in self-pity. I—" He stopped there. "May I get you a drink?"

"No drink, thank you," Louella said. "Sit down, Paul." And now it came, and the part of her mind that watched seemed to alert itself to miss no smallest nuance. "I won't say anything about Roz," Louella said. "I'm not being intentionally brutal, Paul. But I refuse to say what we both would know was a lie."

Paul said, "Hyprocrisy was never one of your vices."

"Don't crawl," Louella said. "I don't want that, either."

He seemed to gather himself then. "What do you want, Louella?"

"That's better." And she paused, choosing her words, her approach. "Are you going to keep the child?"

"Naturally. My daughter, Louella."

"Is she?"

There was a silence. Paul said finally, in a different voice, "I don't think I like that."

Louella said nothing.

Paul said, "Did you come here just to make the implication?" He shook his head. "It isn't like you." He paused. "What are you getting at?"

Louella said, "Do you want to continue as my publisher, Paul?"

He studied her, searching for the meaning behind the words.

"You know the answer to that. I've always taken pride in publishing your work."

"And considerable profit," Louella said. "That is not accusation, Paul. I'm merely stating a fact to be considered."

Paul said, "You bought this house. You rebuilt it. You furnished most of it. Is that what you want me to say?"

"Not say. Just remember." Louella was silent for a moment. Then, "The child may be yours, Paul. It may not be. I don't think you know now, or will ever know." She paused. "I will be happy to adopt the child. Sam and I will give her a home, love, everything a child—"

Paul said, "You're joking." She was not, and he knew that she was not; and he tried, and failed, to find a way of reaching her, of penetrating that assurance. "People don't do that kind of thing, Louella."

"I'm not people."

"Of course you're not. But there are rules that everybody—"

"We'll make it perfectly legal," Louella said. "You're a widower—"

Paul said suddenly, "I never realized before how cold-blooded you are. You're offering me a trade, is that it? I let you adopt the child, and you let me go on as your publisher, *quid pro quo*, don't you see how ridiculous it is? My God, it's straight out of *East Lynne*." And, "Why, Louella?"

"I have my reasons." Louella stood up. "Think about it, Paul. In all of its ramifications."

Paul watched her from the door as she walked down the steps, got into her car, drove away. She did not look back.

15

THE PICTURE of Madge stood again on the easel. George studied it, scowled at it. Gladys was gone, and he was alone now, and it was time, perhaps past time that he did some thinking. When the knock came at the door, he was tempted to ignore it, but he did not. He took the picture down and set it with its face to the wall before he went to answer the knock. It was Martin, and George did not so much as glance in the picture's direction as he held the door wide.

"I want to talk to you," Martin said.

"That would be the obvious inference."

"What does that mean?"

George said, "You understand the words. You're an educated—" He stopped. He said suddenly, "Oh, hell. Forget it. I'm edgy today."

Martin nodded slowly. "We all are."

"The club members," George said. And then, "You want a drink?"

"I do," Martin said. He watched the immensity of George's back as George walked to the buffet. Martin said, "That was quite a Mona bit last night."

"Which one?"

Martin's voice was matter of fact. "About Madge's being pregnant." He paused. "Where would she have gotten that?"

"God knows." George came back with the two glasses, handed one to Martin. "Where Mona gets her ideas—"

"Maybe God knows," Martin said. "But the question is, do you?"

There was silence. Then, "And what does that mean, friend Martin?"

Martin said, "Am I just being stupid? If I am, I'd like to know."

"To paraphrase you," George said, "your lucidity seems to have come unstuck. You'll have to make it plainer than that."

"Madge had an appointment, Friday, Mona said."

"So?"

"Was it with you?"

George said slowly, "Is that the direction your mind is snuffling?" And then, "No, friend Martin, it was not with me." He was conscious of the picture against the wall. "I saw Madge later, had a drink with her—"

"After she'd seen Roz?"

George's eyebrows rose. "You know about that?" He nodded. "After she had seen Roz."

"Do you know why she went to see her?"

"That," George said, "is something you'd better ask Madge. I told you I wasn't God."

"In a way," Martin said, "you are." There came a time when words would not stop, when they seemed to say themselves for reasons, motives that were beyond comprehension. "You're the ubiquitous observer, the omniscient judge. You see all, know all, and are unaffected. Like the gods on Mount Olympus you watch, and smile. You—"

"Ben Pierson," George said, "Paul Warren, Mildred, now you." He understood the cause, and he did not like it at all. He said, "What is this, Hate-George-Hanks-Week? Take a suck of your drink and relax. And then come right out with what's on your mind." The phone rang. George set his drink down and went to answer it.

Bob Lewis's voice, overloud, said, "Old George buddy-boy. Busy? No matter. Drop what you're doing. Rush right over. The wassail bowl is set out in celebration. We're drinking Ben Pierson's health—"

George said, "Why?"

"You didn't know? Why, old Ben has given himself up, confessed, told all. And so the rest of us are, like Caesar's wife, above suspicion."

George said in disgust, "For Christ's sake." And he dropped the phone into its cradle. He turned slowly to face Martin. "You heard?"

"I knew," Martin said. "About Ben, I mean. I didn't know about that." He pointed to the telephone. And then, "A little sick-making, isn't it?"

"To the strongest stomach." George picked up his drink, took a long swallow. He said, without humor, "Do you remember that cartoon, Steig, I think, of the man glaring out of what looked to be a doghouse? The caption was, 'People are no damned good.' Maybe he had something."

"I remember it. And all the other sick jokes."

George studied his drink for a time in silence. "Ben," he said at last, merely that. And then he shrugged his big shoulders. "So." He looked at Martin. "You had something you wanted to say."

It was strange how quickly the feeling in Martin's mind had changed. He said slowly, "Forget it."

"No," George said. "These things fester."

"Now," Martin said, "it's George Hanks, lay analyst?" He was not sure from what source the sudden annoyance sprang, but it was there. He felt a kind of recklessness powered by the annoyance. "How are you on reading palms?"

"You're working yourself up, friend Martin," George said. "Don't." He was silent for a moment. "There's a contagion to hysteria whether the head-shrinkers believe it or not. Now it's gotten to you. You were going to ask if there's anything between Madge and me. There isn't. There hasn't been. There won't be." And he found himself wondering where the George Hanks puckishness had gone; he was not even faintly tempted to take the picture from its place against the wall, set it on the easel in front of Martin and really tear the rag off the bush. "You can believe that," he said.

Martin was embarrassed. He felt deflated. The annoyance remained, but its force was gone. It was as if the rug had been jerked out from under the annoyance. He felt almost cheated, as if he had wanted, actually wanted George to say—

George said, "Are you disappointed? I think you are. I think you hoped I'd say, hell, yes, Madge and I hop into bed every chance we get."

192

Martin stared at him.

George said, "I told you once that there was a kind of built-in bitchiness here in the county, a sort of miasma that comes up out of the ground. Roz wasn't a cause. She was a symptom. Get that through your head. Her living here, in this community, was the perfect juxtaposition of talent and opportunity, if you see what I mean. If she had lived on Park Avenue her scope would have been limited. Here it wasn't, and that contagion of hysteria is the result. Joy Lewis flips her lid and screams. Bob just gets drunk. Mona calls the police, actually summons them, and sicks them onto Wally, scares him half to death, but he'll get over it when the hysteria passes; Wally's resilient; he's a pro. What I'm saying is that it's gotten to everybody. Ben gives himself up. Now you're doing it too. Because you were a bad boy with Roz, you actually want to believe, for Christ's sake, that Madge has been bed-crawling, too. Then she'd be no better than you are. Do you think that would make it all right? It wouldn't. It would finish everything. I think you had a set of standards when you came out here. Maybe they're not my standards. That's unimportant. I try to proselytize no man. But they were your standards, and where the hell are they now?"

Martin was silent. He said slowly, in wonder, "A good question." He set the drink down. "I don't know the answer." He started for the door. George's voice stopped him.

George said, "If you'd had another question in mind, the answer might have been different." He paused. "Am I in love with Madge?" He shrugged those enormous shoulders again. "I don't know. I may very well be. Comical, isn't it?"

Martin opened the door. He said, "The funeral's at eleven tomorrow. Madge made the arrangements." He paused. "Are you going?"

"I'll be there," George said. "Now beat it. Get off my back."

When, later, well after dark, knocking came at his door again, George thought it might be Martin returning, and afterwards he was glad that it had not been because he might have been tempted too strongly to do something irrevocable. He jerked the door open. He stared at Mildred Pierson who stood there, almost gaped at her. "Oh, no," George said.

Mildred came in slowly, making her entrance. She faced George. Her voice was deep, vibrant. "I haven't the right—" she began.

And George said, "Mildred, for Christ's sake, either get down off the stage or turn around and go away. I'm not highbrow enough to be one of your audience." He walked to the buffet. He busied himself mixing a fresh drink. When he turned around she was still there.

She said, "You hate me, don't you, George?"

"That's better," George said. "You sound mortal now. And the answer is no, I don't hate you."

"I was nasty last night. I apologize."

"Paul Warren said once," George said, "that I had probably been insulted by experts. I have. There's no need for apology. You didn't bother me. I'm sorry if that disappoints you, but there it is."

Mildred said, "May I sit down?"

"Of course."

"And may I have a drink? Scotch, and a little water."

George hesitated. Then he turned back to the buffet. He brought her her drink, sat down on the raised hearth to face her. "Shoot," he said.

She held the glass in both hands as if it were a chalice. She said, "It wasn't easy to come here. It isn't easy being here. You're not a very nice man, are you, George? You enjoy—shocking people. You laugh at them. I expect you're going to laugh at me. I won't even be able to—fight back."

George said, "Ben?"

"Of course. Do you want me to plead? I will. I'll—"

"You're going dramatic again," George said. "Relax. Just tell me what you think I can do."

Still holding the glass in both hands she sipped at the drink. Her hands were not quite steady. She said, "He didn't kill her. He couldn't have. Not Ben."

"He tried to kill me." He saw the denial forming in her face. He said, "You can believe that, Mildred. He came at me with a steel jack handle. He was quite serious about it. He was also completely off his rocker."

Mildred shook her head.

"He did something else, too," George said. "He came in here when I was away and he slashed a picture to pieces because he thought it profaned Roz. He said only two words to me down in that parking lot. They were *lecher* and *idolator*. I wouldn't invent things like that, Mildred. I don't think I could."

Mildred's tongue came out between her lips, moistened them, fled back into her mouth like a small frightened animal.

George scowled into his drink, and for a long time there was only silence. He said at last, "Maybe you have something, Mildred. It isn't much, but maybe it's something. Maybe what he did to me, what he tried to do to me is, in itself, a kind of indication that he didn't kill Roz. I don't know. I'll try it on the lieutenant and see. Maybe it won't do any good at all, and if it doesn't what you need is a lawyer, a good one."

Mildred said, "He won't—cooperate. He says he's guilty and he wants to be punished."

George stood up. "I'll try." And then, "Why in the world did you come to me?"

"Why," Mildred said, and it was the dramatic voice again, "where else would I go, George? For help?"

George said merely, in disgust, "Jesus H. Christ."

"I tried Him, George. I prayed. On my knees."

George opened his mouth. He closed it again in silence. He said finally, with gentleness, even smiling faintly, "Curtain line, Mildred. Go home now."

16

BOB LEWIS said, "You thought I'd done it, didn't you, old girl, didn't you? Well, I didn't. You know why? Because I wouldn't have the guts. Good old gutless Bob. That's me."

Joy said, "It's late. And tomorrow is Monday—"

"But no office. Monday, and no work. How about that? Vice presidential prerogative. Office boy says he's going to his grandmother's funeral, actually goes to ballgame. Not a VP. VP says he's going to the funeral of an old—friend. And he goes. Vast difference between office boy and VP."

"Please, Bob."

"Going to scream again? No police around this time. Just me."

Joy said, "What do you mean?"

"Did you kill the fair Roz? I wonder. You were there. I saw you driving there. And you're not like me. You have the guts."

"Bob. Ben—"

"Old Ben confessed. Good old Ben, took us all off the hook, didn't he? But old Ben didn't do it. Not Roz. Old Ben would go down on his hands and knees to Roz. He'd kiss her feet. Wally was there when she jilted old Ben, told him to go away. Wally knows too. But old Ben says he did it, and that's good enough."

Joy said, "Oh, God."

"No good screaming now."

"I'm not going to scream."

"Good girl. You know what? Funeral tomorrow. I have a suggestion. Idea. I'm good at ideas. They're my job. I'm good at my job. Did you know that? I'm good, and I'm getting better, bigger. No guts, maybe, but I'm going a long way. You coming with me? Trips to Europe, big house not like this, clothes, furs, jewelry, whatever you want—you coming with me?"

There was a pause. Then, "I'm coming with you."

"Good girl."
"What was your idea?"
"Oh, that. Glad you brought it up. It's a good idea. Tomorrow we find a crossroads. That's where we bury fair Roz. With a stake driven through her heart. That's what you do with witches."

17

MONA SAID, "Honestly. Ben, of all people. Do you think he actually did it?"
"No," Wally said.
"Why," Mona said, "that's simply silly. He confessed, didn't he?"
"That's what they say."
"Why would he confess if he didn't do it?"
"I don't know."
"There. You see? So he did do it. You just said so."
"I don't believe it."
"Honestly, Wally. Sometimes you make me so mad. Now the police won't bother you any more, although I still simply don't see why you were so upset. Nothing happened, did it?"
"Nothing happened."
"And it's all over and now you say he didn't do it. Honestly. Sometimes you reason just like a—woman!"

18

LOUELLA WORE again the Bergdorf nightie that emphasized the rich curves of her body, the secret shadows. The door to Sam's dressing room-study was ajar. She opened it wide. Sam was at the fine polished desk, his back to her, and she walked quietly across the room, and rested her hands on his shoulders. She stood this way for a few moments, looking down at him in silence. She said then, "Do you wish we had a child, Sam?"

"Louella, please. I don't want to talk about that."

"All right, Sam. We'll talk about something else. Do you want to talk about Ben Pierson?"

"No. Not that either."

"He didn't do it, you know. It isn't in character."

"Louella."

"Hush." She was smiling now. It was a gentle smile. "It doesn't matter. Stop worrying about it, about everything. I'm here." And she dropped her hands from his shoulders, moved around to the side of the desk where he could see her. She watched his face, his eyes, and what she saw brought a glow into her mind. She said softly, "I'm here, Sam. And you need me. That's all that's important. Look at me, Sam. You do need me, don't you? Say it."

"I need you," Sam said. And he added, silently, "God help me."

19

LIEUTENANT FRED PARKER was in, sitting in the small back office of the police station. There was a paper cup on the desk, and two cigarette butts floated in the last half inch of coffee. Two ashtrays were full. The room itself seemed weary. "Sit down, George," the lieutenant said. "Tell me what's on your mind."

George straddled a chair. "Ben Pierson, of course."

Fred merely looked at him.

"Maybe," George said, "I can tell you a couple of things you don't know about him, like, for instance, that he tried to kill me Thursday night." He went through the scene in the parking lot in detail. Then he went back and reconstructed the vandalism of the picture. Then he went back farther, to Ben's intrusion on him and Gladys. Then he sat and waited.

Fred said, "He adds up to a pretty violent character, doesn't he?" He paused, "Or wasn't that what you intended to show?"

"It was," George said, "and it wasn't. I don't know if Ben carries a pocket knife—"

"He doesn't. At least, he didn't when he walked in here. So?"

"Then he probably used mine to cut up the picture. There's one right there by the easel. I keep it sharp."

Fred shook his head. "I don't see what that proves."

"Lack of premeditation," George said. "He came in, saw the picture, went into a frenzy, picked up the knife that was handy and hacked the picture to bits."

Fred thought about it. "Go on." And then, "He followed you all the way to the Jersey bar. That's premeditation."

"But when he got there, he came at me with his bare hands."

Fred smiled faintly, wearily. "That, I'd say, was just plain damn foolishness."

"I told you, he was completely off his rocker. I jolted him. He hit the car hard. I thought then, and I still think, that he intended to call it quits when he walked around and opened the car door. I think he was going to get in and drive away. But the jack handle was on the floor, and he picked it up and had another try."

"Most people," Fred said, "carry their jack handles in the trunk. Maybe he had it handy knowing he was going to use it."

"Then why didn't he? Why did he come at me all spraddled out with only his bare hands?"

The little office was silent. Fred picked up a cigarette package, poked a finger into it. It was empty. He crumpled it and threw it at the wastebasket. "I smoke too much anyway." And then, "Look. I'm just a village cop. Spell it out for me. I think I know what you're getting at, but spell it out anyway."

"All right," George said, and he was silent, setting his thoughts in order. Then, "Has he said anything? Has he said, for example, that he went to see Roz, Mrs. Warren, on Thursday? Say Thursday morning?"

"He went to see her. He ran into Peters who'd gone to see her too. As far as I can tell it was like a couple of dogs chasing after a bitch in heat. I'm not making wisecracks."

"The analogy is sound," George said. "So he saw her. It had to be that way. And what she said to him pushed him close to the edge. He took off like a big bird in my direction. *My* direction. He didn't go for her when she hurt him. He went for me. Everything follows from that."

Fred said, "Tell me why."

"I don't know," George said. "I'm just guessing. But you can't have an idolator unless you have an idol. And when the idol is profaned, you don't destroy the idol, you go after the person who committed the sacrilege. That's the first point."

"I'm listening," Fred said. "I'm not liking it a bit, but I'm listening. Go on."

"The second point," George said, "is the way he went about trying to punish me for profaning his idol. All he had was the urge. He didn't stop to think how he'd go about it. He just went berserk."

"I still say," Fred said, "why you? Why not Peters, or any of the others? They—profaned her just as much as you did."

"I'm not a psychiatrist," George said. "But in a vague sort of way I think I understand it. I think he chose me because I'm the only one who's—formidable. Martin Fuller, maybe, but Martin was in London and out of reach. The rest are not very much. I think he picked me because I'm what I am, physically, I mean."

Fred said, "The little drunk trying to pick a fight with the biggest man in the bar?"

George shook his head. "The little drunk is trying to prove something. This is different. I think Ben in a vague, murky way was trying to destroy himself, as well as me."

Fred pushed his chair back. He stood up, walked wearily to the door. To the desk sergeant he said, "Send out for some cigarettes. And some more coffee. Black." He walked back to his desk and sat down heavily. "You're talking about things I don't pretend to understand." He sighed. "But I'll have to give you your two points. Maybe they mean something. He went after you, not

Mrs. Warren. And a man who goes after you with his bare hands may not be the kind of man who carries a gun to a house and goes upstairs and shoots a woman in the back. Is that what you're saying?"

"That's it," George said.

Fred spread his hands flat on the desk. He studied them. He said, "Maybe it's because I've been wondering too that I'm still here, that I've been here all afternoon and evening. He says he did it. He won't see a lawyer. His wife tried to bring one all the way out from the city. He, Pierson, was either there in her bedroom, or else he sees visions, because he described the room as it was—her purse on the dressing table, her jewelry. And he described her—what she was wearing, where the bullet hole was, exactly the way she was lying."

"Oh," George said, merely that.

Fred nodded. "Exactly. There are characters who do confess, of course, when they've had nothing to do with a crime. In the city it happens all the time, they tell me, whenever a crime gets a big play in the papers. But usually you can trip them up, because they don't know enough and have to guess about details and get them wrong, and you send them away and hope maybe they'll find the rest of their marbles. But Pierson knows exactly what that room was like. He knows exactly what Mrs. Warren was like when we found her." He opened his desk drawer. "Look here." He tossed four glossy photographs across to George, the four photographs taken in the morgue.

George stared at them. He had a feeling of revulsion, and the sense of waste was strong, bitter in his mind.

"There's where the bullet went in," Fred said. He touched the dark spot on the naked back. "There's where it came out. Here, with the brassiere on, you can see it. It looks like a second nipple." He paused. "I couldn't even catch Pierson on that. He said he didn't know where the bullet came out, or even if it did come out. He said she fell face down, which she did, and he didn't turn her over, so he couldn't possibly have known about the bullet stuck in the brassiere. Maybe that sounds funny, reverse twist thinking, but it's on precisely that kind of point that the screwballs who confess get caught up. They try to guess. Pierson doesn't. He says the right things, and that's all he says."

George said, "But you've been wondering."

The desk sergeant came in. He set down a package of cigarettes and a paper cup of coffee. He looked at both men and at the pictures on the desk, and walked out. "Yeah," Fred said. His hands were busy opening the cigarettes. "I've been wondering. Because he says he wants to be punished. That's part of his statement, an integral part. He killed her; and this is how it was; and he wants to be punished. Does a sane man say that, and keep on saying it? That's why I've been wondering." He had a cigarette free of the pack. He lighted it. He worked his mouth. "Tastes awful. Like a hangover mouth." He looked at George and waited.

"Normally," George said, "I don't hold much with psychiatrists. But you'd better call one in, hadn't you? See what he says?"

Fred said, "We can send him over to the state hospital, have him looked at there. I don't think he'll cooperate."

George said, "Can't you bring someone here? Someone in private practice, someone with stature? He'd be more likely to cooperate then."

Fred smiled faintly, sadly. "The looney boys come high. And this isn't Westchester County—"

"I'll pay the bill," George said. He stood up, and his eyes went again to the pictures. "That's all that's left," he said. "Just something lying on a slab, to be put in a coffin and lowered into the ground."

"I know how you feel," Fred said. And then, "Thanks for coming in. Thanks for your—ideas." He watched the broad back move towards the door, stop suddenly.

George turned, walked back to the desk. He picked up the photograph of Roz supine, wearing the brassiere and panties. He frowned at it. "Why the safety pin?" He held the picture down for Fred to see, pointed with a large forefinger at the pin in the brassiere strap.

Fred said slowly, "I'll be damned. I hadn't seen it." And then, "Maybe there are a lot of things I haven't seen."

"Funny," George said. He dropped the picture on the desk and turned away. This time he did not come back.

It was later, considerably later that night when he sat up in bed with a start, jerking himself out of the half-sleeping, half-waking state when the mind, somehow freed, seems to float, to soar, to see things with unnatural clarity and comprehension.

He sat there for only a moment, and then he threw back the sheet and got out of bed. He wore only the bottoms of his pajamas, and he hitched them up as he padded on bare feet out into the studio, turned on the studio lights.

From the wall he took the picture of Gladys's face on Roz's body, and set it on the easel, locked it in place. He stood in front of it for a long time, studying it, memorizing it. And then, at last, he sighed, and sat down, and picked up a sketch pad and pencil and began to sketch in his quick, accurate way.

It was not easy to achieve exactly the effect he wanted. He wished Gladys were here to be posed, but she was not, and that was that. So he worked on alone, pausing occasionally to study again the picture on the easel.

By the time he went back to his bed, the sky was light, and the floor was littered with crumpled sketches that had not satisfied him; but, to the best of his ability, the job was done. He lay awake for some little time in a kind of cold fury. And then, at last, sleep came

This was Sunday.

Monday

1
•••••••

IT BECAME fashionable later to say that that Monday was not like other days, that there was in the air the kind of tension that comes when the Weather Bureau gives local hurricane warning and the time of waiting begins. It simply was not so.

On Main Street and along the few business blocks of Broadway shops and stores opened as usual, and customers arrived, also as usual. The New York papers carried the story of Roz Warren's death—the coverage in the *Daily News* was spectacular—and many people read the accounts at breakfast or on the bus on the way to work or in the luncheonette over mid-morning coffee; but many, too, remained ignorant of the entire affair until the local paper came out that afternoon, and by then quite a few things had happened.

Oh, the fact of the funeral was fairly well known, and discussed. There were those who considered the haste indecent, and said so—dead Saturday night, to be buried Monday morning; was somebody trying to get something covered up as fast as he could? But that attitude was not widespread, and someone in the luncheonette expressed the general view when he said, "Nothing they do would surprise me. Some of them are nice people, but they're all a little nuts."

This is not to say that the village and the county were ashamed of the eccentricity; they were not. They took pride in Louella

Bloom's books, in Mildred's appearances on stage or on television, in George Hanks's magazine covers and illustrations, although they looked upon them in somewhat the same manner that parents view the accomplishments of a precocious child—accomplishments that are not quite real or understandable but do seem to attract considerable attention.

The funeral was looked upon as just another funeral, probably more expensive than most because Paul Warren with that big house and all could certainly afford it, but not to be compared in importance, or even spectacle, to the funeral given a year ago for the local fire chief, or the one for old Mr. Haskins when he passed away. As it turned out, there was not even solid attendance at the funeral by the hard core who disliked passing up any service, regardless of religion or acquaintance with the deceased.

And yet, later, the myth sprang up that there had been portents.

2

MARTIN PLANNED to drive into the city early. Over breakfast Madge said, "I thought you'd stay, Marty. I mean, the service is at eleven, and you are going to attend, aren't you?"

"I'll be back. I promise. But I have to go to the office first." And, looking at her across the table, finding her still a stranger, and himself a stranger too after that scene with George, he said, "You're worried that there won't be enough people."

"Yes."

"Funerals," Martin said, "aren't for the dead. They're for the living."

"That doesn't make any difference, Marty. We owe her—respect."

"I could be cynical about that."

"Don't." She stood up. "More coffee?" She went to get it.

When she returned, Martin said, "You and I are going to have to have a long talk." And then in surprise, "What's funny about that?"

"Your tone," Madge said. "It's the one you use to Johnny." She sat down. She was unsmiling now. "Maybe we'll have a talk, Marty. But not now. And maybe there isn't even anything to say, so talk would just confuse things."

"I think there's a lot to say."

Madge picked up a spoon, looked at it, set it down again. Then her eyes returned to his face, and remained there, steady, calm. "All right, Marty. What is there to say?"

Martin said, "Look. I knew Roz—"

"You slept with her. I know."

He was a trifle off-balance, still he went on. "It was over six months ago—"

"I knew it then. Is talk going to change it? Would talk have changed it then?"

Martin shook his head, puzzled, baffled. "I can't get to you."

"Not with words, Marty." And then, "If you have to go in, you'd better go."

He was started now and he could not now stop. As during that time yesterday afternoon with George, the words seemed to say themselves. "You went to see Roz on Friday. That was your —appointment."

"Yes."

"Why did you go to see her? Was it to talk about me?"

"Yes."

"Oh, my God," Martin said. "Girls together. Is that funny, too?"

"It wasn't. But it is."

"Did you cut me up?" He was being ridiculous, and he knew it, but this, too, he was unable to control, male pride outraged. "So much of me for the wife, so much for the—mistress, perhaps a neutral zone between that both parties agreed would remain inviolate? How did you split me, vertically or horizontally?"

Madge said, "Hadn't you better go now? If you're going, that is."

"I'm going." He stood up, walked around the table and bent automatically to kiss her. Her lips were cool. Her voice stopped him at the door.

"You will be back, Marty, won't you?"

"I'll be back. To pay my respects."

And so he was in town early, ahead of the commuter rush, the first person to reach the office. He took a long time and great care in composing the telegram. It would not be delivered at the factory in California until noon, New York Time, at the earliest, but he wanted to get it on its way. It represented no panacea, but at least it was a start, a step in the right direction. He hoped.

3

SAM, TOO, planned to go into town. Louella said, "The exchange doesn't open till ten, and you'd have to leave then to get back here by eleven." She paused. "Unless you aren't planning on going to the funeral."

"I—wasn't."

"That's up to you, Sam."

"Funerals are—"

"Barbarous? Yes, I think they are." They were in his dressing room-study, and the picture on the chest-on-chest caught Louella's eye. She looked at it in silence.

Sam said, "Are you going?"

"Yes."

"Why?"

Louella shook her head. Her eyes were still on the picture. "I haven't tried to analyze my reasons. I don't think I want to." And then, "Maybe it's a feeling of guilt that drives most people to funerals. Maybe they go because they wish they had been a little more pleasant, a little more friendly, a little more—understanding when the dead person was alive. I don't know, Sam."

"Usually you're more decisive than that."

Louella smiled faintly. "Dogmatic, you mean, Sam? I guess I am dogmatic usually, but not this morning."

"Do you want me to go with you? I will, if you like. You know that."

Her smile turned gentle. "You're sweet." And she was silent for a moment, still studying the picture of herself. "Do you remember that summer in Switzerland, Sam?"

"Of course I do."

She turned then to face him. "Did you enjoy it? All of it? Or did you begin to fret towards the end, find yourself anxious to get back here to the routine of work. Don't answer yet, Sam." And she was silent again, watching his face. "How important is your work to you?"

"That's an odd question."

"I know it is," Louella said. "It's a question no woman should ever ask a man, because it seems to belittle him. But I'm asking it."

"Why," Sam said, "I don't think I know the answer, Louella. Is it important that I know?"

She took her time, watching him still, studying him, drawing upon all of her knowledge of him. She said at last, "Yes, Sam, I think it is important that you know. Think about it. I won't tell you the reason yet."

4

THE COLD FURY was with George still when he awakened. He showered, shaved and dressed even to a necktie, and went out to the kitchen, his sleeves rolled up on the blacksmith's arms. He brewed a pot of the special coffee and poached himself an egg while he thought about things. He had to go back a long time in memory to find another occasion when the emotion of anger had gone quite so deep.

There had been a tackle once, playing his first year in pro

ball. The tackle had taken pride in his press clippings that said he was quite considerable of a terror, and he had set about demonstrating his particular brand of terrorism in wanton fashion. He was warned. He was warned a second time, and even a third, but his transgressions continued, and George had watched, and waited, feeling then as he felt now, the fury under tight control. He had stood it as long as he could. They carried the tackle off the field and away to the hospital not too many plays later.

One of George's teammates, watching the departing stretcher, said, "You should have killed the son of a bitch."

And George answered in simple truth, "I tried."

It was at times like this, George thought, that man demonstrated the fact of his animal antecedents. Man flattered himself that he was a rational being, even invented a God conceived in his own idealized image. And most times man's behavior was more or less rational, prompted by reason rather than emotion. And, paradoxically, it was when man was confronted by reasoned evil, rational viciousness, that he reacted in pure animal fashion, powered by emotion, sometimes blindly, as a wounded rhino charges, but sometimes with cunning, a wounded buffalo rather than a rhino, circling and stalking, waiting patiently for the opportunity to destroy.

The law took cognizance of this; a crime committed in the heat of passion was bad enough because man was supposed to be able to control himself; but when a man distorted the reason his ancestry had endowed him with, twisted it and used it for ignoble purposes, then the crime became magnified into an affront against the entire human race. Ben Pierson, reacting in frenzy here in the studio and down in the parking lot, could be forgiven, even pitied. Someone who maimed or murdered in cold blood had closed out his membership in human society.

George was tidying up the breakfast things when Madge came along the path to the kitchen door. Her eye caught the necktie. "You're going to the funeral."

"Of course," George said. He wiped the small frying pan dry, hung it up on the stove hood, took off his denim apron. "Coffee?"

"Some of yours?" Madge smiled faintly. "I'd love it."

George poured two cups. "You could duplicate it, you know." It was faint accusation.

"No," Madge said. "I wouldn't take the trouble. Few people would. Few people have your determination to get what they want, whether it's superlative coffee, or position, or anything else." Always she could be at ease with this big man, and she did not understand why. She said, "I want to ask a favor, George. It's about that picture."

"It won't be shown," George said. "It would just cause more talk, and we've had enough of that."

"I'm asking a lot, am I not?" Madge produced that faint smile again. "Asking an artist to destroy his work, I mean."

"I won't destroy it," George said. He watched her smile fade. "But it won't be shown. Drink your coffee."

She sipped slowly. She set the cup down. Her eyes had not left his face. "Are you angry with me, George?"

"No."

"With someone." It was a statement, no question.

"I guess I'm more transparent than I thought."

Madge was silent, thoughtful. "Did Ben kill her, George?"

"No."

Madge waited, but there was no more to the answer; there was only the simple, definite, flat denial. "Do you know who did?"

"I have an idea."

"It could have been any one of us, couldn't it?"

"It could." And then, and he was not quite sure why he said it, "It wasn't Martin."

"Dear George." She was smiling again. "Thank you." Her eyes went to the necktie again. "The funeral's not until eleven."

"I have some things to do first."

She stood up then, smiling still. "I can recognize dismissal when I hear it. Thank you for the coffee. Thank you for everything." She was gone.

George rinsed and dried both coffee cups. In the studio he

collected the crumpled sketches, tossed them in the fireplace and touched a match to them, watched them burn. And then he made his bed with his usual meticulous care, put on his jacket and went out to his car.

His first stop was the hospital where, in a patient way, he satisfied hospital officialdom that his request for knowledge was neither unethical, illegal, nor immoral—not an easy task, this, nor had he expected it would be; built into the walls, permeating the corridors of every hospital was a vast reluctance to tell any outsider anything at all. But he got his information at last, and he drove around to the large house converted now into apartments, and rang the bell of the one marked Lucille Spencer, R.N.

Miss Spencer was in, wearing white stockings and white shoes and a housecoat instead of her uniform. There was about her a stolid, no-nonsense attitude as she stood at the door, holding it open, but not too wide. George said, "I understand it was you who went to the Warren house Saturday night to attend the baby." And he paused, smiled. "The hospital told me. I convinced them I was harmless."

"What do you want?" Miss Spencer said.

"I'd like to talk to you. It will only take a few minutes."

"What do you want to talk about?"

"The baby," George said. "Only that."

Miss Spencer hesitated. And then she held the door wide. "I don't see any harm in that. Come in."

5

LIEUTENANT PARKER arrived at the station a little before ten. He had, he figured, more than made up for the tardiness by the long hours spent yesterday trying to gather facts that would stand up. And maybe he had just been wasting most of his time, because after that visit from George Hanks he, Fred, was not at all sure of much of anything.

The day sergeant said, "The Pierson character wants to talk to you."

"So?" Fred said. "About what?"

"He won't tell me. I think the guy's batty."

"And you may be absolutely right," Fred said. "Bring him in." He walked into the tiny back room. The ashtrays were still full. He emptied them into the wastebasket, crumpled the two paper cups and threw them in too. And then he sat down at the desk and waited.

Ben held himself tall and straight. He still wore the dark glasses. He said in that fine deep voice, "I have a favor to ask, lieutenant." He paused with an ingrained sense of timing. "I'd like to attend the funeral services."

Fred looked at the sergeant. The sergeant rolled his eyes. Fred said, "That's an odd request."

"Why, lieutenant?"

Fred began to smile. He shook his head. "I'm damned if I know."

Ben said, "I killed her. I want to be punished. But I also want to—pay my last respects. Is that incredible?"

"I don't know that, either," Fred said. He got out a cigarette, lighted it. He studied Ben's face through a cloud of smoke. "Are you sorry you killed her, is that it?"

"I have no regrets. She was evil. She had to be destroyed."

Fred thought of George Hanks. He said, "She was your idol."

"She was a false idol."

"I guess," the sergeant said, "you don't need me, lieutenant." And he added under his breath as he walked out of the office, "Jesus!"

Ben said, "I give you my promise, lieutenant, that I will make no attempt to escape."

Fred stifled a smile before it could appear.

"Nor will I cause a scene."

Fred leaned back in his chair. He asked himself where was the harm? And if George Hanks was right in what he had said last night, and this one was merely a character without all his

212

marbles who had given himself up for reasons, dark motives beyond a sane man's comprehension, then it followed that the guilty man, or woman, was one of the others, and where was a better place or time to watch them, observe their actions and reactions than at the funeral where emotions could be expected to lie not far beneath the surface? And another point: would not Ben Pierson's presence, his unexpected, if only temporary, release from custody be something of a jar to anyone who, knowing of Ben's confession, might very well consider himself safe, home free? He turned all this over in his slow careful way. The clincher was, of course, that single question: where was the harm? He said finally, "I guess it can be arranged."

Ben said, "Thank you, lieutenant. I shall need clothes. My wife can bring them here."

Not that, Fred told himself. He wanted no more of the Eliza-crossing-the-ice act, the husband and wife team in impromptu dramatic performance. "I'll have one of the boys pick them up," he said.

6

WALLY PETERS, in a dark summer suit, said, "For God's sake, aren't you ready yet? They aren't going to hold up the festivities for us, you know." And he shook his head. "I think you'll probably be late for your own funeral."

Mona giggled. "That's silly. How on earth could anybody be late for his own funeral? Tell me that. It simply isn't possible. Honestly."

7

ON THE PHONE Madge said, "I'll swing around and pick you up, Paul. There's no need for you to drive."

"That's very decent of you," Paul said. "Most considerate. I haven't told you yet how grateful I am for—"

"Please," Madge said. "Don't thank me, Paul. I—wanted to do it." Strangely enough, it was true.

8

THE ORGAN played quietly, interminably there in the large room of the funeral home. Madge had said yesterday to Paul, "Is there anyone who should be notified? Friends? Family?"

And Paul had said, "No one. Roz had no family. Father and Mother both dead. She was—alone."

And so it had seemed better not to have even a screen to separate the attendance. The coffin, banked with flowers, and closed by Madge's decision, was at the head of the room. The crew-cut young minister waited behind the scenes, in the wings as it were, and what he thought about while he waited nobody ever found out. He was young and eager and thoroughly out of tune with the entire situation. When his time came, he tried; he has to be given that.

Louella and Sam were first to arrive, and they waited in the small entry until Madge and Paul Warren came, and then the four of them walked in together with only low words of greeting among them. Louella's face was impassive in enforced repose. She noticed with satisfaction that Paul seemed to have hold of himself. Sam was uncomfortable, and wanted to fidget, but dared not. He wore what George Hanks called his banker's face. When Joy and Bob Lewis arrived, Bob's color not good and his hands a trifle unsteady, everyone nodded solemnly at everyone else, and there was no sound but the ceaseless organ music.

Mildred Pierson came in alone and took her place. She wore no make-up. Even sitting, unmoving, she managed to be dramatic;

her hands, folded in her lap, conveyed a kind of silent martyrdom.

Wally and Mona, for a wonder, arrived in ample time, and Mona managed a whispered, "You see? We're early. Honestly," as they walked to their seats.

A few other people, mostly female and identities unknown, took seats near the center of the room which was far and away the best vantage point.

George and Martin met on the sidewalk and went in together, Martin to sit next to Madge, George on the aisle. The funeral assistant caught Madge's eye and looked his solemn question, and Madge glanced around at the assemblage, checked her mental list, and was about to nod, when Ben Pierson walked in, still wearing his dark glasses. He took the seat next to Mildred, and Mildred took his hand and held it in both of hers.

Louella's face lost none of its impassivity. Sam opened his mouth, closed it again in silence, and scratched briefly at his ear. Madge looked at Martin, who was looking at her, and then they both faced front again. Mona nudged Wally with her elbow. Wally gave the faintest of nods. George turned clear around to see, as he had expected, Fred Parker inconspicuous in the rear of the room. Bob Lewis leaned close to Joy's ear. "For God's sake, don't start that screaming again." From Joy there was no sign that she even heard. And then the organ music stopped and there was only heavy silence, and the young minister walked to the portable lectern.

"We are gathered here," he said, "to mourn the loss of a beloved friend untimely plucked from the womb of life."

Martin closed his eyes. He thought that Macbeth, and distorted Macbeth at that, was considerably out of place. He opened his eyes and glanced at George and saw that George thought so too.

The young minister had his notes, and he referred to them. "Rosamund McCartney Warren was a gentle soul, wife and mother in all of the fullness that those wonderful words connote . . ."

Wally wondered who had ghosted the minister's script, and

Mona was convinced then, and maintained later, that the minister wasn't talking about Roz at all, it was somebody else he had in mind all along.

". . . in her gaiety and warm friendliness . . ."

It was becoming apparent to the minister that he was not getting through to his listeners, that something, somehow was wrong. Louella took a deep audible breath. Sam looked down at his hands in embarrassment. George's shoulders stirred gently; it was the only sign of restiveness that he gave.

". . . she was unselfish, placing others always before herself . . ."

Paul stared straight ahead, unseeing, unhearing, no faintest flaw showing in the veneer of calm. Madge glanced at Martin, a helpless, hopeless plea.

". . . her footprints in the sands of time—"

It was suddenly too much. George Hanks stood up and the minister's voice quavered and stopped. George walked up the aisle. He said gently, "I'll take over. I knew her a little better than you." One large hand closed on the minister's arm, assisted him away from the lectern. George faced the gathering. There was neither sound nor movement, and for a few moments he watched them all, studied them, the fury under tight control in his mind.

He said slowly, distinctly, and with a stiffness that was utterly unlike George Hanks, "This was a woman. I knew her well. I called her friend." He paused there, to give the words emphasis.

"In death I will assign her no other qualities than those she possessed in life. That would be dishonest, an affront to our friendship. The qualities she did possess were enough. She died for them, and with them, and left the world a poorer, less exciting place for her passing. She had the ability to make colors glow, minds sing, and such was her force that she stirred us all. Of how many persons can that be said?"

He singled out no face. He watched them all, as they watched him. "I will not judge her," he said then. "I am not competent to judge. And neither is any one of you. If judge you must, then judge yourselves, measure your own actions and words and thoughts. Each of us knew her. Each of us felt her influence. Some of us, I think, are better for it. Some of us are unchanged."

He paused there and looked from face to face, drawing them to himself and his words, holding them in the silence. It was a strange tableau, and although later telling of it, remembering it, Mona would always giggle, she felt no inclination to giggle now.

George said, "At least one person has, in destroying her, destroyed himself. He has taken away something that cannot be replaced, and for the rest of his life that knowledge will plague him. Wherever he goes, however he tries to hide that knowledge will be with him. Him I judge, not her." The fury emerged briefly. "Him I damn."

The young minister, listening, flinched. So did they all. There was only silence.

"She was what she was," George said then in the quiet voice. "She was, as we all are, a mixture of strength and weakness, good and bad, black and white and all the spectrum colors between. She lived her life as she thought best, as we all do, in the end accountable only to ourselves. She is gone. Her passing leaves a void. It will not be filled by any other."

He was done, no more words left to say. He walked back down the aisle to his seat, and the minister, trepidation plain, moved slowly to the lectern. The minister moistened his lips and took what seemed to him the safest course. "Let us pray. 'Our Father who art in Heaven' . . ."

9

ON THE drive home Bob Lewis said, "That was quite a show old George put on, wasn't it?"

From Joy there was only silence.

"And Ben walking in like Banquo's ghost. That means he's

repudiated his phony confession? If that's it, it puts us right back where we started."

"Bob." Her voice was calm enough, and when he turned to look her face showed nothing. And yet the words had a strange, unreal quality. "I was there," Joy said. "I rang. There was no answer. I walked in, went upstairs. She was there on the floor, dead, and the baby was crying down the hall and I didn't know what to do. So I ran." She paused. "At the party, waiting, knowing—that was the worst time of all." She was silent.

For once Bob could think of nothing to say.

10

MARTIN'S PHONE CALL came a little after noon. He took it in the study, the door closed. Howard Post, who was Vice-President and General Manager of Coast Aircraft, said, "I have your telegram, Marty. It means what?"

"I hoped I'd made it plain."

"Not plain enough. We don't shuffle people without reasons."

"I have reasons, Howard, personal reasons. I can't stay here. I'm sorry."

"You'll have to do better than that, Marty. You're valuable to us right where you are. You're the best man we have for that job—"

"I'm sorry, Howard." He had thought it over carefully, with as objective a logic as he could muster. That talk with George yesterday had been the trigger, of course, but unless the charge had already been built up in his mind, ready and waiting for the spark there would have been no detonation.

"You had standards when you came here," George had said. "Where in hell are they now?"

Martin didn't know the answer, and he even doubted if there was one. In a year many changes took place, small, subtle changes, and it was not possible for a man to go back in his mind and try to isolate each one. Nor, probably, would it be profitable even to make the attempt, because the fact of the big change within himself was real, and could no longer be ignored, and what did it matter to know exactly why and how it had come about?

And the change was there in Madge, too, and his understanding of that was as imperfect as his understanding of the other.

He did not for a moment give credence to George's concept of a miasma that seeped out of the ground here in the county. And yet, as an analogy which was the way George intended it, the concept was almost exact. You thought that you could remain unaffected, aloof, and you found that you were wrong, that the built-in bitchiness—also George's phrase—was in the air you breathed, and you absorbed it and retained it, and it became a part of you.

Oh, there were people—Mona and Wally Peters came to mind—who could breathe the air and thrive; just as there were some people who could live their lives in the tropics and never contract malaria. But he, Martin, was not one of those. He lacked the antibodies that produced immunity. He understood that now, and he hoped that the understanding had not come too late.

He had thought of a simple move of residence, across the river, say, where the air was not quite the same. He had rejected it. In a year a man built up a pattern of life, and if that pattern was bad, then it had to be altered completely, a new pattern established in a different locale lest any remaining familiarity produce the same familiar response.

Roz, George had said, was not a cause but a symptom, and that was true, too. It was futile to place blame on Roz. He, Martin, had known all along what he was doing, and he had known that it was wrong. What he had not known, understood, was that a physical act produced a mental change, that by the nature of things no man remained unaffected by his transgressions. At least this was so with Martin, and if the theory lacked universal applicability he did not care.

To the disembodied voice on the phone, he said again, simply, "I'm sorry, Howard."

"That sounds like an ultimatum." And the voice had altered.

"I don't mean it quite that way."

There was silence. Then, "I think you do, Marty," Howard Post said. "Whether you realize it or not, you're putting your abilities, your value to us right on the line. You're telling me that this is how it is, and I either fish or cut bait. Isn't that right?"

Martin had not thought of it this way, and yet he supposed that it was so. He was, in effect, standing up and spitting in the corporative eye, telling them what he wanted, whether they wanted it or no. He said, "I guess, Howard, that that's what it boils down to. For personal reasons I can't stay here—"

"You mean you won't, Marty."

"If you want to put it that way."

Howard Post said, "We have, we had great hopes for you. You came out of engineering with the broad view that not many engineers manage to acquire. You've broken the cocoon of specialization, and you're learning to see the picture as a whole, the corporation as a whole—engineering, the shop, sales, service, policy, planning and all. Do you want to jeopardize a big future by an ultimatum at this point?"

Martin had not intended it to be like this, and yet, viewed logically, how else could it have come out? In exchange for paycheck and position you gave up at least a portion of your freedom of choice. That was axiomatic. And so, in attempting to exercise that mortgaged portion you produced conflict. And yet, in a larger sense, the freedom remained. In the end you did what you most wanted to do. This was the ultimate truth. "Howard—"

"I think," Howard Post said, "that you'd better give this a little more thought. Will you do that, Marty? You're at home with nothing to distract you—"

Martin said, "I attended the funeral of a friend. That's why I'm home, Howard."

"Marty. Do I ask you to punch a timeclock? You run your

show as you see fit. You run it well and so I have no complaints or even questions." There was a pause. "I repeat, you're home with nothing to distract you. Think this over a little more. Talk with Madge. Then call me and tell me what your decision is." And, with finality, "Goodbye, Marty." The threat was there, unmistakable.

11

MILDRED PIERSON was on the telephone too. Her agent said, "I've been trying to get you, darling. I read about Ben in the papers this morning—"

"Ben didn't do it," Mildred said. "He couldn't have. I know Ben."

"What can I do?"

"I don't know. I don't know what anyone can do."

"He has confessed, as the papers say?"

"Yes."

There was a pause. Then, "Let's face it, darling, Ben takes life pretty hard sometimes. He tends to carry the woes of the world on his back. It's you I'm worrying about."

Mildred said, "I'll be all right."

"Of course you will, darling. But there's a decision to make, remember? We've got to give the Coast an answer."

"I can't think about that now."

"Baby," the agent said, "you've got to. Thirteen weeks, two thousand a week, and a good part in a vehicle they're aiming right at Academy Award contention. This one you've got to make up your mind on—"

"Do you think I could leave Ben now?" It was the full dramatic delivery.

"Baby doll, what can you do for him? Answer me that."

There was no answer.

"Study on it, darling. Give it the full intellectual treatment. Call me back this afternoon. Okay?"

"I'll—call," Mildred said.

12

GEORGE SAT again in Fred Parker's little office. Fred said, "Tell me why you want the pictures."

"Not yet," George said. "I don't want to go off half-cocked."

Fred leaned back in his chair. He said, "That was quite a speech you made at the funeral." He paused. "It wouldn't be that you were aiming it at somebody? Somebody particular?"

"It could be," George said.

"Not Pierson."

"No."

Fred was silent for a little time. "I watched them all. I didn't see a thing. You think you got to somebody?"

"Maybe," George said.

"Last night you opened up with me. What's wrong now?"

The fury pushed at him. "I got mad. It doesn't happen often. Now—" He stopped, reached inside his jacket pocket and took out the folded sketch, the one he had done last night that had finally satisfied him. He unfolded it on the desk.

Fred sat up. He studied the sketch. It was two views of the same figure, Roz Warren in brassiere and panties and mules. She was standing, and bent over. The first view was three-quarters rear, from the right side; her right breast showed in profile. The second view was three-quarters front, from the left side. Fred nodded slowly. "It could be. She was in that position when she was shot, that's what you mean?"

"Yes."

Fred opened the desk drawer and took out the photographs, shuffled through them. Then he studied the sketch again. "It looks right. So?"

"That's why I want the pictures. I want somebody else to check them, and me."

"Want to tell me who?"

"No," George said. "Not yet. I'm still guessing. I want to be sure."

Fred sighed. "Stubborn, aren't you?" And then, "I owe you something for last night, for yesterday." He flipped the photographs with the backs of his fingers. "Help yourself." And he waited until George had reached the door. Then, "When you think you're sure, you come back here to me, that's understood."

George said, "There may be no proof. There probably won't be."

"I'll be the judge of that.

George merely nodded as he walked out.

13

THE PLEASANT white house seemed strangely empty now, as it had not seemed during the six months that had ended last week with Roz's return. It was not empty, of course. There was the woman upstairs, and the baby. But there was no Roz, and there would never again be Roz. There was the difference. It was now, thinking clearly for the first time since Saturday, that Paul comprehended fully the sense of loss.

He was not, and he had never been, a deeply emotional man. Anger was rare, and he preferred it so. In anger one said things that could not be recalled, did things for other than logical reasons. And the man of reason was Paul's ideal. And yet, on Thursday evening, and again on Friday, he had been caught by emotion too strong to resist.

Thursday evening, of course, it had been George Hanks who had set him off, and until now Paul had not understood why his reaction to George had been so bitter. Granted the man was abrasive; a scoffer; he had always been abrasive. Granted, too, that George's size and strength and assurance were a constant affront; they had been no more so Thursday evening. And yet he, Paul, had let himself go, spoken words that had lain mute in his mind for months, years. Why?

In a vague way he did understand, of course, and he had to admit it, and the admission was not pleasant. Sitting listening to George at the funeral, watching him, the explanation had come unbidden into Paul's mind.

In front of them all George had allowed the depth of his affection for Roz to show, just as, in a more subtle way, he had allowed it to show that Thursday evening. And it was that Thursday display that had triggered the anger. George had broken the rules. He had shown to Paul what Paul did not want to see. He had been unfair, demonstrating what should not have been demonstrated, brought to mind thoughts that should have been ignored. And there was the cause of the anger—the sense of unfairness. And now Roz was gone, dead, and God, how he missed her!

Friday's experience, Louella's visit to the office, had been, in its way, even more shattering, more destructive of Paul's aplomb. The woman was unbalanced, of course, and irresponsible. The dreadful part was that her irresponsibility could not be controlled; her illogical logic could not be refuted. Because Roz and Sam had allegedly committed indiscretions and thereby given offense to Louella, he, Paul, was to be punished—was ever argument more monstrously distorted?

He had tried to reason with Louella. Reason was futile. He had tried appeal to their friendship, their publisher-author relationship built up over the years. It was a waste of breath. He had said at last, "You want your pound of flesh, is that it, Louella?"

And she had answered, "I'm glad you understand." God!

He had gone to the office Saturday driven by a compulsion against which there was no defense. He was not an accountant, he was a bookman, but no deep knowledge of accountancy was necessary to demonstrate to himself in figures, dollars and cents, what the loss of Louella Bloom's name from his list would mean. Oh, it was not ruin, nothing so spectacular as that. And wherever her new book was published, if it was successful, as it would be, then reprint sales of her previous books would again be stimulated to Louella's and Paul's profit; they were still bound together by that contractual umbilicus whatever happened. It was not ruin, or anything like ruin her defection threatened, but it was loss, substantial loss, the difference between ease and security on the one hand, and perpetual scramble on the other, a prospect that was intolerable. And yet what could he do?

First George Hanks, then Louella; and now Roz gone, dead, and the house empty-seeming, desolate.

He thought of the baby upstairs, and of Louella's madwoman suggestion, which was, of course, entirely out of the question, and probably not even intended seriously, merely an irresponsible whim. Or, was it? The new thought struck him with almost devastating force. Was it no whim, but all part of vengeance, of punishment? Was that what the woman had in mind? To strip him of everything?

It was then, in the emptiness, the desolation, the full comprehension of Roz's loss that the fear began. Dressed, he felt naked; secure, he was without defense. And he was alone.

14

FRED PARKER did not really want to listen at all, but he supposed that he ought to because something might be said that would cast a little light into the darkness. And it was not even necessary to strain; Mildred and Ben, playing a renunciation scene to the hilt, could be heard clear out at the sergeant's desk.

"I can't," Mildred said. "To leave you, now, in your time of need—"

"You must." Ben was in fine voice, deep, mellow. "You can't

help me. No one can help me. From now on you must live your own life."

"Ben—"

"Listen to me. Believe me. I'm at peace. For what I've done, I'll be punished, and that is just. You aren't involved. I don't want you involved."

"Do you actually think I could leave, go out to the Coast, act? With you here just—waiting?"

There was a long silence. Fred sat uncomfortable at his desk. There were times when he disliked police work. He supposed every policeman did, except perhaps the few who took pleasure in pushing people around and there was a name for that kind of person whether he was a cop or not.

Fred was strongly tempted to call out to Mildred and Ben, tell them that their histrionics were not necessary, that he didn't believe Ben's confession, and that he wished Ben would repudiate it and get it over with. The two of them were acting, of course, but that did not mean that their suffering was any the less real, and Fred's sympathy went out to them. Murder was always nasty, vicious business, and there was never any telling who all might be hurt, innocent or otherwise. It was hard to control the anger he felt at that concept.

When Mildred came out, she carried a handkerchief rolled up into a little ball. Her eyes were red. "Thank you, lieutenant," she said.

And Fred, standing, said, "Any time you like, ma'am." And he added, "I'm sorry. I really am." But what in hell was a man to do?

15

MARTIN TALKED, and Madge listened quietly, gravely. "That's it," Martin said. "Howard suggested I talk it over with you. He was saying in effect that you're involved, and of course you are. So's Johnny, but we have to make the decisions."

"You make the decisions, Marty. You always have."

"This time I want your help." He shook his head. "No, that's wrong. This time I need your help. Because when I call Howard I'm going to have to be definite."

Madge said, "You already are definite, aren't you, Marty? You think that no matter what happens this place is—"

"It's bad," Martin said. "It's unhealthy. Maybe not for everybody, but for me, for us. That sounds silly. Maybe it is silly. But it's true."

Madge said, "Are you blaming the place, the county for what happened between you and Roz?"

In a way he was, and in a way he wasn't. He tried to explain. "She was what she was, as George said today. But the point is that she wouldn't have existed anywhere else except in a place like this."

"I know what she was," Madge said. "She was incredible." And then, "She's dead now, Marty. You're free of her."

"I was already free of her," Martin said. "That was why I went to see her Saturday. I wanted to tell her that I was free."

"Maybe the person to tell was not Roz, but someone else. Me. Had you thought of that?"

Martin said slowly, "No, I hadn't. I should have. I'm sorry." He spread his hands. "Where does that leave us?"

Madge shook her head. She smiled faintly, without amusement. "We're going around in circles, aren't we? Maybe I'm not being fair. No, hear me out, Marty. Friday when I went to see Roz, to ask her to leave you alone— Yes, that was what I asked her, girls together, as you put it this morning. I shouldn't have gone, but I did. In a way I'm glad I did. But the point is that if she had agreed to leave you alone, I would have been content, and I would never have said a word to let you know that I knew about you and Roz. I'm glad it didn't happen that way. It's better like this, out in the open. Maybe that's immodest or immoral. I don't care. You can't push something under the rug and forget about it. You have to look at it and make up your mind."

Martin said, "You told me this morning there was nothing to talk about, remember?"

"I remember. And I was wrong. I was playing the role of outraged wife. Now I'm not. George said if we had to judge somebody to judge ourselves. I'm trying. I find myself guilty as an accessory, a complaisant wife who knew what was going on and tried to pretend it wasn't and hoped it would stop, and did nothing. I suppose I ought to feel that I've been cheated, robbed, betrayed because you went to bed with another woman. The funny thing is, I don't feel that at all. I don't feel anything. I'm still me. You're still you. I just don't care what happened between you and Roz. Maybe I should, but I don't." And then, "Will you answer one question, Marty? I think I know the answer, but I want to hear you say it. If there had been any way to do it, would you have left me for her?"

"Good God, no."

"Then," Madge said, "I'm still in first place, and that's all that matters."

And it was then that George Hanks walked up the porch steps and rattled the front door.

He glanced at them both as he came in, and he looked as if he were about to say something and then changed his mind. He dropped the glossy photographs on the coffee table. He gave Martin and Madge a few moments to glance at them, look away. George said then, "I'm not just being ghoulish. I want your help. I want to pick your brains."

He took out the sketch he had shown to Fred, the two views of Roz standing, bending down, her arms reaching. To Martin he said, "You have an eye. You can see things in three dimensions. Do I have the position right for the bullet to go in where the pictures show, and come out where it did?"

Martin took his time over the photographs and over the sketch. It was easier now, a problem to be examined; it was no longer

Roz he looked at, it was merely a human body. He straightened at last. "I'd say it was right," he said. "She was standing, bending over something—"

"Sit down," George said, "and I'll go through it for you, hypothesis, theory, whatever you want to call it. I want your reactions." He talked for some little time, and when he was done he looked at both of them, studied their faces. "If it fits," he said, "and I think it does—" He paused. "Name me a name. You first, Martin."

There was silence in the room.

George said, "Go ahead. You're thinking a name. Say it."

Martin said it.

George said, "Madge?"

"The—same name," Madge said. "It—has to be. But—why?"

George stood up. He collected the pictures and the sketch. "The why doesn't matter. The fact does. We all agree on the name."

Martin said, "You've got to have proof."

"There is no proof."

"Then you can't—"

"I can," George said. "I will. I'll find a way." He was gone, off the porch, down the steps.

Madge stood for a long time, her back to the room. She watched the broad shining river, the green of the hills beyond and she remembered how strange and refreshing that green had seemed after the brown of California. Only a year ago. She said, "I loved it here when we first came. It was new, exciting. Now it's horrible." She turned then. Martin was watching her. "You're right," she said. "Any place, any place at all except here. It's not for us. Call Howard. Tell him. It is an ultimatum. It's—got to be."

16

SAM BARNES OPENED his mouth and then closed it again. He said, "You don't, you can't mean that, Louella."

"I can. I do."

"I won't let you," Sam said. "Why, it's inhuman."

Louella watched him, studied him; as that dispassionate part of her mind studied her, scrutinizing words, actions, feelings, everything. "Is it, Sam?" she said, merely that.

Sam said, "Taking the book away from him is your privilege—"

"But," Louella said, "you wouldn't have done it? Is that what you're saying?"

"I wouldn't have done it," Sam said.

It was as if she were on stage in the spotlight glare, acting for a critical audience of one—herself. She had listened carefully to the eulogy George had delivered, and she had found it strangely moving. She tried now to find words to match the honesty of his. And the audience of one watched, and waited. She said finally, "Tell me why, Sam." And she smiled faintly. "I seem to have misplaced my dogmatism today."

Sam said slowly, "It was a cruel thing to do. I was the one who hurt you. The fault was mine. Not his, not hers, mine."

"You're a gentle man, Sam. I've always liked that in you."

"Hurt for hurt," Sam said. "What does the Old Testament concept accomplish?"

"Satisfaction," Louella said. And she added, "Sometimes." And yet she was not sure that even the qualification made it so. On that bare stage in the spotlight glare she found doubt beginning.

Sam said, "As I said, Louella, it was your privilege. But this other, no." He paused. "Tell me why. Is it further—punishment you have in mind for him? Is that it? Are you deliberately dangling just beyond his reach what you've already taken away from him?"

There were times, Louella thought, when it seemed pure miracle that there was any human communication at all. One wrote a sentence, read it a dozen times, found it unambiguous; and then on the thirteenth reading discovered that it was susceptible to two, or even three different interpretations. One acted, and the action had many sides and it was sometimes impossible to turn towards another the side you wanted him to see. She said, "Is that really what you think, Sam?"

"You don't want the child, Louella. And if you did, buying it is not the way. What else can I think?"

It was uncomfortable on the bare stage in the pitiless glare of the light with more doubts gathering in the shadows beyond. "I don't know, Sam." And she was silent then, thinking again of George's words, putting her own interpretation on them. She was conscious that Sam watched her, and waited. And this was new, and different, too; in his quiet patience there was a kind of dignity she had never found in him before. She said, "What would you have me do?"

Sam shook his head. "I'm not competent to judge."

And so Sam, too, had listened to George's words. It was strange that they had carried so much weight. "Carry rancor to the grave," Louella said, "and no farther?"

He was silent.

"Would you like me to phone Paul, tell him that what I did was done in anger? That I retract all of it?"

Sam said slowly, "It would be generous, Louella."

17
●●●●●●●

FOR THE third time George sat in the small office with Fred Parker. "I'm as sure as I can be," he said. "There is, as I told you, no proof, only theory." He spread out the photographs on the desk, laid the sketch beside them. He talked as he had talked with Martin and Madge; and Fred listened and heard unmistakably the ring of conviction, of truth, and then, at last, leaned back in his chair and stared at the far wall.

There was only silence in the office for a long time. Fred sighed. "You're smarter than I am," he said. He didn't mind in the least that it was so, because the job was the important thing, the only thing. He raised his voice to the desk sergeant. "Bring Pierson in." And then he looked at George. "Now we can see how good he guesses." He gathered pictures and sketch and turned them face down.

Ben glanced at George as he walked in. He said nothing. Fred Parker said, "Mind taking the dark glasses off?" He watched Ben hesitate, and then comply. Ben's eyes were solemn, dark; they seemed filled with vast sorrow. Fred said, "How was Mrs. Warren standing when you shot her?"

"You doubt me still," Ben said. In the deep voice there was sorrow too, and more; even a kind of compassion for the interrogator who knew not what he did. "And yet I tell you—"

"How was she standing?"

Ben was silent. He looked down at George. "Are you enjoying this mockery?"

"No," George said.

Fred Parker said, "You've had time to remember. How was she standing?"

"She had turned away from me," Ben said. "I shot. She fell. I waited to be sure that she was dead. Then I left the house. I threw the gun in the river and went home to get dressed for the party."

George watched and listened, and was silent, finding no words to speak.

Fred Parker said, "She just turned away? That was all?" And, "Why did she turn away?"

Ben's face was set, masklike.

"Was there something she was going to do? Had she been doing something when you came in?" He was not a cruel man, and he took no satisfaction in leading from strength with the sure knowledge that he could not be answered. But it had to be done.

"What does that mean, lieutenant?"

Fred shook his head. The silence grew, stretched taut.

Ben said, "I have nothing more to say."

Fred sighed. "I know. And that's not good enough."

"I killed her—"

"And you want to be punished," Fred said. "I know that, too. But I'm afraid we can't oblige."

"I went there—"

"Yes," Fred said. "You went there. You saw and remembered everything just as it was. But as it was after she was dead. You didn't see her alive—"

"I tell you, lieutenant, I killed her. She was evil. She had to be destroyed. I told her—"

"Whatever you told her," Fred said gently, "she didn't hear. She was already dead."

"I don't remember each detail—"

"No. It's not good enough." There was finality in the words, the voice. "You can go now. Your wife will be glad to see you."

Ben's mouth worked, but no sound came out. He lifted his hands in silent plea. And then, slowly, helplessly, he let the hands swing down to his sides. He looked at them both with his solemn dark eyes. His shoulders were bent as he turned away without a word and walked out.

Fred stood up, and moved wearily out into the front room. He was not gone long. He returned, settled himself in his chair again. "I told one of the boys to follow him, see that he gets home all right. I wouldn't want him walking in front of somebody's car." He paused. "That's all I can do." And then, in a different, harder voice, "So now where are we? You're right. We haven't any proof."

"Maybe I can get it," George said. His voice was quiet, ominous. "I can try." And the fury in his mind was difficult to control. "If you'll play along."

Fred took his time. Then, "Tell me what you have in mind. I'll probably play."

18

THERE WAS glare from the pavement, and the dark glasses were still in his hand. Ben put them on without thought, without even the knowledge that he had done so. There was no anger in his mind. There was only the deep sorrow out of which forgiveness sprang. The police lieutenant and George Hanks knew not what they did. In their mundane, narrow way they mistook the form of truth for its substance, which was what came of the habit of scoffing.

They were rootless people among whom he had lived too long, and he found pity for them now because it was their ignorance of *order* that confused them, led them astray, drove them like witless monkeys from one enthusiasm to the next in ceaseless haste. They deluded themselves that they were free; it was the freedom of hysteria, and, although Ben doubted that they thought so deep, the basis of the hysteria was, had to be, fear.

He, Ben, was not afraid. He had found *order* again, and it was comforting. The Rules had been there all along, ineluctable, and he had avoided them for a long time, but now, returning to their protection, the shelter of their unyielding rigidity, he felt only relaxation, and peace. His world was secure once more, as it had been so long ago, so far away. One transgressed, one was punished. It was as simple as that. And his had been the ultimate transgression. He had worshipped an idol, and the idol was false, and what did it matter whose hand had actually destroyed? This was the basic truth that people like the lieutenant and George Hanks could never, never comprehend. Ben felt compassion for their ignorance.

19

HOWARD POST'S voice said, "I hope you've changed your mind, Marty. We'll forget all about that telegram."

Martin said, "I'm sorry." The study door was closed, but Madge sat with him now, perched on the arm of the large chair, her eyes fixed on Martin's face.

"That means what?" Howard said.

"I'm not sure," Martin said, "that I can explain the reasons. They're tangled—"

"Untangle them."

"No," Martin said. "They're—personal. They affect me, us, the part of me and us that has nothing to do with Coast Aircraft, Howard."

Howard Post said, "Wrong. Whatever affects you has to do with Coast Aircraft."

Martin's eyes were on Madge. "I don't want to argue, Howard. But I don't accept that. A paycheck doesn't buy a—soul." He paused. "I'm going about this in the wrong way, I know. I should have planned it carefully, worked out logical reasons to show you that it would be to the company's advantage to move me. I understand that, Howard. That's the way things are done. Maybe I'm being inept, but I'm also being honest. I can't stay here."

"You've talked with Madge? She's a sensible girl."

"Madge," Martin said, "feels as strongly about it as I do." He watched Madge nod.

Howard Post said, "So far, Marty, every move you've made has been up. That's the way we like it to be. We like to plan for our people, train them, move them along—"

"Howard," Martin said, "do you think you're God?"

There was a short silence. Then, "What was that?"

"A question," Martin said. "Shall I repeat it?"

"Don't bother. But I didn't expect that from you, Marty. I'm disappointed."

Martin said, "It's trite, it's hackneyed, it's also true, Howard, that people aren't automatons to be shuffled here and there like so many machines. They're sentient. If they weren't they could better be replaced by machines. I'm me, with all that entails, or I wouldn't be of any value at all to you. And being me I retain my own feelings and my own judgment and my own freedom of choice. I am free to choose, Howard. There are no puppet strings controlling me."

"You can always leave the company," Howard said, "if that's what you mean."

"That," Martin said, "is precisely what I meant. I wouldn't like to. What I might find elsewhere would probably be less than I have now in salary, position, responsibility. But the choice is there. And if there is no other way, then that is the choice I'll make. I'm sorry. But that's how it is."

There was more, but none of it important, and he hung up the phone, his hand not quite steady, and he looked at Madge with a small, sad smile. "I guess I really tore it, didn't I?"

Madge nodded. "I think you did." And then, slowly, "It's silly, illogical, childish, I guess—" She stopped there. "All of a sudden everything's a mess." She paused. "There's only one thing." She paused again. "I don't think I've ever been quite as proud of you, Marty."

20

GEORGE WAS in no haste driving away from the village center. The cold fury was with him still, but buried deep now, overlaid by other currently stronger feelings. There was a sense of regret that events had reached this penultimate point and that he, George Hanks, had become the logical instrument of what man was pleased to call justice. And there was sadness, too, because although waste generated anger it left also a sense of loss. And there was reluctance and even a faint disbelief at the enormity of what he was going to attempt. Added to everything else there was the knowledge that he might very well accomplish nothing.

It did not occur to him that he might turn back, that he had, after all, done more than his share in explaining to Fred Parker what must have happened in that room where Roz had been found dead. Nor did he attempt to analyze his motives for going forward. There were times when a man was caught up in the flow of events, carried along inexorably, and at such times it was best to concentrate only on what lay ahead, anticipate, if possible, what might be waiting around the next turn. The time for questioning, for the weighing of moral and ethical niceties was before you became involved. Once committed, you went ahead to the best of your ability, to the limit of your strength. He knew no other way.

He carried the glossy photographs and his own sketch with him as he got out of his car and walked up the steps to the porch of the pleasant white house. He knocked and heard the echoes inside. He was standing immobile, large and solid, unsmiling, when Paul Warren opened the door. "You," Paul said, no more than that.

"I have some things to show you, some things to tell you."

Paul said, "I'm not interested in anything—"

"Oh, you'll listen," George said. "And you can do it however you like, sitting up in the normal way, or flat on the floor with me on your chest. You can believe that, Paul."

"Reverting to Neanderthal type, is that it?"

"That's it," George said. He walked through the doorway, closed the door behind him. He took Paul's arm in one large hand, turned him towards the living room.

Paul jerked his arm, tried to free it. Surprisingly, he succeeded.

George said, "Thinking of calling the police?" He nodded. "Suit yourself. They'll be interested." He walked past, into the living room, took a seat on the sofa.

Paul followed, stood looking down at him. "Say what you have to say, and then get out. And don't come back. Ever."

"Fair enough," George said. He spread the four glossy photographs face up on the coffee table. "You might as well look at them."

Paul merely glanced, looked away, looked back again in slow disbelief. He said, and his voice was low and not steady, "Even from you I wouldn't expect this kind of ghoulish—"

"You'd better sit down," George said. "This is only the beginning. These—" he gestured at the photographs, "—are just for reference. That was the way she was when she was found." And then, again, "Sit down, Paul." He spread his sketch on the table. "This is how it happened. You'd better look at this one, too."

Paul said, "I didn't believe that people like you existed."

"Your mistake. We do. Roz could have told you I was real." He had a pencil in his hand. He touched the sketch lightly. "The bullet went in here." The pencil moved. "It came out here. She was bending over, as I've drawn her. That's how it had to be to make the bullet path a straight line." His voice was quiet, normal. He concentrated on the facts, the theory arising out of the facts, shutting his mind to all else. "The question," he said, "is what was she bending over, and why was she bending at all?" And for the third time, "You'd better sit down, Paul."

The backs of Paul's legs found a chair. He sank into it. He watched George with incredulity, shock written plain on his face.

George said, "She was lying near the bed. She had fallen there and she had not been moved. But there was nothing on the bed. The dress she was going to put on was over a chair clear across the room. So why was she bending? What was she reaching for?"

There was silence in the room.

George said, "The police lieutenant asked me, and asked Martin Fuller, too, whether Roz would be more likely to be dressed this way in front of a man or another woman. Independently, both Martin and I said she would not allow herself to be seen that way by anyone. In a way we were right. We knew her that well, Paul. But we were wrong, too, because under one set of circumstances, and only one that I can imagine, she might allow herself to be seen that way by someone and do nothing about it."

Paul said slowly, distinctly, "A monster. There is no other word."

George looked at him, watched him steadily for some little time in silence. Then he picked up one of the photographs, held it out. It was the view of the woman lying supine, and clothed. "There's a safety pin in the bra strap, Paul. Nobody noticed it at first, but it's important. I know why it's there, why she put it there. I know why she was bending over, and why she didn't bother to put on a robe when one particular person came in. What she was doing was more important to her than the way she looked."

He had the sketch in front of him now, and he was bending over it, working with the pencil in sharp, clean strokes. He talked on with no change in the quiet, even flow of his words. "I went to the hospital this morning, Paul. They gave me the name of the nurse who was sent here that night. I talked with her. She remembered. She also gave me help, instruction in something I didn't know much about. I doubt if you do." He paused, studied the sketch, added a line or two. Then, satisfied, he looked at Paul, held him with his eyes.

"I don't know when they changed technique," George said. "Diapers were always three-cornered as far as I knew. They aren't these days. They're folded in a rectangular shape, brought up between the baby's legs, and pinned at the sides. Two pins, one at each hip. Safety pins, of course. When the nurse got here and went up to the nursery to see about the baby, the baby's diapers had been kicked off. There was only one pin in them, and that wasn't enough. The nurse didn't make any fuss about that. Why should she? It meant nothing to her. She had no way of knowing where the other pin was—in Roz's brassiere. She had no way of knowing that that explained why Roz was bending over when she was shot. She had no way of knowing that that explained why Roz didn't care about being seen in her underclothes because taking care of the baby was far more important to her than her own appearance."

He held out the sketch. "Here's the way it was, Paul. I've sketched in the bed. I've sketched the baby on the bed. Roz was bending over it. She had put one safety pin in the diaper. The other was still fastened, and closed so the baby couldn't possibly grab it and be hurt, in Roz's brassiere strap. Some women do it that way, the nurse told me; some women hold the pins in their mouths, not that that matters."

His hand holding the sketch was rocklike in its steadiness. Paul watched it in a kind of fascination.

George said, "You couldn't leave the baby on the bed after you shot her, of course. Babies kick and squirm and have to be watched lest they fall off things like beds and injure themselves. And so you took the child back to the nursery, back to its crib without noticing that her diaper was held by only one pin." He leaned forward and laid the sketch in Paul's lap. Then he sat back on the sofa, and for a time his eyes scanned the photographs, and the cold fury began its slow bubbling rise in his mind, forcing its way through the other feelings that had overlain it.

"Why you killed her," George said, "I don't know. With all the faults you may attribute to her, she was worth an infinity of you. Perhaps that was the reason. Perhaps there were other, more immediate reasons. Perhaps I'm at least partly the cause. What you felt when you found me here Thursday night must have burned deep or you wouldn't have said what you said. I had seen her before, Paul. I came to see her on Wednesday, to welcome her back. I told her then that she had given a hostage to fate. The baby, I think, is the beginning, just as the baby is the means to the end. Make out of that what you will." He gathered the photographs. He picked the sketch from Paul's lap. He stood up.

Looking down, holding the man with his eyes and with the new, unfeigned depth to his voice, he said, "I'm going to the police now, Paul. I think they'll believe me. Ben's confession doesn't stand up. Everything points straight at you now—the one person Roz would have ignored while she went on with what she was doing, taking care of her baby. You were at your office all Saturday afternoon? That will be examined and re-examined, and it will be found that it was quite possible for you to leave the building, and return, without being noticed. I don't know how you did it, but the police will find out. They'll find where your car was parked, and the attendants will be sifted. They'll check the roads, the toll stations, the parkway police. You can't anticipate all of the loopholes, Paul, nor even begin to plug them. It was diffuse before. Too many persons were involved, each one with a possible motive. It's focused now. Now the police can concentrate their efforts. I said today that whoever destroyed her destroyed himself as well. You did, Paul. You're damned."

George turned away. As he started for the hall the telephone rang, rang a second time. He looked back from the front door and saw Paul pick up the phone; and Louella's voice said, "Paul. I want to talk to you—"

Paul dropped the phone into its cradle. He stood there looking down at it. When it began to ring again he did not touch it. It was still ringing, and still untouched, when George opened the door and walked out into the sun.

He drove slowly down the long drive. Around the first turn on the county road Fred Parker sat waiting in the police car. George stopped. He handed the photos and the sketch to Fred. He said, no longer in fury, merely in emptiness, "I did the best I could. I don't know how much it shook him. Give him fifteen minutes or so to think about it. I think the effect may be stronger then." He put the car in gear and drove off. He did not look back.

21

THE PHONE had at last stopped its ringing, but Paul still stood looking at it as if it were something malevolent and sentient, something to be feared, as if its clamor might start up again, heralding Louella's voice. "Paul. I want to talk to you."

Words were merely words, innocent enough. Who should know that better than he? And yet, of course, it was not so; it was at best no more than half-truth. Because words, spoken, became more than mere sounds. They took on the intent of the person who spoke them. In their color and accent was knowledge of what was to come, secret knowledge shared only by the words and their speaker. The listener could only wait until the secret was revealed, because from the preamble inference was futile.

"Paul. I want to talk to you." No more than that, but it had been enough.

George's opening had been even more innocent-seeming. "I have some things to show you, some things to tell you." The words had betrayed no hint of their secret shattering knowledge.

'Friends, Romans, countrymen, lend me your ears . . .' Who, hearing that beginning, had seen where the ending would be?

Or the Moor's final speech with its gentle, 'Soft you; a word or two before you go.' Hinting at nothing. Could the listeners have guessed at the words that would follow? '. . . then, must you speak/ Of one that lov'd not wisely but too well;/ Of one not easily jealous, but, being wrought,/ Perplexed in the extreme; of one whose hand,/ Like the base Indian, threw a pearl away/ Richer than all his tribe . . .'

The phone rang again. It startled him. He stared at it, listened to its clamor. Slowly he turned away. It was strange how Othello's words kept repeating themselves in his mind. '. . . of one whose hand,/ Like the base Indian, threw a pearl away/ Richer than all his tribe . . .'

George was no Shakespeare. He had put it differently, but his words, too, would not be silent. "With all the faults you may attribute to her, she was worth an infinity of you."

And she was gone now. And the phone continued to ring, Louella, behind the innocent beginning, waiting to continue her unbalanced vengeance and strip him of everything. First George, then Louella—even, perhaps, acting in concert? He felt naked again, defenseless, alone. And the phone rang on and would not stop. He walked to the window, wanting sight of the sun, the sky, reality, a little time to think.

The police car was coming up the drive.

22

FRED PARKER got out of the car. He carried the photographs and George's completed sketch in his hand. He was a gentle man and he did not like what he was doing, but there was no hesitation in his mind. A job was a sacred thing, and if people wanted to laugh sometimes at the concept of a village cop with this attitude, why, that was all right, Fred didn't mind; Fred knew better than they how it was, how it had to be.

He walked up the broad steps neither fast nor slow, merely deliberate, giving the approach the best that was in him. He had no idea what was waiting for him. Almost certainly there would be denial. Maybe there would be laughter, too. He had encountered both before. He heard the phone ringing, and he wondered at that, even waited a moment or two, his hand on the wrought iron knocker, giving the man inside a chance to answer the phone.

But the ringing continued. And then, distantly, muffled, he heard the new sound. It seemed to come from the cellar. He had heard gunshots before. There was no longer deliberation in his manner as he dropped the knocker, reached for the doorknob itself. The door was unlocked. He went in quickly.

Upstairs the baby began to cry. The phone at last stopped its ringing. Fred found the cellar door, and hurried down the steps. He was pretty sure what he would find.

23

LOUELLA SAID, "He answered the first time, and hung up. Now he won't answer at all. Why, Sam?"

"I don't know, Louella. Maybe he has his reasons."

"For not talking to me?" And then, slowly, "Yes. I suppose

he has." She stood up. She turned. "Will you come with me, Sam?"

"Where?"

"To see him. To explain—no, to apologize." She smiled faintly. "Picture Louella making apology. Do you find that ironic, Sam, or amusing?"

Sam shook his head. "Only gratifying, and admirable."

And so, amongst the group immediately affected, Sam and Louella were the first to know what had happened. Fred Parker told them in perhaps unnecessary detail, but, then, there was a kind of angry sadness in Fred's mind and this may explain the casual brutality. "He shot himself when he saw me coming," Fred said. "Or maybe he didn't see me, but he knew I'd be along. He put the barrel of a Police Positive .38 in his mouth and pulled the trigger. It's probably the same gun that killed Mrs. Warren, and if it is then we've proved that he did it, although we knew already."

Louella had no words, none, and that horrible, watchful part of her mind took careful note that disbelief came first, and then a kind of guilty weakness that was akin to terror, and for a moment she thought she was going to be sick. But the moment passed. That detached part of her mind watched, and waited. But where was grief?

Fred said, "The phone was ringing, somebody trying to get him. I wonder who it was."

It was Sam who said, "Is it important, lieutenant? I don't think it is now." He led Louella back to their car.

24

GEORGE HEARD the news over the phone, also from Fred Parker. "I thought," Fred said, "that you'd rather hear it from me than from the grapevine."

"Thanks." Then, "Are we proud of ourselves, lieutenant?" And quickly, "Don't answer that."

George sat for a long time in the pleasant studio after that phone call. It was growing dark when he walked out to his car and headed south, towards that Jersey bar. The record of his activities that night is a trifle confused, but the end result was that George and two truck drivers all showing signs of wear and tear appeared before the local judiciary Tuesday morning charged with a considerable breach of the peace. They were found guilty and fined fifty dollars apiece. George paid the three fines, shook hands all around, and drove back home feeling better, somehow purged.

25

WHEN THE phone rang in Martin's study, both he and Madge went in to answer it. Madge closed the study door, thereby shutting out the rest of the world, or trying to. The voice on the phone was that of Martin's assistant in the New York office, and the voice was loud enough for Madge to hear too. "A TWX in from the factory, Marty. It's signed Howard Post, and I think you'd better hear it."

"I'm listening," Martin said, and years later he was to look back on that moment and remember how time stood still.

"It says, 'TO ALL BRANCHES. EFFECTIVE SOONEST FOLLOWING PERSONNEL CHANGES IN CUSTOMER RELATIONS: MARTIN FULLER TO LONDON TO ESTABLISH CUSTOMER RELATIONS DIVISION FOR EUROPEAN AND AFRICAN COMMERCIAL AND MILITARY OPERATIONS. NEW DIVISION TO REPORT DIRECT TO THIS OFFICE.' How about that, Marty? And the rest of it turns this office over to me. How about that?"

Martin was watching Madge's face. She was smiling, with her lips, with her eyes, with all of her. Strangely, tears rolled unheeded down the sides of her nose.

The voice in the phone said, "Hey, Marty. For God's sake say something."

And now Martin too could smile, even relax. "Congratulations," he said.

"In spades," the voice said. "To both of us. What do you suppose got into the old man?"

It was not until later, much later in the day, that Madge heard the news of Paul Warren, from, of course, Mona.

26

MONA CALLED Joy Lewis, too. And then Mildred Pierson. And then she flew upstairs and hammered, simply hammered on the study door. "Wally! Wally! Open this door. Honestly. Paul Warren killed himself. Isn't that—exciting?"

27

THERE WAS one more thing of note that occurred on this day, although it was actually night. Ben Pierson did not even try to sleep. He waited with solemn patience until the sleeping pill Mildred had taken produced its results. Then, quietly, he got his long thin body out of bed and went downstairs where he spent a long time composing a letter which he sealed into an envelope and attached the envelope to the front of his pajama coat with a paper clip. He used a heavy silk necktie and a kitchen chair and the waste pipe that ran overhead through the cellar. He died shortly before midnight.

This was Monday.

E P I L O G U E

IT WAS A STOUT CRATE the lorryman delivered to the London flat. Martin opened it carefully, one slat at a time. Madge watched. What was inside was wrapped securely in heavy brown paper, and when Martin untied it and began to peel the paper down, the deep frame appeared first, and then Madge's face, smiling, glowing, and then her bare shoulders, and Madge wanted to scream, but merely closed her eyes instead.

She heard the paper tearing on, and then there was a long, long silence. Martin's voice said at last, "God, you're lovely."

Madge opened her eyes. She looked, stared at the picture. She wanted to laugh, but only a giggle came out.

Martin said, "You don't have a dress like that, slinky-type." He turned to smile at her. "But I must say it looks pretty special on you." He faced the picture again, studied it once more. He said slowly, "George is good, isn't he? I mean really good."

"Understatement," Madge said, and she couldn't help it, she just had to giggle again.

It was some days later that the letter arrived. It said, "For the picture, *de nada*. I wanted to do it. I did it. My pleasure.

"You'll want county news, to set against your own imaginings if for no other reason, bearing firmly in mind, as you read, what I am pleased to call the Hanks Unified Theory. Reduced to its essence the theory states: *And this too will pass*.

"Sam and Louella have come forward, if that's the phrase, and offered to adopt the Warren child. Offer has been accepted by the county court. Louella has turned fiercely protective and maternal with two children to rule. There is, of course, a considerable disparity in their ages, but Louella takes that in stride. She has plucked Sam out of Wall Street. They have sold their house. They are headed for Switzerland to set up permanent residence. The reason, as given, is to enable the child to grow up away from memory of, and gossip about, Roz and Paul. And the reason, I admit, is sound. Still I wonder if that is the entire story. I think the seventeenth century must have been pretty lively up in the Alps. Louella's new book, incidentally, *Fire and Wind*, is bounding up the best seller ladder, as anticipated. It is dedicated to Paul. Again I wonder.

"Mildred, in stunning widow's weeds, has gone off to Hollywood. The newspaper coverage of her departure would nauseate you, so I do not enclose. Think the worst, and you will have it exact. And yet I think she misses him. I do. Buster Keaton cast as Savanarola no longer strikes me as funny.

"Bob Lewis has changed agencies and, by accounts, taken a good share of the billing along with him. He has a lofty pinnacle in mind, and I think he'll reach it. I wonder what he'll find when he gets there.

"Wally works. Mona giggles.

"The Warren house has been sold. People named Warwick—Luke and Buzzy, and you call her Buzzy or she pouts. They are in trade—their term—and determined to sublimate the profits from a string of specialty shoppes into sensitive support of the arts (whatever the hell that means). Swimming party this Sunday, a planned amalgam of mercantile stuffiness and BOHEMIANISM (whatever the hell that is) I plan to attend. With Gladys. Remember Gladys? I have told her to bring her Bikini, the transparent one. Mustn't disappoint Buzzy.

"Once you've felt the charm of the tropics you'll always return —who said that, or something like it? No matter. Not true of the county, anyway. Except, maybe, for some of us, who would find the county wherever we went, or, more accurately perhaps, would take it along with us. So why move? QED. *This too will pass.*

"Bless you, children."

G. *Hanks.*